Quotes about *The Postcard in the Window*

"I'd love it to be the start of a series…"

Karen Louise Hollis

"Genuinely a joy to read."

Ahone Lane

"All the place descriptions were so vivid…"

Jodie Homer

To Rebecca,
Happy reading !
Best wishes
Sarah
X

About Sarah Scally

Sarah lives on the south coast of the UK with her family and works for the NHS.

She has written in a freelance capacity for magazines and business journals and writes scripts collaboratively with two friends.

In 2013 she won a competition to write a 45-minute radio play. This play was the beginning of The Postcard in the Window and in 2020 it was one of twelve manuscripts longlisted for the Comedy Women in Print prize (CWIP) for an unpublished novel.

The Postcard in the Window

SARAH SCALLY

First published in Great Britain in 2023

A CIP catalogue record for this book is available from the British Library.

ISBN: 9798396143227

To my family, with love.

🪧 Chapter One

*E*DDIE LIFTED her hand and gave the skipper of the boat a wave. With most of his face hidden behind a bushy beard he looked more pirate than pleasure boat day-tripper. A woman popped up next to him in a flowery apron and round glasses; Eddie was reminded of a meerkat. The woman waved enthusiastically, and Eddie felt obliged to increase the speed of her response. Why did people wave from boats anyway? You didn't from any other form of transport. Eddie didn't begrudge waving but, with hundreds of boats a day during summer, she worried about repetitive strain injury. For several seconds they continued, maintaining eye contact, until the cruiser finally rounded the bend. With a sigh of relief, Eddie stopped. She smoothed her wavy hair away from her face and returned to sipping her morning coffee.

Eddie Maguire - or *Edwina Ann* to use her full name - liked to tell people she lived in an upside-down house. It wasn't *actually* upside-down, but with bedrooms on the ground floor and living space upstairs she could sit in her lounge and watch the river flow past for hours. Cradling the warm coffee cup, her attention wandered to a family of ducks near the opposite bank. The mother duck chased one of her brood trying to make a break for freedom. Roughly, she nudged it back to its siblings like a sheepdog with a bothersome flock. They all had a purpose. If they didn't peck at weed or chase lumps of bread, they would go hungry. Eddie had no such purpose. At just ten to nine in the morning her day stretched endlessly ahead. Draining the cup of its last dregs she crossed to the kitchen and rinsed it out. In the cul-de-sac below she spotted Sophie from number one. In her young mum uniform of jeans and trainers, Sophie herded her three youngsters into the car. Two were in and buckled tightly but the little one was distracted, hopping on the lawn. In one swift move Sophie scooped her up and belted her in the car seat. Expertly done. She slammed the door and puffed out in exasperation. With a rev of the engine she was gone, and Eddie let out a slow breath. Someone else with something to do. Sophie would probably love to have some of the time that Eddie now found weighed heavy on her hands. The cul-de-sac was quiet again. The day was grey and still. Eddie remained motionless, staring out. She sniffed, came back to the present and wiped her eyes, noticing the photo on the windowsill. Taken in 2008 at her daughter's graduation, it always made her smile. Heather's mortarboard balanced precariously on top of her curly, dark hair as she stood between her parents. They oozed happiness, playing at happy families on the Town Hall steps, as Heather's friend had captured the day. Eddie's smile fell. A lot had happened since then and she calculated the years that had passed. She'd get another photo with Heather next time they met - whenever that might be. On a whim she fetched the phone and dialled Heather's number. It rang just twice before being answered. Breathing quickly into the receiver, Heather sounded as if she was running.

"Yes."

"Heather?"

"Mum, you okay?" Heather's anxiety was palpable down the line.

"Yes, yes. I'm fine. I just thought I'd give you a bell."

"Oh right," Surprised, Heather paused. "I'm just on my way to work. Should have been there half an hour ago, but the traffic's a nightmare. You know how it is." Another pause, Heather probably remembering that her mum didn't know how it was anymore. "Anyway, I'm sorry mum, but I need to dash. Can I call you this afternoon, I should have more time?"

"Of course, love, whenever you can."

"Bye mum."

"Bye love, look after-" Eddie looked at the phone. There was no one there. She exhaled slowly and replaced it on the cradle. "This won't do," she whispered into the silence. "Won't do at all." She recognized the signs – lethargy, weepiness, loss of appetite – and was determined not to stumble back into the fog that had enveloped her for months after Rex had died. She'd get moving, talk to someone... anyone. Should she go for a walk? She paused, unsure. Would she be able to cope outside? Walking had been her saviour after Rex. Every day, striding along the riverbank as her pedometer clocked her steps. But that had been a while ago. Now she needed to be realistic. She could head to the shop and pick up a gardening magazine for ideas. Yes. With renewed energy she went downstairs and prepared to leave the house for the first time in four weeks.

Eddie followed the river for a mile, slowing to take a peek at one of the larger houses on the opposite bank. Work was happening to build a mooring jetty and it looked quite different after just four weeks. Most of the properties on that side of the bank had similar, supposedly for their private canoes or day boats. As she peered through her scratched sunglasses the reality was that the Simonton Mute swans were already using them for nests. Bad news for the homeowners, as taking on a swan wasn't to be advised. There was a story of someone having their arm broken by the flap of one wing, or was that an urban myth? She was sure she'd read it somewhere. The white swans, on this stretch of water, were a local attraction and not to be messed with. They added to the genteel nature of Simonton.

Leaving the river behind, Eddie branched off down a residential road. Her fluorescent-signed destination, nestled in a small parade of shops, came into view. As she stepped over the threshold, an electronic beep announced her arrival. She raised a hand to Amir, slumped behind the counter, and pasted on a grin to hide her disappointment. She'd been hoping to see Janet. Of a similar age, she considered Janet a friend. She was fun and if the queue wasn't too lengthy, they'd have a good chat. Amir, on the other hand, never said a lot.

"You alright Amir?"

He rewarded her with a grunt. At least he was aware that someone had spoken.

"Lovely day." She tried again and pointed out the window. She felt a minor victory when he raised his head. "Nice out. What time you on 'til today?"

His eyes flicked to the cheap wall clock. Its second hand clunked heavily round the seconds, and he puffed out his cheeks.

"Six to six." His tone was flat. He wasn't happy. "A long one."

"Just think of your pay packet." She tried to be upbeat. "All that money rolling in."

"Ppphh." He slouched onto the counter. "I'm tryin' to save, but just paying off my debts." He returned to his phone and Eddie took that as her cue to go shopping. Conversation over. She ambled to the magazine rack and leafed through the tattered offerings. She settled on two and glanced round, her eyes drawn to the chocolate. A few squares of Bourneville after dinner would be just the ticket - it was Friday after all. Picking up a bar she approached the counter and stood patiently, waiting for Amir to look at her rather than his gadget.

"Pfhh." He made a noise like an old man getting off a low chair as he straightened to punch the amounts into the till. "Seven ninety-three." He held his hand out, but his eyes flicked back to his phone. Pulling a ten-pound note from her purse Eddie held it between her thumb and forefinger and waited. Eventually he glanced up.

"Please."

She nodded and handed it over. "Thank you."

"Sorry," Amir mumbled, "need more change, don't I?" He locked the till, leaving her with her hand outstretched, and disappeared into the back of the shop. She sighed and ran her finger along the edge of the counter. With no Janet available for a chat, this trip was going to be a quick one. She glanced to her left where a large red noticeboard was stuck with creased cards and scraps of paper in orderly columns. In the bottom corner, someone had written the dates of when they were to be removed.

Experienced gardener. Friendly, with up-to-date DBS check.

For rent - Double room in shared house. £360 per month. Suit professional person/ couple. Call Dougie for more information.

An image of a slum landlord dressed in vest and grubby trousers, sitting on a stained sofa, popped into Eddie's head. She shuddered as she recalled some of the places her Heather had lived as a student. Dougie was probably a lovely, tidy man and she was being mightily unfair. Probably.

The Happy Wanderers rambling group. Informal weekly walks: every Saturday, rain or shine. New Members Welcome. Telephone Colonel Tucker (retired) for further information.

She used to enjoy hiking. Amir re-appeared and nodded when he saw her looking.

"Only came in yesterday." He tilted his head at the notice, and she saw they'd paid for a fortnight.

"Funny." He chuckled then stopped, taking Eddie by surprise. She couldn't remember seeing him smile before let alone laugh. "He came in with a teenage boy, real moody." Amir's shoulders slumped and he hunched forwards in imitation. "He didn't want to put the card up, but the man got cross… waggled a stick. I think it was his grandad."

Eddie frowned. She wasn't following.

"The man, this man here." Amir jabbed at the card. "Colonel Tucker. I think he was his grandad. Wasn't taking any nonsense from the boy." Amir's nose wrinkled as if he'd smelt something unpleasant. "He was wearing bright yellow trousers."

"The boy?"

"No." Amir looked at her as if she was stupid. "The Colonel." He nodded at her. "Why don't you do it? I would if I wasn't stuck here."

Now she really was confused. "You would what?"

"Go hiking."

"You would?"

Amir didn't strike her as the type to enjoy the great outdoors. Good looking, in a brooding way, his gelled black hair and well-groomed stubble seemed more city slicker than countryside romper.

"Yeah man. Loved my Duke of Edinburgh." He hitched up his low-slung jeans and started walking on the spot, swinging his arms backwards and forwards, his face lighting up.

"You've done the Duke of Edinburgh?"

"Don't look so shocked." He glanced at her, affronted. "My dad got me into it. We spent most weekends away." His face clouded, "until a couple of years ago anyway. They were good times, man," he added quietly.

"Why don't you do it then?"

He blinked. "I would, believe me. But my dad's like 'work and study, Amir.'" He rubbed the back of his neck and shrugged. "But go on, you do it." He scribbled something on a post-it note and held it out. She saw the phone number and shook her head.

"Oh, I don't know," she hesitated but he jabbed the yellow square at her.

"I heard you tell Janet." He stared at the post-it note as it hovered between them.

"Tell her what?"

"That you, er…" he wouldn't meet her gaze. "Need something to do."

"Oh."

"And you used to walk," he added quickly. "I reckon this could be your thing."

Eddie's cheeks heated up. She thought that conversation with Janet had been private. Had he been eavesdropping or had Janet told him? Either way she felt a prickle of embarrassment and wanted to go home. She whipped the square of paper from him and put it between the magazines.

"I'll think about it," she replied curtly and pocketed her change. She didn't want to appear ungrateful but then she didn't need life coaching from this youngster either. As the electronic beep sounded her departure, she heard him shout.

"It could be fun!"

📷 Chapter Two

OLONEL B. Tucker (retired) couldn't understand what had happened. One minute he'd been in the living room of his beautifully furnished bungalow, watching the golf on TV and waiting for his lunch to heat up. Next minute there'd been a bungalow-shaking explosion and he'd hobbled through to investigate. Now, standing just inside the kitchen door the scene before him looked like a bloodied battlefield. The walls and ceiling dripped with bolognaise sauce and the microwave was a blackened box that continued to spark and hiss in the corner. It was missing a door. As his eyes looked round the room he found it, embedded in the side of the fridge.

"What the...?" He leant against the table and rubbed his eyes, defeated. The stubble on his chin rasped as he ran his hand over it. He'd forgotten to bloody shave as well. Now he couldn't even heat up a sodding microwave meal. There was a knock on the back door and, before he could compose himself, it opened. His grandson stepped into the kitchen, eyes down, staring at his phone.

"Jack, don't –"

Too late. Jack stepped on a sheet of lasagna and daintily slid into the centre of the kitchen as if performing Torville and Dean's Bolero. He careered into his grandad and together they glided, before hitting the side of the fridge and falling to the floor.

"Good God, Jack. You and that bloody phone."

"It wasn't my fault."

"Of course it was your fault!"

The fridge bounced against the wall sending shockwaves up to the ceiling, dislodging a dollop of pasta sauce. It fell with a 'splat' on the Colonel's head. Jack choked down a snigger.

"Do not dare." The Colonel held up his hand. He was *not* in the mood.

"Sorry."

For several seconds they sat in silence. The Colonel moved and, with a wince, levered himself up to sitting.

"Shit, grandad. You okay?"

"I'm fine," he snapped.

"But your hip?"

"I'm fine." The Colonel carefully stretched out his leg.

"You sure?"

"Jack, will you shush." He continued to point his toes and flex while Jack watched in silence.

"Alright?"

He knew Jack was worried, but he did wish he would stop talking. He couldn't feel any pain, but he wouldn't know for sure until he stood.

"Can you help me off the floor?"

Jack hopped up and, putting his arms under his grandad's armpits, manhandled him to standing. Once on his feet, the Colonel steadied himself then gingerly wiggled from side to side. He pushed his hips out, first to the left then the right, before rotating in a circle.

"Disco dancer," Jack quipped but was silenced with a look. This was *not* the time to be flippant. Satisfied there was no lasting damage to his new hip the Colonel turned to survey the kitchen.

"What happened anyway?"

The Colonel shrugged. He didn't know. "One minute I was watching Tiger Woods going for glory and then I heard an almighty bang." He sighed. "I've no idea what happened… I was getting on so well too."

Jack raised his eyebrows.

"I *was*," the Colonel insisted. "Believe it or not I can look after myself, Jack." He rubbed his chin and instantly felt the stubble. He rolled his eyes. It was no wonder Jack didn't believe him. "I was going to have a bath and shave after lunch," he explained, and Jack nodded slowly. Well, *he* knew it was the truth. He didn't have to justify himself.

"Mum doesn't mind cooking for you. Why don't you just stay with us a bit longer? Just 'til you're mended."

"I am mended, Jack. Besides, I like my independence."

"God, grandad. You are *so* stubborn." Jack pulled his phone from his pocket and started typing. The Colonel watched his grandson's fingers flying across the tiny letters and tutted loudly.

Jack glanced up. "What? S'mum. Asking if you're okay"

"You've been sent to spy on me now?"

Returning the phone to his pocket, Jack looked to the ceiling as if praying for patience. "No. Just making sure you're okay. She'll drop a stew off later." Jack pulled a chunk of pasta off his trousers, examined it, then flicked it in the swing bin.

"I don't need feeding."

Jack looked around the room in an exaggerated fashion. "I'd beg to differ." He paused. "Just accept a little help, grandad. It won't be for long."

The older man nodded. He felt well and truly defeated - at least for today.

"I still don't understand what happened."

"It was a microwave lasagna. I took it out the cardboard sleeve and put it in for four minutes-"

"A plastic container?"

The Colonel nodded, frowning.

"Did you make holes in the lid?"

The Colonel narrowed his eyes at a splat of sauce on the wall, then looked back at the boy. "Oh… maybe *that's* where I went wrong." A strip of lasagna caught their attention. It slid down the window, leaving a trail of tomato sauce, before coming to rest on the windowsill.

"Come on."

He felt the weight of Jack's arm around his shoulder.

"I'll help tidy up then can I make a sandwich? I'm starving."

Half an hour later and the kitchen was back to its former glory; albeit the microwave was missing a door (now standing by the bin outside, ready to go to the tip) and there was a huge dent in the side of the fridge. Returning the dustpan and brush to its place under the sink, *everything in its place,* the Colonel caught his breath as he straightened up.

"Grandad, go and sit down. I'll finish up."

He was about to argue but felt Jack's hand on his back, gently pushing him towards the door.

"What you got in for sandwiches?"

The Colonel stopped and thought. "Ham in the fridge. There might be salad too." He pointed to the high cupboard. "Crisps up there, help yourself."

Jack nodded. "I'll sort something. Might not be pretty." His grandad gave him a thin smile.

The Colonel was carefully lowering himself onto the floral sofa when the telephone rang. Hovering over the cushions, his bottom sticking out behind, he pushed himself back up and reached over to the occasional table for the handset.

"Simonton 456899. Colonel Tucker speaking. Who is calling?" Affronted by a whistling noise, he held the receiver away from his ear and bashed it. "Hello, is anyone there?" He was about to hang up when a quiet voice came down the line.

"Hello, is that Colonel Tucker?"

The voice was faint. He could barely hear it. "Yes, it is. Who is calling?" He spoke louder, hoping the caller would do the same.

"I was phoning about the advert in the Simonton shop. The rambling club?"

"Oh yes." His voice grew frosty as he pictured the postcard. He'd done it to help Jack, secretly hoping that the boy's father might offer. He eased himself onto the sofa and waited for the caller to get to the point. There was silence.

"Are you still there?" He barked down the phone line.

"Er yes." She was awfully timid. "Maybe this wasn't such a good idea."

"I can't answer that for you," he replied gruffly, "but with regards to the Wanderers, I'm helping my grandson train for the Duke of Edinburgh. He was going to give it up as he missed the school practice last year… he was rather poorly." He stopped and rubbed his hip. She didn't need to know *that* much information. Bloody walking group. He wouldn't be able to make more than a couple of yards with this throbbing pain. He looked around for his paracetamol.

"Okay. When do you meet?"

"Saturday mornings. Zero nine hundred hours. Rendezvous point, Visitor Centre by the harbour. Do you know it?"

"Yes. I know where that is," she paused. "And how far will you be going?"

He sighed impatiently. "Along the coast to Gabriel's wood and back to the Visitor Centre. Provisional recce suggests approximately four miles."

"Oh, okay." The voice was unsure.

"Is that too far?" His voice was snappier than he'd intended, but he really needed his pills.

"No. I can do that," she replied equally as snappy. "I used to go on hiking weekends with my husband."

"Oh, two of you then?"

"No just me," she hesitated, "*if* I decide to come."

"Righto. Well, it's up to you," he replied rudely. He could not bear dithering. You made a decision and followed it through. He levered himself off the sofa with a grunt. "I'm sorry. I really need to go. Maybe see you one Saturday." He put the phone down and limped back towards the kitchen.

Jack was on the other side of the door with two plates of sandwiches. He swooped them out of the way just in time. "Watch it grandad. Who was that?" Then he noticed his grandad's face. "You okay?"

"Fine. Just need some bloody pills." The Colonel made towards the cupboard that housed the first aid box, but Jack intervened.

"You go and sit. I'll bring them."

"I'm alr-"

"Go grandad, you need to rest."

Even though Jack was polite and didn't make a fuss, the Colonel couldn't help but feel he was becoming a burden. And he didn't like the feeling one little bit.

Eddie stared at the phone. "Well, what a rude man!" She replaced the handset and clicked the kettle on. How *not* to persuade someone to join your hiking gang. Standing by the counter she peered out at the cul de sac. She wasn't going to join now. He could stuff it. She scrubbed her lunch dishes and jammed them onto the drying rack. She made a cup of tea and moved to the table where she flicked through her magazines. Turning the pages and concentrating on the pictures soothed her. After a few moments she forgot about the obnoxious little man and concentrated on the design for her garden instead. By late afternoon she'd ordered four flowerpots and drawn a sketch for Charlie, her odd job man. She'd call him next week. Satisfied, she sat on the sofa and watched as the afternoon gave way to evening. Her mind wandered back to the phone call. She pictured the Colonel as a short, pompous man, with a large round belly and ruddy cheeks. She considered the walk but screwed up her face, dismissing the idea. She was alright here on her own. The phone rang and broke her out of her thoughts. As she held it to her ear, she could hear traffic in the background.

"Hello?"

"Hi mum, it's me."

"Heather." She immediately brightened at the sound of her daughter's voice. "Thanks for calling back, love. How was your day?"

"Yeah alright, thanks. I'm just on my way to a meeting, so I can't be long -"

"Now? It's nearly the weekend."

There was a snort of laughter. "Weekend? You must be joking. I'll probably be working on this McCormack's deal. Weekends aren't really a thing at the moment."

Eddie searched her memory. She vaguely remembered hearing something about a deal.

"It's all about to kick off next week. There will be press interest, lots to do and not enough time. Sorry." She paused, and Eddie heard her breathe deeply. "I'm wittering."

Eddie walked through to the sofa and sat down, glancing at the photos on the mantelpiece.

"It's nice to hear you witter," she chuckled. "We haven't spoken for a while."

She heard Heather's footsteps stop.

"I know, it's been so crazy trying to find any free time. Listen, I've just reached my car so I can't be long. Why don't you come for a visit? Text me some dates-"

Eddie leaned into the phone, keeping her mouth clamped shut.

"-we could take in a show."

Eddie did want to see her. She missed her. But going up to London? "Oh, I don't know, love."

"Why not?" Heather grew impatient. "I could show you around. I'm not sure when I'll get-"

The line went dead. Eddie waited. She looked at the phone expectantly but when it didn't ring again, she returned it to the cradle. She'd call Heather later when she wasn't so busy. What would she tell her anyway? It wasn't like she'd been doing anything exciting. Eddie stared at the phone. The red light of the answer-machine glared back. She couldn't remember the last time it had flashed with a message. Without thinking, she pressed the button.

"You have no new messages." A voice like Joanna Lumley's chastised her for having no social life. Being a glutton for punishment, Eddie pressed it again.

"You have no new messages."

The carriage clock on the mantelpiece chimed loudly and made her jump. Five o'clock on a Friday afternoon and the whole weekend stretched out in front of her. Maybe she *should* give that walk a go? At least she'd have something to report to Heather, if she ever got hold of her again. Moving to the hallway she opened the under-stairs cupboard and peered in. Her walking boots were there somewhere and, switching on the light, she wondered if she could find them in time.

Heather gunned her car down the dual carriageway. Her first meeting had been at seven that morning and she now had a blinding headache having guzzled too much caffeine. Braking, she approached a junction with four-way traffic lights. Her eyes scanned the lanes, as she weighed up which would be the quickest. She still had so much work to do and hoped another couple of hours would be enough. She chose the right-hand lane and joined the line. The engine ticked over and, irritably, she picked at her thumbnail. The lights changed to green, and she inched forwards.

"Come on!" she growled. The queue stopped moving. Some idiot was trying to turn right. A green P plate was stuck to the car's bumper. Why was a new driver out on the busiest road in bloody London, at rush hour? Heather blasted her horn. She swerved round and glared at the driver. She instantly felt a rush of shame when she saw a young girl hunched over the wheel, sobbing.

"I'm sorry," Heather whispered as she pulled away. She blew out her cheeks as the knot of worry in her stomach inflated, now with an added layer of shame. She needed to chill out a bit. And just… be nicer.

She pulled into the car park at Mercury Consulting, still consumed with guilt. As she switched off the engine, her mobile started to trill. She sighed. *Be nicer,* she repeated as she fished it out of her bag and smiled at the familiar name on screen.

"Georgie! How you doing?" She brightened at the thought of her old Uni friend.

"Good thanks. Listen, I know you're busy, so I won't keep you long-"

"-it's fine. Always got time to speak to you-" Heather picked at her thumb.

"-What? You not beavering away at work?" Georgie's girlish voice sounded incredulous.

"Well," Heather laughed. "I'm just going back in actually, but I've got ten minutes for you."

Her friend sighed heavily down the line. "You're going in *now*? Have you had the day off or something?"

"No, I've been working. I've just returned from a meeting." She climbed out the car and rolled her shoulders, grateful for the stretch.

"Jeez Heath, they're taking the mick. What time will you finish?"

"I don't know. Seven? It's not a problem." It wasn't *that* late. Plenty of people worked hours like her. Besides, she didn't exactly have a lot else to do. She had no friends in the capital.

"You should be getting your glad rags on for the weekend; single, city-girl like you."

Heather laughed. She couldn't remember the last time she'd worn anything other than a work suit, or her jogging pants at home. It was a far cry from the corporate parties she used to attend in Dubai. She stared at her reflection in the wing mirror. *Another* spot on her forehead and without thinking she started to pick it. She needed some healthy stuff; vegetables, water… she'd get some this weekend.

"Anyway," she smoothed down her side plait. "To what do I owe the pleasure? Or have you just called to tell me how sad my life is?" She grinned at her pasty face reflecting back. She'd read somewhere that if you smiled it relieved stress. It didn't work.

"Heather, I didn't say that." Now her friend was exasperated. "Actually, I'm calling to thank you for your lovely painting."

Heather smiled with genuine affection, pleased that her friend appreciated her gift. "You are very welcome." It had been a labour of love for Georgie's new arrival, Mabel.

"You're so talented. John framed it yesterday and I shared a photo with two mums from NCT. You should do more."

Heather grabbed her bag and clicked the car's lock. "I loved doing it for Mabel, but it takes time." She walked towards the office block's grand entrance. "And that's something I'm short of, at the mo." The idea for 'Twinkle twinkle little star' had come to her at four a.m. as she'd been in bed, wide-awake and panicking about work. Rather than fret about the insomnia that had started to plague her, Heather had got up and toyed with her old painting kit instead. She'd enjoyed it, surprisingly so. She'd since come up with a list of other nursery rhymes to paint, when her job didn't take up *all* her energy.

"These women are loaded, you could name your price," Georgie whispered. "Just saying."

Heather laughed. She loved how, even years after university, they were still skint students at heart. "Thanks, that's very flattering." She played down her talents.

"Not flattering. It's true."

"How is Mabel anyway?" Heather kicked herself for not asking earlier. "Are you getting any sleep yet?"

"Sleep isn't too bad. She's so beautiful, you'd love her. She's nearly six months old. You. Must. Visit!" Georgie said the words staccato, for additional emphasis.

"I know, I'm sorry." Heather meant it. "Let's get a date arranged and I'll come for the weekend."

"Pinky promise?"

"Pinky promise," she smiled.

Chapter Three

As soon as the birds started singing on Saturday morning, the Colonel was out of bed and preparing breakfast in the kitchen. After the lasagna incident, and the subsequent deep clean, the kitchen was now spotless. Sun shone in through two orange patterned blinds, giving the room a warm glow. As the Colonel made a pan of porridge, with a pinch of salt, he switched on the small TV. Breakfast news: North Korea, the latest political scandal, and another knife crime. He tutted and turned it off again. While the porridge simmered on the stove, he did gentle stretches, scanning his body for aches and pains. At 08:00 hours, when Jack rang as arranged, he'd been able to declare he was fit to walk (albeit he had a tiny twinge when he stood at a certain angle) but he didn't mention that, for fear of Jack cancelling.

At 08:50 hours precisely he stood to attention on his drive. The bungalows of Deronda Close were pristine. Immaculate flowerbeds brimmed with primulas and tulips, all reaching up to the sunshine. The Colonel surveyed his own front garden, and his shoulders sagged. He should be tidying this rather than spending time out hiking. There *were* several splashes of colour in his flowerbed but, unfortunately, they were clumps of dandelions. They would need pulling before they set to seed. Maybe Jack could help - for a price of course. It wouldn't be for long as he sincerely hoped to resume full duties soon. He glanced at his wristwatch. 08:55. They were five minutes late. He tutted. Sloppy practice. His eyes kept drifting to the entrance of the Close.

He was becoming agitated when, at 08:58, a puffing metallic-blue Micra screeched around the corner and swung to a halt. 08:58! This wasn't acceptable.

"Morning dad," Diana Tucker hopped out.

"Afternoon!" He replied pointedly. No apology and what was she wearing? He scowled at her patterned leggings, scruffy t-shirt and flip-flops. She hugged him and kissed his cheek. She ran a finger over his chin. Uncomfortable, he stepped back.

"Not having a shave today?"

Bugger. He'd forgotten again. See, sloppiness. Now he'd let himself down. At least he'd ironed his khaki knee-length shorts. He'd even used a quick spray of starch to keep the pleats neat. He still had standards and tapping his pocket, he checked he'd remembered his Mint Imperials.

"Y'alright?" She frowned at him and ran a hand through her wild, greying hair.

"Fighting fit. Thank you," he replied stiffly. "What about you? You look…"

"I know, I know." She flapped her hand and took his rucksack, shoving it on the back seat. "I've been up since early, trying to finish a painting which is proving problematic… don't panic, no one will see me." They climbed into the car. "And if they do, I won't let on I'm your daughter-"

"- In-law," he corrected, and she glanced across.

"Yes, of course." She fired up the car and slung it around the corner, "I meant, how is your hip? Jack told me what happened. Sorry, I didn't call but I knew I'd see you this morning."

"It's fine. I took paracetamol and had an early night."

"And now?"

"I've been awake since sunup, ready for action. No need to panic."

She narrowed her eyes at him. "I know you don't want to let Jack down-"

"I don't mind cancelling," Jack glanced up from his phone. He was on the back seat, squashed between rucksacks and his mum's painting paraphernalia.

"I wouldn't dream of it," the Colonel insisted. "I dubbined my boots last night in preparation-"

"I noticed."

"-and we might have a new member joining us." He glanced sheepishly over at Jack, who clamped his lips together grimly.

"Might not as well," his grandson replied in a low, yet audible voice. Diana glanced in the mirror and caught his eye for an explanation.

"Grandad was rude."

"She caught me unawares," the older man explained quickly. "I might have been a bit…brusque," he conceded, as Jack raised his eyebrows. The Colonel fished the tin of mints from his pocket and handed them round before popping one in his mouth. "For your information I feel extremely guilty and if she turns up, I'll apologise. Satisfied?"

The car chugged on. "In addition, I couldn't cancel the day as I didn't want to disappoint Mike. He's also coming."

Jack groaned loudly from the backseat.

"Don't be like that, Jack. I know he's not to everyone's taste-"

"He's a prat!"

"Jack!" Diana's voice held a warning.

"He's got a new Sat Nav system he wants to trial," the Colonel continued over their petty squabbles.

"How exciting." Jack's voice dripped with sarcasm and earned him a glare from both of his relatives.

"He told me about it yesterday-"

"But grandad-"

"-I know. You've got to use your map."

Jack humphed. "I knew this was a waste of time. I should just forget it."

"I did explain to him that you're learning to use an OS map. He was impressed by the way. He asked if you would do a session with the

Cadets one evening." He saw Jack's sneer and realised this was going to be harder than he'd anticipated. During a distinguished career the Colonel had prided himself on a firm, but fair, command of his troops. Unflinching in the face of danger, he'd always led from the front. But now…well, he just felt old. And too weary to be taking on this obstreperous teenager… even if he was his own grandson. "You can navigate. Mike will use the Sat Nav as secondary intel." He gripped his seat as the car slewed round a corner.

"Sorry! I'll slow down-"

"Good idea," he murmured, tensing as pain shot through his hip. He turned away, not wanting Diana to see his discomfort. "Anyway," he continued, "I'm intrigued to see this gadget. It warns of dangers with terrain, has multiple languages-"

"-yeah, most phones do now," Jack cut across him, seriously unimpressed, as the Micra turned onto a bumpy track. Known only to locals, this short cut was pitted with crater-sized potholes and despite slowing to a crawling pace they bounced around like rubber balls.

"Ow!" Jack banged his head on the roof as they hit a large dip. It was with a collective sigh of relief that they crested the hill and spotted the single-story Visitor Centre in front.

"Look at that!" The Colonel forgot his discomfort and drank in the view. The stone building contrasted against the backdrop of azure blue sea and sky. For the first time since his hip operation, he felt a bubble of excitement at the thought of the day ahead. Diana yanked on the handbrake and his bubble popped.

"I'll drop you here." She hopped out, releasing Jack from the backseat, and passing them their rucksacks. "Right, I'd better get back to work. Give me a call when you're done, and I'll come and fetch you." She planted a sloppy kiss on the Colonel's cheek then one on Jack's. "You boys have fun, eh?

Chapter four

EDDIE SCANNED the area as she approached the Visitor Centre. Satisfied she was alone, she tugged at her wedgie. Her hiking trousers didn't use to ride up this badly, she must have put more weight on than she'd realised in the last couple of years. At least she could still get into them and do the button up, even if the waistband threatened to cut off her circulation. She straightened and sucked her stomach in, simultaneously wiggling her toes. Could feet put on weight too? Her boots, dragged out from under the stairs last night, felt snug. Rooky error. No doubt the pompous Colonel would despise this lack of preparation. Approaching the Centre, she wondered if she had time to pop in and see if they sold plasters, but a man was already standing outside. Was that him? He looked ridiculous, but much younger than she'd expected. He was dressed in camouflaged jacket and trousers, his face smeared with... mud? Twigs stuck out from his black woolly hat. They gave him a 'just crawled through the hedge' look, although the creases in his clothing contradicted that, suggesting they were fresh out of the packet today. Frankly, he looked like a signed-up member of the SAS - but one who'd been dressed by his mum. But he was rather attractive, and the muscular outline of his torso was visible under the jacket. He obviously kept himself fit and as Eddie approached an involuntary giggle escaped from her lips.

"Gosh, I nearly didn't see you there." She waved at his camouflage as he stood to attention.

"Highly effective, isn't it?" His voice was higher than she'd expected and at odds with his tough-guy façade. "Easy to spot here on the coast path, but when I get in the woods… poof." He flicked his hands in front of her face, "invisible. Worked a treat when I was isolated in the Black Forest for ten days."

"Germany? Why were you out there?"

He turned to stare at her. He sniffed. "If I told you, you'd become a target. It's safer I don't."

She laughed, not sure if he was joking. His clear blue eyes stared out from under the waggling branches; he was serious. "Stealth gloves," he held up a hand. "All clothing is combat proven and rigorously tested."

"And your face blends in too. Army issue paint?"

He shuffled and looked at his feet. "Er no, actually. This one is from Boots makeup counter, but it works though, doesn't it?" He turned from side to side to give her a better view. Was he pouting? He was either really into war games or just a tiny bit mad.

"Well, pleased to meet you," she held out her hand. "I'm Eddie."

Remembering his manners, he shook her hand. "Hello Eddie, I'm Mike."

"Oh. Not Colonel Tucker?"

"No," he snorted, "I wish. They should be along shortly."

Feeling a flutter of nerves Eddie wracked her brain for more to say, as Mike lifted his wrist to examine a huge military-style watch. What was she letting herself in for? This looked far more serious than her old boots and hiking trousers were prepared for. She needed to back out now and make her apologies.

"Actually Mike," she took a step back and began patting her pockets as if she'd lost something. "I think I'm going to have to return home, I seem to have forgotten-" *What? What had she forgotten?* "-I need to check something, I'm not sure I-"

"Ah, here they are now." Mike waved enthusiastically and she turned to see two people approaching from the back of the Centre. There were visual similarities between them, despite the fifty years age difference, but it was obvious which was the Colonel. The knee-length khaki shorts, sturdy leather boots (polished to an incredible sheen) and walking socks folded around his shins gave it away. He looked like he'd just stepped from the set of 'It Ain't Half Hot Mum.' With an air of confidence, he marched straight towards them, a stick in one hand and the other swinging backwards and forwards. Eddie could almost hear the 'left, right, left, right' bark of a drill sergeant and was disappointed when he didn't click his heels as he stopped.

"I almost didn't see you there, Mike." His cool grey eyes swept over the younger man dismissively as he drew himself up to full height. With a straight back and his chin out he was tall and slim, with an unmistakable air of superiority. He reminded Eddie of Rex; he'd also looked people up and down in that way, and Eddie felt her hackles rise as she watched and waited.

"Crikes, its Rambo," deadpanned the younger version as he sauntered over. "Are we expecting trouble?" He was several inches shorter, with a low-key dress sense of jeans, sweatshirt, and hiking boots. He peered out from under a thick mop of hair and tutted as Mike performed a strange curtsy, turning full circle to show his outfit.

"Effective, isn't it?"

But the Colonel had already turned his attention to Eddie.

"Are you the lady who phoned?"

"Yes. Eddie Maguire." She held out a hand and pulled herself up to her full five feet three inches as she looked him squarely in the face. "Pleased to meet you."

He shook her hand firmly, holding her gaze before slowly releasing it. "Pleased you could make it Eddie. And er," he hesitated, at a loss for words, "apologies for being so… brusque on the telephone." He leaned in. "You caught me at rather an inconvenient moment."

"Don't worry." She smiled thinly, now intrigued as to what had made him *that* bad tempered. The younger man watched their exchange with interest and Eddie turned to smile at him.

"And this is my grandson, Jack."

She reached out her hand and the teenager gave it a quick, limp shake without saying a word.

"Just the four of us then Mike?"

Mike nodded like an enthusiastic dog taking instructions from its owner, the sticks in his hat bouncing up and down.

"Well, I suggest we get on then. Give the coordinates to Jack and he can plot the route to the first checkpoint."

Mike nodded and held up a black gadget, the size of a sturdy mobile phone. "This is the latest in high-tech satellite navigation systems. Ladies and gentlemen, I present the GoRamble." He stroked it and paused to get their attention. Eddie waited expectantly whilst the Colonel stared out to sea. Jack wasn't even pretending to listen as he smirked at something far more interesting on his own phone.

"Programmable in fifteen languages." Mike upped his volume. "*Fifteen*" he repeated, and Eddie felt obliged to respond, "Oooo". This made the Colonel turn round.

"*And* it's accurate to within one metre. I've put the route in, and we'll use it as back up as Jack leads out."

"Excellent." The Colonel turned to his grandson. "Jack, get the coordinates. Remember what we've been talking about."

Jack put his phone away and looked at his grandad.

"The map? Coordinates?"

Jack frowned and swung the backpack off his shoulder. "Have I got the map? I thought you were bringing it."

The Colonel closed his eyes and took a large breath in. "No. I told *you* to get it from the kitchen table when we packed yesterday."

Jack dug in his bag and reached down to the bottom. He pulled his hand out, the frown now a deep furrow as he pushed his floppy hair away from his face, flustered. "I haven't got it, grandad. Can you just check your bag, please?"

The Colonel sighed and bent over. Keeping one leg straight while the other bent, he looked uncomfortable as he began to unload his bag. Out came a waterproof jacket, a tiny camping stove, a kettle, two mugs, several loose bin liners - Eddie frowned - and two pairs of woolly socks. He pulled himself upright and dropped his hands to his sides. Nothing. Eddie shivered. She'd been standing for a while and despite the sunshine the sea breeze was cooling. She rummaged in her rucksack for her cagoule. She reasoned she had a few moments while the men got themselves sorted. She brought out a tartan flask of hot water, hot chocolate sachets, a huge packet of egg sandwiches – she'd made enough to feed the five thousand, let alone four people. Ah, there it was. Repacking her bag, she watched the others in silence. With a hint of satisfaction, she felt less of a rookie now as she noticed the Colonel starting to panic. She caught Mike's eye and he shrugged, pushing the volume button on the GoRamble. With each push the device beeped louder.

"Mike," barked the Colonel, "I think that's loud enough, don't you?" He gave his hip a brusque, no-nonsense rub then resumed the search of his bag. Mike sneered over the top of his head - a small round bald patch just visible in the otherwise full head of hair - and Eddie bit her lip to stop a smile appearing. The dynamics of this little group were certainly interesting.

"Well, I've not got it." Miffed, the Colonel shoved the contents back in his bag. "That's a SNAFU, Jack. Good job Mike's here. Operation 'Map Reading Practice' will have to wait until next time. Right! Shall we get on? Mike, good to go?"

"Yes! Colonel!" He pressed a button, and the screen sprang to life with a map of the surrounding area. A robotic, Birmingham accent issued forth.

"Leaving. Visitor. Centre. Simonton. Return. Journey. Turham. Village. Total thirteen point two nine four five kilometres."

"Very precise," Eddie whispered as the machine paused to recalibrate.

"Proceed. Easterly. For three point four six kilometres. Press. To. Begin."

"It *is* very precise, Eddie, tracks via satellites," Mike wore a huge grin.

"Wow," Jack whispered in a sarcastic tone. "Pretty much everything *does* nowadays." With a sigh he shoved his pack on hunched shoulders and scuffed at the floor. "This is going to be sooo much *Fun!*"

The Colonel frowned and spoke in a low voice. "It'll be as much fun as you want it to be, Jack. Now," he took a sharp intake of breath, "can we advance on the first checkpoint? *Please?*"

Chapter five

OR OVER three kilometres they tramped along the gravel coast path. The crunching from underfoot provided a soundtrack to the cinematic, one hundred- and eighty-degree views. Fluffy clouds skittered across the vast blue and Eddie found it difficult to see where the water stopped, and the sky began. Her face was in full sun, its rays heating up her skin. For the first time in a while her body seemed weightless. It moved freely, loosening, and releasing long-held tensions. She felt like a flower opening up to the sunshine. Polite chitchat was the order of the day and the group stopped frequently to marvel at the nature around. Even Jack appeared to have taken his grandad's comment to heart as he walked up front with Mike. He wasn't exactly blown away by Mike's technology, but Eddie heard him ask several questions; the two of them frequently pausing to check something on-screen. The Colonel walked behind them, and Eddie followed, trying to match his long strides. Still convinced he was a pompous… well, she didn't like to swear … she remained peeved from their earlier interaction. She wasn't inclined to talk so kept her own counsel, relieved that her trousers weren't riding up as she'd feared they might. Like a lecturer let loose with a telescopic pointer the Colonel occasionally raised his stick to direct her attention towards a point of interest. He explained where a ship had run aground on treacherous hidden rocks and, using his stick, pointed to the white ripples out to sea where the waters swirled over the wreck beneath.

"Tallest point along this coastline."

The stick directed Eddie's attention to a flat-topped cliff. It was interesting. Another factoid she didn't know despite living in the area for years. She listened and he took her silence to be interest. Relaxing into the walk she found she was waiting for the next snippet, begrudgingly acknowledging that he knew a lot about the area. He could probably make an interesting travelling companion, if you could get past the shorts and rumpled socks. Then she told herself off. She, more than anyone, knew of the battles that some people were fighting, and he could have his own. She'd spent so much time on her own recently that she'd stopped seeing the good in people - she'd stopped seeing people altogether! Perhaps this was her wakeup call.

The path narrowed abruptly and became overgrown on both sides. The Colonel slowed and waved his hand for her to do the same, using his stick out front to move the brambles away.

"Careful," he warned over his shoulder, "it's getting narrower". He held some scrub back for her to sidestep through.

"Ow!" Something pulled at her skin. He held out his arm and she grabbed it to steady herself, lifting her trouser leg. A deep scratch on her ankle began to ooze blood and the Colonel tutted in sympathy.

"Bad luck, old thing, that looks nasty." He called the others to stop, and Mike came bouncing back. "Shall I take a look?"

"Good idea, she needs first aid."

Mike frowned. "Oh, I'm not trained in first aid."

"Why did you offer?"

Mike looked puzzled. "Um, to reassure her."

"What? By offering first aid that you can't administer. How very reassuring," he said sarcastically as he pulled himself to his full height and scowled. Taking a deep breath the Colonel exhaled slowly, obviously channeling his inner Zen. Still balancing on one leg, Eddie wobbled, and the Colonel turned back to her. "Eddie, sorry. Please, sit here and

I'll see what I've got in my bag." He led her to the side where a line of large boulders marked the edge of the path. He eased her slowly down to one of the rocks and waited for her to remove her boot. She peeled back her sock and winced as she uncovered a bleeding scratch.

"Ah, that's not bad." Jack sounded disappointed and, unimpressed, his attention wandered back to the sea. The Colonel edged him out the way and handed Eddie a plaster. "Here, use this."

She smiled weakly and placed it over the scratch, pressing the edges firmly in place.

"Would you like a mint imperial?"

She looked up to find the Colonel holding out a tin of sweets.

"Bit of sugar, for energy? I swear by them. Or I've got Kendal mint cake in my bag?" She pointed to the mints and took one gratefully. She popped it in her mouth while he offered the tin around. She took a swig from her water bottle, a trickle escaping down her chin, and wiping it, she looked up to find Mike and the Colonel watching. Her cheeks flushing, she stood up and stamped her foot to get the trouser leg back in place. "Come on then," she made a shooing motion, "this isn't going to get us far, is it?"

The Colonel nodded and Mike restarted the gadget.

"Ay, recalibratin'." A broad Liverpudlian accent shouted, and Eddie half expected Steven Gerrard to jump on the path in front.

"Did you change its settings?" Jack tried to grab the GoRamble, but Mike fended him off with a hand. He shook his head, as mystified at the change as the rest of them.

"Ay. Continue in an easterly direction for a lorra metres," it ordered. "After one hundred metres do ten staaar jumps."

"Hold on, I've got notes somewhere." Mike pulled off his rucksack and was unzipping the pocket.

"STAAAR JUMPS!"

They all stared, open-mouthed.

"Ay. No activity detected."

Blimey, it was angry.

"Shut down commencing in thirty seconds. Thirty. Twenty-nine. Twenty-eight…"

"It's shutting down. We need to move." Mike shoved past the Colonel. "Come on! I'll sort it later." Taking huge strides in time to the countdown, he set off.

"Ministry of Funny Walks," Eddie suppressed a giggle. "Come on, you heard him." She waved at the others to follow.

Eddie was breathing heavily and although the sun was cooling, sweat still prickled the back of her neck. Endorphins whizzed round her system making her feel 'buzzy' and whilst the walk was more frenetic than she'd expected, she was rising to the challenge. It was nice to be out the house and it felt good to be alive-

"Turn left!"

-if it wasn't for that flipping machine. The GoRamble's scream snatched her from her happy place as Mike stopped abruptly at a fork in the path. Surprised by the sudden halt, Jack careered into him sending the machine spiraling to the floor. Like a set of dominoes, the Colonel barged into Jack followed by Eddie, who added an elbow to Mike's kidneys for good measure. Pushing them roughly away Mike bent to retrieve the black box from a clump of gorse as Jack turned to fuss over his grandad.

"I'm alright Jack, leave me alone." The Colonel started to grumble then paused. "Er… Eddie?"

"Oh my god, I'm so sorry." She had her arms wrapped around him. She whipped them away as if she'd been scolded, losing herself as she enjoyed the impromptu cuddle. She turned to hide her blushes. As they shuffled apart, back to a more appropriate personal space, Mike wiped the machine. "It says to turn left and head up to those woods." His eyes wandered to a copse in the distance then, holding the gadget outstretched, he took the left turn and walked towards the trees.

"Stupid bloody machine." The Colonel had been grumbling for the last half hour and Eddie hoped they could all have a break soon.

"Should we follow him?"

"I suppose we'd better," the Colonel replied wearily and smiled. It was the first genuine smile she'd seen from him. It reached his pale grey eyes and made the edges crinkle. She found herself smiling back. She turned to follow him, appraising his outline as he marched on, swinging his stick. His left leg seemed the stronger and gave a more forceful forward movement. The right in contrast seemed to linger, waiting for the stick to offer it support. He dodged a muddy puddle and paused to point it out. He was taller than Rex had been and slimmer, almost too slim and Eddie found herself wondering about his home life. Would there be someone to look after him when he got back tonight – if they ever got back! She sighed as she too skirted the puddle and landed in one of his footsteps. He seemed less stressed since they'd been walking, and she felt herself warming to him… a little. She remained wary, as she was with all men, but he must have looked handsome in his uniform, before the pomposity took over. Her mind wondered to the first time she'd seen Rex.

Eddie had worked in London for two years once she'd finished University. She had 'flitted' (as her parents had called it) from one job to another as she'd tried to find something to maintain her interest. Finally, and much to her parent's delight, she'd moved back home to attend the local teacher training college. She'd been a few weeks into the course when one evening she'd attended a photography event. It had been a pilot session, arranged for a couple of hours to see whether there was an appetite amongst the students to learn about different professions. On that occasion, twelve of them attended to hear a talk from an up-and-coming photojournalist, Rex Maguire. The talk was followed by a tour of the facilities and the college's state of the art Dark Room. They'd crammed into the room with the lights turned off and in the darkness the photographer's voice had floated out to them as he'd explained the process of converting film into physical print. Eddie had been very aware of the man's tone, his choice of words and the delivery of his talk. She'd heard him swallowing during pauses as he'd searched for the right descriptions to use. It had been a life changing evening for differing reasons. When the lights came back on the group had shuffled in a line towards the exit, thanking the speaker as they left, as if he was the vicar at a church door. Eddie had rehearsed a quick, neat 'thank you' but as she'd drawn level with him, she'd tripped and Rex, tall and solid, had put a hand out to steady her. Thanking him awkwardly she'd hurried out to catch up with her friends, but not before she'd glanced back and caught his eye. He'd been so much older than her, with a 70s beard and flares - the height of sophistication at the time. She really hadn't stood a chance once their eyes had locked. Cupid had shot an arrow and she'd been hit. But she hadn't known then that she was just the latest in Rex's growing line of admirers.

The ground became softer as they cut across the corner of a rapeseed field. The cheerful yellow stretched in the distance filling acres of farmland, but today it didn't make Eddie smile. She looked ahead to see how the rest of the group was faring.

"Are you sure this is right?" The Colonel turned a full 360 degrees to take in the sea in one direction, flat fields and woodland in the other.

"The sat nav seems to think so," Eddie said quietly, hoping the Colonel would stop shouting. It was probably good to be loud in the theatre of war, but not when talking at close distance. "I'm sure he knows what he's doing."

"I wouldn't bet on it," he shouted.

Mike glanced back over his shoulder. "I can hear you, you know? You're very loud."

Eddie pulled a face and waved the Colonel on. Jack languished behind, staring at his phone as he typed with two thumbs.

"Jack! Keep up, love. We don't want to lose Mike."

Putting his phone in his back pocket, Jack jogged towards them.

"Actually," he whispered, "we could find a nice pub, have a roast dinner."

"Pub! You can't do that on your Duke of Edinburgh, son. You'll have to carry everything you need, live on your wits-"

"It's a two-day hike, not a trek into Patagonia," Jack laughed.

"Well, the principle's the same. The Army teaches you to be prepared."

"Isn't that the Scouts?"

The Colonel's eyebrows knitted together. "Well, whoever it is, it's a good motto to live by."

Jack nodded towards their leader and tutted in disbelief. Mike was jumping up and down, trying to see over a hedge. Each time he landed, his backpack rose up and hit the back of his head. Eddie shook her head in exasperation, why didn't he just walk the extra ten feet to where there was a gap in the hedge?

"Do you think he was ever a Scout?" Jack whispered.

The Colonel looked appalled. "Dear God, I hope not," he growled, "even the Scouts wouldn't have been prepared for that!"

The Colonel was keeping an eye on Mike. The directions didn't seem right to him, heading inland towards the woods when they really needed to stay on the coast path. This was turning into a nightmare. As they stopped for a breather, he surreptitiously swallowed two painkillers. He tried to be quick, but not quick enough. Jack spotted him smuggling them back in his bag and the Colonel shook a warning. He didn't want a fuss in front of everyone and anyway, Mike was waiting at a stile for them to catch up. As they approached, Mike coughed to get their attention. "Here's one for you," he chewed his bottom lip. "What do you call-"

Jack groaned, interrupting, so Mike started again. "What do you call a soldier who's survived mustard gas and pepper spray?"

The Colonel exhaled, looking up to the sky. "Good Lord, Mike, is this one of your stupid jokes?"

Mike nodded and waved his hand, encouraging them to answer.

"I don't know, Mike. What do you call a soldier who's survived mustard gas and pepper spray?"

"A seasoned veteran." Mike laughed out loud and looked eagerly at their faces. Eddie smiled weakly. "I thought that was a good one," he said huffily but when no one spoke he pointed to the stile. "Colonel, will you bring up the rear?" Without waiting for a response Mike climbed over and led from the front. The Colonel held out an arm to help Eddie over. He steadied her as she wobbled on the third step, then she landed on the other side with a thump. Jack followed, hopping over the rickety steps in two bounds, then turned.

"You alright, grandad?"

"Fine, thanks. You two carry on." The Colonel paused on the top step and shooed them away. He wanted some privacy. Taking a deep breath he swung his right leg over, shifting uncomfortably as pain flared. The pills needed to kick in soon and gingerly he stepped back onto terra firma. He paused to give his hip a good, hard rub and closed his eyes, massaging as the heat from his hand provided some respite.

When he opened his eyes again there was already a considerable gap between him and Eddie and Jack. They were oblivious to his pain and, gritting his teeth, he swung his stick and carried on.

Up front, Jack was explaining to Eddie that he'd started training for the Duke of Edinburgh with his college the previous year. When he'd been laid low with glandular fever he'd missed the training, and fundraising, and had almost given up. He smiled. The college had subsequently announced another event this September, and that was why he'd been prompted to start training again.

"Grandad thought he'd help." He rolled his eyes, shoulders hunched. "He *made* me put the advert in the shop."

Eddie wondered if he was enjoying the day. He didn't seem quite the sullen teenager he'd been that morning, but it couldn't be much fun being out with oldies for a whole day.

"My husband and I used to hike a lot," she said. "In fact, I've got all sorts of camping equipment you could have." She had a garage full of stuff and none of it had seen the light of day for several years. It might be just the thing for a beginner. She was hardly going to be using it.

"Didn't he fancy it today?"

It took Eddie a moment to realize he was talking about Rex. Hadn't she mentioned she was a widow? "Oh, he died. Two years ago now." Glancing across she saw Jack blush bright pink and turn away. He rubbed at his shoulder, and she felt a surge of sympathy for him and his teenage awkwardness.

"Sorry," he mumbled into the ground.

"It's fine, Jack. It's nice to talk about him." And it *was*. She rarely did. Most people skirted around the subject altogether, assuming it was easier for her if they avoided it. The trouble was she'd been with him for such a huge chunk of her life that by *not* talking about him she didn't talk about the majority of her life so far. Maybe she needed to talk.

Perhaps she should see a therapist, someone neutral to talk through her issues. Goodness knew she had plenty; the guilt of stealing him from his first wife for starters, and her anger at what he'd done after.

"You okay?"

Jack's voice brought her back to the present.

"You went all…" he flapped his hands in front of his face to indicate she'd zoned out.

"Sorry, just thinking," she shook her head. She didn't want to think about Rex just now. These were her new friends, and these walks were for her. "Anyway, the camping stuff. You'd be welcome to have a look."

"Um, maybe."

She chuckled at his reticence. "It's all fairly new," she added. "I think you'd be pleasantly surprised."

He nodded, glancing at her through his eyelashes. He was a good-looking lad, nice olive skin albeit his floppy hair could do with a cut. It would stop the nervous habit he had, of pushing it off his face.

"I'm enjoying today," she said, "it's been a long time since I was out and about." She sighed deeply. "I needed to get out, meet people, make some friends." She heard him snort and looked over to see him smiling.

"And you found me, grandad and Mike! Bad luck."

"Umm, when you put it like that…"

He swiped playfully at her arm.

"Talking of which, where is your grandad?" Eddie looked behind, lifting her hand to shield her eyes from the sun. Jack stopped and squinted.

"I thought he was behind us. I'd better go and check." He jogged back to where the path bent around the corner, then turned and signalled.

"Panic over, he's coming… slowly."

Chapter Six

TWO HOURS later the Wanderers were exhausted, cold and hungry. "Hansel had the right idea," Jack muttered to no one in particular, "… or was it Gretel?

"What are you talking about?" Eddie squinted over at him, the shadows in the wood making it difficult to see.

"A trail of breadcrumbs. Be more effective than that old gadget we're following," He tilted his head towards Mike, as Eddie caught up. Only half listening, she realised she was still wearing her sunglasses and swapped them for her spectacles.

"Oh, for Christ's sake!" Ahead, Mike bashed the gadget against his leg. "Ow. Now I've got no bloody signal."

The Colonel stopped. He wiggled slowly from side to side.

"D'you need more painkillers?"

He nodded once and pulled a blister pack from his pocket. Taking a swig of water, he gulped two down.

"Bad back?" Eddie could sympathize. She'd had sciatica once and it had floored her for weeks.

"Hip op." He wiped his mouth. "Last month. Still recovering." He rolled his eyes, disappointed by his slow recovery.

"Last month! Goodness, Colonel, should you even be out?" Eddie pointed to a fallen tree trunk and motioned for him to sit.

"Don't fuss, old girl," he paused. "Sorry." He held his hands up. "Apologising again. I don't mean to be rude."

She waved away his apology, understandable if he was in pain. Then something clicked in her head. Was that why he'd been so grumpy on the phone?

"Anyway," he interrupted her thoughts. "Please don't call me Colonel. My name is Bristol - Tolly to my friends."

She was flattered that he considered her a friend. She was about to comment on his unusual name, when Mike appeared beside her and thrust the gadget in her face.

"I'll go back, get a signal. I won't be long." Without waiting for an answer, he hopped over a clump of ferns and jogged back the way they'd just come.

"He's an idiot," the Colonel growled. "I knew this was a mistake, putting him in charge."

Eddie shivered and looked around them. The temperature was definitely starting to drop. "I'm getting chilly. Let's make a hot drink and warm up, while we wait."

Tolly produced three bin bags from his rucksack. With a pair of woolly socks on top, it made a comfy seat on the tree trunk. He eased himself down onto the softest one while Eddie and Jack set about getting the tiny stove to work. Before long they each had a mug of hot sweet tea and were huddling together on the makeshift seat.

"Perfect," Eddie whispered, taking a sip. "Egg sandwich?" She offered round a foil packet. "Help yourselves, I made loads" and they sat silently eating and drinking.

"Are you warming up?"

She nodded, touched that he was interested in her welfare when he was the one who'd had an operation. He pulled another bin liner from his bag and ripped it down its side before opening it out. He wrapped it round her shoulders and tied the two ends under her chin.

"Ha." Jack's mouth was full of egg sandwich. "The new superhero."

"Not quite London Fashion Week, but it'll warm you up." Tolly smiled and held her gaze. A warm glow did indeed flow through her body, but whether it was the cape or something else, she wasn't sure.

"Well, what do we look like?" Her voice sounded unnatural, and she glanced away. "Me in a bin bag, you with your poorly hip and Jack... well, you're fine." She looked him over. "But Mike, that's another story."

"If he's got lost we could be here for hours." Jack's wide eyes surveyed the darkening woods. "At the mercy of the elements, prey to hungry animals that stalk the forest by night-"

"We'll be fine Jack." Eddie patted his knee and handed over the foil packet. "We've got enough sandwiches to last us for days. But we'll be tucked up in our beds before dark. Besides, I promised to report back to Amir."

Jack paused chewing and raised an eyebrow.

"The young man who works in the 7-11."

"Oh, him. He didn't say a lot."

Jack resumed his attack on the egg sandwich and Eddie watched him quietly. They'd probably have a bit in common if they were introduced properly.

"He's done the Duke of Edinburgh."

They both turned in surprise.

"Really?" Tolly held his mug suspended, impressed.

Eddie nodded. "Uh-huh. Couple of times actually. He's keen to come out when he's got time."

"Good for him." Tolly slurped his tea, holding the mug between both hands. "You'll have to give him a glowing report. We could become a band of five, the start of something big." He held his mug out and Eddie reached to clink it. Despite being lost, in the middle of nowhere, she realised she'd be sad if they didn't do this again.

After draining his mug Tolly stood and swayed his hips from left to right several times. He did a full circle, hula hooping with an invisible ring, then stretched up. He fished the tin of mints from his pocket and offered them round, waiting patiently while Eddie took one. Jack declined.

"Right, I might just go and have a look round." Tolly tapped the side of his nose. "Reconnaissance."

Eddie stood too, but he backed towards the surrounding bracken.

"I just need to… I won't go far."

Eddie shook her head, sucking the sweet. "I think we should stay -"

"Eddie," whispered Jack. "Grandad needs to go into the woods."

"Yes, but I think-"

"Eddie. Grandad needs a wee."

Her eyes widened as her cheeks flushed. "Sorry. Why didn't you say?"

"I was trying to be polite," Tolly whispered, rubbing the back of his neck awkwardly. For a few seconds, they held each other's gaze. Then Jack coughed noisily and thumped his chest.

"Sorry, swallowed a bug." He cleared his throat several times, coughing loudly before finally announcing that it had gone. He looked rather disgusted, so Eddie pointed out that it was extra protein in his diet.

"If you get lost in the wilds on your Duke of Edinburgh you might have to eat bugs and forage."

But the look on Jack's face suggested he'd rather die from starvation than do that. He hopped up to follow his grandad.

"I need to go too. What?" He returned his grandad's glare. "She didn't understand when you were subtle," he said, waving his hand at

Eddie as they started to walk away. He stopped when he saw that Eddie was following.

"I need to go too. Don't panic, Jack, I'll go the other way," she laughed. "See you back here in five?"

Chapter Seven

"TWENTY GREEN bottles, hanging on the wall…" Eddie hopped off the path and brushed aside the ferns, searching for a suitable place. She saw a nice dense clump of ferns. *Perfect*! "There'd be nineteen green bottles hanging on the wall. Nineteen green bottles…" She squatted among the greenery and continued to hum the next verse. Finally, zipping up her trousers, she stood and belted out another verse with gusto. "Sixteen greeeen," she extended the vowels operatically and flung out a hand as if on stage.

"Oi, you."

She caught her breath. Who was that?

"Can you be quiet?" A man's voice was coming from somewhere nearby, and his west-country twang didn't sound happy. Eddie crouched down.

"Who's there?" Her heart hammered against her chest. "Can you see me?"

"No, but we can blinkin' hear you."

Crikey, he sounded angry.

"We were wondering whether you could *kindly*," he lingered sarcastically, "keep it down?"

She crept around, peering through the trees. "Where are you?"

"Over 'ere."

Hold on. Even with her old glasses, one clump of vegetation didn't look quite right. The colours weren't as bright. As she crept towards it a door creaked open and a man stepped out. She shrieked.

"Shusssshhh." He put his finger to his lips and beckoned her over. Well, he put a finger to where she thought his lips would be if they weren't covered in an enormous grey, wiry beard. With his huge growth of whiskers rising up, and his bushy, overgrown hair encroaching on his face, she could just make out his eyes. They flicked from side to side as they scanned the vicinity.

"Who are you?"

"Shusssshhhh."

As she walked closer, she saw it wasn't a bush at all. He had, in fact, climbed down from a large shed. It was covered in camouflaged netting which hid it from the outside world. Eddie had to admit, it was extremely effective. She would never have noticed the structure in a million years and, climbing three steep wooden steps, she followed him in.

"Well, I never."

It opened out into a garden shed, only much, much bigger. Benches ran along two sides and large plate glass windows above gave uninterrupted views out to the woods. "This place is practically invisible."

"That's why they call it a hide," he said, barely concealing a smirk. She wasn't warming to him at all.

"Oh, I've seen them on Springwatch." She nodded to each of the other bird watchers sitting inside. One, two… five, plus Grumpy pants. Two were women and all of them wore an array of dark, outdoor gear. They seemed very polite… and quiet.

"Nice to meet you," she whispered. "Are you bird watching?"

"Trying to. When they're not being scared away by noisy hikers." Grumpy raised his binoculars and looked into the distance.

"Sorry." She tried again. "If I'd known you were here…" she trailed off and he nodded. He seemed to accept her apology and motioned for her to sit on the bench.

"I love bird watching." She took his seat while he remained standing. "I leave mealworm and peanuts out on my bird table-"

"Sshush."

She stopped and bit her lip. They stared through their binoculars, all trained in the same direction.

"Er ... what are you watching?"

With a sigh, Grumpy handed his over and waited while she turned them the right way round. She glanced at him and smiled, noting how much his beard looked like a bird's nest.

"See the tallest spruce?"

She nodded.

"At the base, there's a pool of water?"

She fiddled with the focus and honed in on a large puddle.

"See the bird drinking from it?"

"Oh yes. Gosh, he's well hidden."

"It's a red spot-chested goose."

Eddie laughed excitedly. "A red spot-chested goose! I've never heard of it."

No longer quite so Grumpy, the man was getting animated. She could see him hopping from foot to foot in her peripheral vision, her attention remaining on the bird. Unfolding from its seated position it stood up, shaking out its wings. She gasped. Its chest was indeed a startling shade of red, with distinctive white circles. Mesmerized, she stared unblinking through the glasses as it bent over to take a long, slow slurp of water.

"It's rare," Grumpy whispered. "Normally lives in North America, but this one flew in from Canada last week."

"Wow, that's a long way-"

"It went to Ireland first, then Wales." His Adam's apple bobbed beneath his whiskers as he gulped. "We got the tip-off that it was here."

She handed the binoculars back. "Fantastic."

"It really is!"

They all lowered their binoculars and turned, nodding in unison. They returned to the bird and the hide fell quiet. She heard a gentle rustling of the trees outside and wondered how long she had to stay before she could politely take her leave. In the distance there was a loud shout. It broke the silence. She cocked her ear. Were people calling?

"Eddie, where are you?"

Oh no. Tolly. She held her breath, willing him to go away.

"Eddie!" He was getting louder. "Are you okay?"

Grumpy narrowed his eyes at her. "You Eddie?"

She pulled her mouth. "Sorry." All faces swiveled towards her, as she tried to curl her toes in her tight boots. "I'd better go." She pointed to the door as Grumpy nodded, his beard hitting his chest as he did so.

"Lovely to meet you all. Hope you have a good day."

The Colonel's voice echoed outside. She needed to move.

"I'll see myself out."

"Quickly," hissed Grumpy, "they're goin' to scare her away."

"Sorry." She moved to the door and pulled it open. "We'll be quiet -" She caught her foot on the lip of the doorway and slid down the steps. "Aargh." Her scream reverberated around the trees, and she landed on the ground in a heap.

"Eddie? Where the heck are you, old girl?"

She lay on the floor, looking at the sky as she did a rapid scan of her body. She wiggled her arms, then legs. She jumped up. She was alright. A movement in the undergrowth made her turn as a loud commotion came from the direction of the pond. Something was stirring. The sound of flapping caught her attention, the whoosh of wind. Coming straight towards her was a huge object, travelling very quickly. Instinctively she ducked. The air vibrated as, whatever it was, narrowly avoided smacking into her. Once it had passed, she looked up to see a large bird soaring away; its distinctive red chest, with white spots, flew up into a grey sky. She paused, then began to back away from the hide.

"Bloody brilliant!" Grumpy's voice boomed out from above, his feet stomping on the wooden boards of the hut. Scared that he was about to come out and throttle her, she moved more quickly.

"Fan-bloody-tastic," he wailed. "Five days sitting here with you lot, and your burping and farting. And what do I get?"

Not waiting to hear the answer, Eddie crouched low and, keeping to the bracken, she ran back to find her companions.

Jack and his grandad could not stop laughing. Big fat tears of merriment rolled down their cheeks and Tolly dabbed his eyes with a starched white handkerchief. Eddie shushed them, motioning to keep quiet. She worried that Grumpy was lurking somewhere in the bushes, out for revenge, and she didn't want to give away their location.

"It was so camouflaged I had no idea it was there." She patted the top of her chest to calm herself, suppressing a chuckle. "Bit weird when you think about it. Anyone could use it to spy on people. He didn't need face paint. Between his hair and his beard, you could only just see his eyes."

"Hey," Jack suddenly looked serious. "Do you think they were watching when we went to take a leak?" He shuddered but Eddie waved away his concern.

"Trust me, Jack, they only had eyes for that poor bird."

Tolly chortled again, deep and sonorous from within his chest. "Well, they must be pretty annoyed. Five days in that hide wouldn't have been much fun. Then you come along, crashing their party-"

"-You two were the noisy ones," she argued, taking a deep breath.

Her stomach was aching from laughing so much. "I wonder where the poor bird is now?"

"In Grumpy's back garden, pilfering nuts from his feeder." Tolly's mouth twisted into a crooked smile.

"Sunbathing on his patio, enjoying some privacy," Jack joined in and Eddie flapped her hand, begging them to stop.

"I'm riddled with guilt as it is." She dabbed her eyes with a tissue and tried to collect herself. "I haven't laughed like that for ages." She blew her nose as both of them watched. "Well, I haven't," she said, a touch defensively. She fiddled with the zip on her trouser pocket. "Since retiring my life's been a bit…" she faded away, but Tolly touched her arm and nodded. "I understand. Work provides structure… friends too. What did you used to do?"

Eddie smiled and explained that she'd been a teacher. Whilst she'd enjoyed the work, it was the young people she was drawn to. She glanced at Jack. "Probably a similar age group to you. I miss seeing people and having a purpose." She bit her bottom lip; she was saying too much. "I just need to get into a routine, that's all. Losing Rex, and then retiring soon after, I've not been able to do that yet."

"Must have been a tough time for you, old thing." Tolly paused. "I remember when I lost Thea-"

"-Grandad! She's not dead!"

"I'm aware of that, Jack. Thank you. I know it's not exactly the same, but when you've had years with someone and then, for whatever reason," he looked pointedly at his grandson, "they're no longer there, it's difficult. Habits built up over years have to change."

Eddie nodded. She wondered who Thea was, but now wasn't the right time to ask. Suddenly a rustling in the woods made them start. A loud voice rang out, shouting and unhappy. It had a broad American accent. "Move it!"

"I'm sorry," a timid voice replied.

"You need to pick up the pace," the American shouted. Mike lurched from the undergrowth, making them jump. He no longer wore his hat, and his cheeks were an alarming, bright red. Beads of sweat ran down his face, but as he spotted them his face flooded with relief.

"Mike," Tolly beckoned him. "Over here, old Bean."

Mike held the GoRamble out. "I don't know what I've done. It won't stop shouting at me."

Jack snatched it off him.

"Come on!"

It wasn't getting any more polite and Eddie tutted.

"Just switch the thing off," she said, annoyed that it had interrupted their chat. Mike glanced nervously at it.

"I don't know how to." He gnawed at his thumb. His pupils were so far dilated that both eyes looked black as they stared out from his vivid pink cheeks.

"Just put it in a pocket for now." Tolly motioned at Jack to shove it in Mike's backpack. "The post office will love you when you return it next week."

"I went miles, needed a signal." Offering no resistance Mike stood meekly while his backpack was zipped back up. "It kept shouting, like Raging Bull. Rain coming, clouds in the distance." He prattled on, flitting quickly between subjects. Eddie held her hand to his forehead. Was he delirious? He was extremely hot.

"Have you eaten anything?"

He shook his head. "Past red flags. No other people. No time to eat."

She exchanged a concerned look with the Colonel. "Maybe you should have a sandwich, Mike? Keep your energy levels up?" She fished out the remaining sandwiches and handed one over. He wolfed it down, hardly chewing, so she handed over the packet. He inhaled another.

"Blimey Mike, you *are* hungry."

He nodded and sank to the floor, clutching a third one. Eddie handed him a cup of water to wash it down.

"Here you go, old Bean. This'll perk you up." Tolly broke off a square of his cherished Kendal mint cake and handed it over. Mike stared, as if unsure what to do with it, so Tolly nodded, as if to a small child. He gestured for it to go in his mouth and when Mike did as instructed Tolly squeezed his shoulder.

"That's it, old Bean. You'll soon be right as rain."

Eddie watched the exchange, oddly touched. She was just starting to relax when a rumble of thunder sounded in the distance and, catching Tolly's eye again, she motioned for them to get moving.

"Not to hurry you Mike, but I think we need to get going. Rain's coming." They coaxed him to standing.

"Right troops," Tolly shouted with authority, "let's move out. Double time. Quick march." Falling in line, Eddie was grateful she was with Tolly, someone trustworthy to share this burden with.

Chapter Eight

AS THEY marched on, Eddie relayed her adventures to Mike. He chuckled quietly as he heard about Grumpy and the goose. By the end of her story he'd perked up considerably. She thanked her lucky stars for the recuperative powers of egg sandwiches. It didn't take long before his face returned to a normal colour, then he spoke for the first time since rejoining them.

"My mother wanted my father to join the Army, but he joined the Navy out of spite." He glanced at Eddie and raised his eyebrows. What was he talking about?

"He was a Petty Officer," he grinned. "Do you get it? *Petty* officer? Spite?" He waited for her response.

"Oh! Very good, Mike." Yep, he was nearly back to normal.

"I've got another."

Tolly rolled his eyes. "I wish you hadn't," but unfazed Mike continued.

"What do you call a military officer who knows everything about everything?" Silence, as they wracked their brains. Unable to contain himself Mike shouted out "General Knowledge" and earned himself a groan from each. As the path narrowed Tolly slowed and waved Mike ahead. He patted Mike's shoulder, and Mike seemed to stand taller. Eddie was watching. She'd been surprised by him several times today; a gesture here, a rallying nod there, despite the pain he was in himself. Approaching a fork in the path her heart sank as Mike pulled the gadget from his backpack. "We *have* to use it," he apologised, "otherwise we've no idea where we are." He pressed a button and the screen lit up.

"Programming…"

He stared as a map loaded. Maybe it would be okay.

"ACHTUNG!"

Eddie jumped out of her skin, the shock making her giggle.

"Jesus." Jack clutched her arm in surprise.

"Valk ahead for precisely zweihundert metre."

"German?" Tolly flustered. "What precisely-"

"SCHNELL!"

Mike did a comical half-skip-run and waved at them to follow.

"EIN, ZWEI, DREI, VIER…"

"This is intolerable!" Tolly whacked his stick against a woody frond of bracken causing thousands of spores to rise up in a cloud. Coughing uncontrollably, he leant on his stick as he searched for his handkerchief.

"Save your breath for walking, grandad. I've a feeling you're gonna need it." Jack bounded after Mike, leaving Eddie to help the older man.

Thirty minutes later Eddie was boiling. Her whole body was sweating – could eyelids sweat? Because it certainly felt like it. Her hair was stuck to the back of her neck, and she wiped it. What on earth must she look like? She realised she didn't care and pushed the thought aside. The surge in activity was making her legs complain. Later she'd treat herself to a nice long bath. There'd be plenty of time for a rest - but, for now, she felt alive. She had entertaining company and was in the great outdoors. She glanced over at Tolly.

"I'm *still* enjoying today," she said defiantly as he swung his stick backwards and forwards.

"What? Despite Mike making it a blasted nightmare?"

"Even with Mike and that annoying machine," she chuckled. "Fresh air, new people, lovely views. It's been a tonic."

"Yes, it has." Tolly looked across. "You're right. Actually, I feel I've been rather rude at times. This ruddy hip operation knocked me for six. I've been feeling… well, *old*." A nervous smile flicked across his face. His grey eyes held hers before casting back to the path in front. Eddie noticed he was leaning more heavily on his stick when putting weight on his right leg. "I just don't like being dependent on my family - even though they're very good to me. I don't think I've even thanked them."

"Well, it's never too late," she suggested. "You could buy them some flowers, or a present."

"Yes, I might do that," he frowned. "Yes, I should."

"So, I meant to ask you," she said as they continued side by side. "Where does your name come from? After the city?"

He shook his head and smiled. "After a car - the Bristol 400."

"Oh, how unusual."

He nodded. "My parents were car fanatics. They had four children so I've got a brother, Morris-"

"Minor?"

He nodded, impressed by her car knowledge. "And Sunny…"

"I doubt it's after the Nissan Sunny?" They both laughed.

"No, a Sunbeam Alpine. They had one when they got married." Seeing the blank look on her face he added, "it's a two-seater. A very beautiful machine, I'll have to show you a picture. Then they had me, Bristol." He paused and took a deep breath. "And then my sister. Netty." There was a twinkle in his eye and for a moment Eddie wondered if he was having her on. "By the time she came along they'd saved and added a Hudson Hornet Hollywood to their collection."

"No!" She took a sharp intake of breath. "She's called Hornet?" She laughed as he nodded slowly. Fancy being called that!

"She rather likes it now. Even carries a photo of it in her handbag. An icebreaker at parties," he chuckled softly. "Now that was a real beauty. It would probably be worth a fortune today." A wistful look came over his face and he explained that when his father died, they'd discovered the family business had been left in a mess. It had debts and a remortgage that his mother knew nothing about. "She had to sell the family home and the car collection was auctioned," he paused, breathing slowly. "It wasn't so bad. She bought a nice cottage, midway between Morris and me. She wasn't exactly destitute. It was more the memories that went along with the cars." Eddie thought about her parents and the happy memories she carried of them. They'd not had two pennies to rub together but they had always been there, a solid family unit. Her face fell as an image of Rex popped to mind, unbidden. Would Heather's memories be as pleasant? She doubted it. Heather had left for university as soon as she could, and she'd not really been back since.

As they approached the bend, they found Jack and Mike waiting for them.

"There are more red flags up there." Mike pointed along the footpath and jogged forwards, "I'll have a quick look."

"It surely can't be far," Eddie asked as Tolly passed around the last of his Kendal Mint cake. Before anyone could respond, a loud crack of thunder reverberated around the trees. Mike had stopped in the middle of the path, holding up the gadget. As they waited Eddie noticed their surroundings. The forest was petering out. Were they finally reaching the edge? Instead of the expected farmers' fields, however, the woodland path had turned sandy. A tall dune rose in front of them and turning three hundred- and sixty-degrees Eddie looked around.

"Do you know where we are?"

Mike shook his head as a spinning disk appeared on the screen.

"Come on Mike, let's have a look." Jack held his hand out impatiently. He raised his eyes to the sky, tapping his foot. Mike just clutched the machine closer to his chest and stared back at the teenager.

"Give it. Don't be so annoying… I'm supposed to be out later."

Eddie glanced over at him. That explained why he seemed so impatient to get on.

"Just hang on a minute, it's still spinning," Mike cradled the GoRamble protectively, keeping a wary eye on the teenager.

Eddie tried to make conversation. "Where are you going, Jack?"

With his head still tilted up Jack closed his eyes and paused. "Nowhere," he mumbled defensively. Tolly caught Eddie's eye and shrugged.

"Come on. This is taking too long." Jack stamped his foot. On impulse he lunged for the machine and, taking Mike with him, they fell to the floor wrestling. They rolled around, sand sticking to their clothes as neither of them showed any sign of giving in.

"Stop it," Tolly shouted, trying to prise them apart. "This is disgraceful behaviour."

With a grunt Jack pinned Mike down and sat on top of him. Eddie was reminded of Saturday afternoon wrestling on TV and was tempted to chant 'Easy! Easy!' Jack ripped the gadget from Mike's hands and triumphantly stood, waving it in the air. After a short run up, he threw it high into the air. Stunned, they watched as it flew over the clearing and disappeared down the other side of the dune. Eddie's mouth dropped - Jack had an amazing bowling technique. If he didn't already play cricket, he should consider taking it up. Mike scrambled over to him, and the two men glared at each other, breathing heavily.

"That bloody machine, it's… it's…" Jack was so incensed he couldn't string words together as Mike stamped his foot and glowered back. Like watching two stags during rutting season Eddie couldn't tear her eyes away, worried that Mike was about to launch at Jack's jugular.

"Tell you what-" but she couldn't finish the sentence before a second loud rumble of thunder ripped through the woods. "Forget it, we need to get going."

"What about my GPS?"

"Well, old Bean, if you're quick you could run and get it. It can't have gone far." Tolly looked into the distance. "In fact," he frowned, "why *are* there sand dunes in a wood?"

Deep, pitted tracks ran along the ground but before Eddie could point them out the sound of revving vehicles caught their attention.

"Was that a tractor?" Jack turned, his eyes wide. "If there's a farm, they could give us a lift."

"I'll have a look while I get my gadget," Mike mumbled, slouching off towards the dune. He was a man drained of energy and, as Eddie watched him go, a knot of tension bloomed in her stomach. "Be careful Mike."

Jack touched her arm. "I'll follow him, I feel really bad now. I just want to get home."

Eddie paused, wondering why he suddenly seemed in a rush. Even if he did have a date, they still needed to look after each other while they were out here. She watched him go then mustered what little energy she had as she prepared to follow.

The dune was taller than she'd first thought, the sand made it hard going. Hundreds of tiny grains came over the top of her hiking socks and rubbed the back of her heels as she crawled three steps up only to sink back two. Tolly was quicker. He powered ahead despite the odd rub of his hip. He was soon halfway up behind Jack, with Mike about to summit, so she gritted her teeth and pressed on. From above a cheer rang out. Lifting her head, she saw Mike's feet disappear over the top. Seconds later a huge boooom rang out around the trees and she screamed, as the ground shook beneath her feet.

"Good God! Everyone down!"

A murder of crows rose squawking in the air. Tolly scrambled towards her and, reaching for her hand, he pulled her next to him. "If I'm not mistaken, that's a bloody Challenger Two," he gasped.

"A what?"

"British tank, in use since 1998."

"A tank!"

But he was already crawling upwards, tugging her to follow.

They reached Jack at the top and peered down into the clearing. Two monstrous tanks faced each other, their turrets inches apart. Mike lay on the ground between, curled in the foetal position with a thumb jammed firmly in his mouth. He babbled incoherently; his eyes squeezed shut.

"Stay here, you two." Without waiting for a response Tolly started an awkward descent, bumping and sliding uncomfortably down the dune as he moved straight into the eye of danger. Below, the hatches on both tanks flew open and two people in Army fatigues clambered out. A tall man, in his mid-fifties, marched towards the other. Eddie's mouth formed a surprised 'O' as the second person, a petite, young woman, emerged. Slim and neat, her dark brown hair was wound in a tight bun at the back of her head. Oblivious to their audience, or the man staggering down the slope towards them, they halted opposite each other.

"Bloody hell Cartwright," the man spoke, "why did you stop so suddenly?" He talked in the plummy tones of an English Army officer and Tolly paused, a dreamy expression on his face. Was he recalling happy memories of the Officers' Mess? Eddie certainly thought so and smiled.

"I stopped because I'd shot you. That means 'Game Over'. I win!" The woman stood to attention and saluted. "Sir," she added, suddenly remembering to whom she was speaking.

"You did *not* shoot me - I shot you!" The man responded swiftly to the salute then added, "at ease, Major." They both relaxed.

"With respect… Sir," she made to salute again but her superior officer waved it away with an air of annoyance. "You most definitely did *not* shoot me. I was obviously victorious."

Eddie choked back a giggle. She held her breath as she watched the woman stand up for herself.

"Not so!"

"Yes, so! I mean I did win."

"Ha, this is classic *you*. Just like at Sandhurst. So defensive."

Tolly reached the bottom of the sand dune and marched towards them, swinging his stick in an authoritative manner. "Sorry to interrupt," he shouted. "You're obviously busy and I wouldn't normally intrude between two warring officers of the King's British Army…"

Disturbed from their argument, the two soldiers turned and stood to attention. Tolly saluted and they immediately reciprocated.

"Sorry old fellow. I didn't see you there." The man spoke first.

Tolly nodded, apology accepted. "Did you see *him*?" He pointed to Mike's quivering body between the two tanks.

"Good gracious, no. I thought it was a bush-"

"Yes, me too-"

"-At least we agree on something," the male officer said pointedly to his companion.

"Oh, he *will* be pleased! Mike, your camouflage had them fooled."

Mike whimpered but didn't move from his curled position.

"But what's he doing down there? Didn't you see the flags?"

"Ah!" Tolly turned as Eddie and Jack approached. "Mike mentioned flags, didn't he?"

They nodded at the two officers.

"I said 'flags.'" A quiet voice gibbered from the ground. Mike's eyes were open now and colour was returning to his cheeks.

"Don't you realize this is M.O.D. property?" The male officer peered at Tolly. "You shouldn't be out here when we're on manoeuvres."

Suddenly the woman jabbed his finger towards her compatriot. "What do you mean, 'this is just like at Sandhurst'?"

"Well," the man turned to her. "You did have a bit of a reputation."

"For what?" Her eyes narrowed and she straightened up to her full height, looking the officer straight in the nipples. "What sort of reputation?"

"For being a stickler-"

"-a stickler? I play by the rules, if that's what you mean?"

The other officer seemed to be thinking of an appropriate response.

"What?" She barked, edging towards him as they both ignored the intruders.

Seeing their opportunity Tolly hauled Mike to his feet. "Eddie," he whispered, "I suggest we get away."

"But this is interesting. I agree with her, rules are there for a reason-"

"It might be interesting now," he hissed, "but it won't be interesting when they arrest us and throw us in prison for trespass."

That got her attention. "Can they do that?"

He nodded emphatically.

"Fine. Let's go," she whispered and slowly they inched backwards.

"So, you're saying I should just agree that you won?"

"Yes, I think so -"

"But that's absurd."

Unnoticed by the two Army officers the Wanderers turned and ran. Slipping round the side of the dune they ducked out of sight and didn't stop running until they reached the edge of the wood.

Chapter Nine

"So, we ran away while they were arguing." Eddie put the last of the shopping in her bag and looked up to see Amir watching, his mouth hanging open.

"No way!" Lifting a box of crisps onto the counter, he paused. "I wish I'd been there, sounds amazing." He sliced through the sellotaped box with his penknife. He was obviously busy and here she was nattering. She drained the last of the tea and pushed her mug over the counter.

"I'd better leave you to it. You look like you've got enough to do."

He carried the box over to the shelves and put it on the floor, crouching to unload the packets on the shelf.

"I'll let you know when we're going again, you should come."

"Yeah maybe."

"Don't sound too keen," she teased, and he glanced over. He stood up, still clutching crisp packets in both hands.

"Sorry. It's just I don't have much free time that's all… I'm either here working, or at Uni."

Her eyebrows shot up. She had no idea he was a student. "What are you studying?"

"Maths," his voice was monotone. He wasn't exactly jumping for joy about his choice of studies.

"How long will you be doing that for?"

"Too long Eddie, and that's the truth."

She remained silent, a useful habit she'd picked up as a teacher.

Everyone loved to fill a vacuum, so if you kept quiet the other person felt obliged to continue. As he put the crisps on the shelf he turned back.

"What are you, the Student Police?" Once again, her trick was about to work. "I'm in my second year, so two more to go, if I want a Masters."

"And do you?"

"God, Eddie," he picked at the hem of his t-shirt. "I dunno."

She left her bags and walked over to him. "You alright, Amir?"

He nodded but his face didn't agree.

"Want me to make you a cup of tea?" She waited and to her relief, she noticed a corner of his mouth twitch into a smile.

"I'm alright, honest. I'm just… fed up." The words seemed to take him aback. Hearing your thoughts verbalised could do that. "I don't really get on with anyone. I'm stuck in limbo, working here, so I can't go out partying and even if I could, I'm so much older-"

She chuckled.

"I *am*! I'm twenty-seven-"

"You're not *that* much older. I spent the day on Saturday with Jack-"

"-And others."

"Yes, and others. But we all had fun." Had Jack enjoyed the day as much as she had? He'd been talking nonstop by the end of it. She wondered if he'd tell his mates about it today. "Anyway," she continued, "if you had the choice, what would you do?"

"I'd be an oligarch wouldn't I, sitting on a yacht off St Tropez."

She rolled her eyes and tutted. "Be serious. What would you like to do?"

He glanced over at the door.

"No one's coming, just say it."

"You'll laugh." He rubbed the back of his neck then folded his arms across his chest, forming a barrier.

"Why would I laugh?"

His tough façade fell away, and his shoulders slumped. "You know that outdoor shop, on the High Street?"

She nodded. She knew exactly where he meant. An independent camping shop, it sold a full range of equipment and clothing and had been there for years.

"I used to go there all the time. Great little place." She'd parted with a lot of money in that shop. Tents, camping stoves, sleeping bags – all from there. "My daughter, Heather, wouldn't have so many fillings if it wasn't for their Kendal Mint cake."

"I know, right. I used to spend all my Saturdays in there."

"Her too. You probably met each other."

He grinned, his whole face lighting up. "Well, I'd like to run something like that."

"What? A camping shop?"

"What's wrong with that?" He looked down and gave the crisp box a poke with his toe.

"But… you *do* know that was for sale last year?"

"Yeah," he mumbled, "I know."

"And no one bought it."

"I didn't have the money, I still don't have the money," he sucked at his teeth. "It just needs bringing up to date. A lick of paint, a change of stock, a website." He puffed his cheeks out. "Anyway, no use. My dad wouldn't allow it."

That had to be the saddest thing she'd ever heard. He sounded so defeated. Adamant that it couldn't be done, before he'd tried.

"Have you spoken to your dad?"

He turned back to the crisps and shook his head sadly. "Not really. It's not going to happen."

Eddie thought about Heather and her work. Was she happy? Because one thing was for sure, Amir wasn't.

"So," he went back to stocking the shelf. "When you out rambling next?"

Eddie recognized a change of subject when she saw one. "We did mention Saturday. But to be honest, it might take the others longer to recover." She pretended to jog towards the door then did a couple of lunges on each leg. "They're not all as fit as me, you know, Amir!" She was pleased to see a small smile return to his face. He was such a good-looking young man; it was a shame he didn't have more to be happy about.

"Hey!"

She stopped at the door and turned back.

"Tell that Jack, if he wants, I could help him with his map reading."

"That's really kind of you Amir, I'll pass it on."

Walking along the High Street Eddie glanced at her reflection in a shop window. Wearing jeans, a sweatshirt and trainers she'd been out walking every morning since the Wander and already felt better for it. She sneaked another look. She wasn't bad for sixty-five years old. She wasn't exactly in the latest fashions and her hair was in desperate need of a cut. Maybe she could get a colour on it, lighten it up. Maybe go blonde. She chuckled, perhaps just a few highlights to start with. Someone got up from a bench in the town's tiny square and she walked briskly over the cobbles to take their place. She closed her eyes and tilted her head towards the sun. It felt good, a moment of calm. Flickers of gold danced across her eyelids as she allowed herself to relax in the warmth.

"Alright for some, darling. Is that how you spend your days now you're retired?" A voice sounded close to Eddie's ear, and she opened her eyes. All she could see was a silhouette, but she'd recognize those gravelly tones anywhere.

"Hello Audrey. Long time no see. Sit down, sit down." Eddie shuffled along the bench and made room for her friend to join her. She was only tiny, thanks to her personal trainer and an aversion to bread, so slotted onto the bench easily.

"I was only talking to Jerry about you the other day."

"Oh?" Eddie was surprised that *anyone* talked about her.

"Don't worry." Audrey put a reassuring hand on her arm and squeezed. Her perfectly polished red nails contrasted against Eddie's grey sweatshirt. "I was just saying that I hadn't seen you for ages… now you're a lady of leisure. How's it going?"

"Oh, you know, takes a bit of getting used to." What a silly thing to say. Audrey wouldn't know. She'd not gone back to work following the birth of their first child. She now had three boys in their twenties who between them had already produced four grandchildren - all boys. She was always tied up with babysitting or childcare.

"So, what have you been up to?"

"Lots of gardening, bit of decorating. I've joined a rambler's group."

Audrey pulled a face. "Ugh, bit outdoorsy for me I'm afraid, but whatever floats your boat." She paused, "and Heather? All shopping trips and cocktails for you girls, eh?"

Eddie smiled, *if only.* Audrey gave a long sigh. "I envy you. I seem to be busier than ever, awash with nappies and formula milk. We hardly have a weekend to ourselves nowadays, the benefits of having family close by, I suppose." It sounded as if she was complaining, but her gooey smile belied that fact, and Eddie envied her old friend.

"How are the boys?"

"Boisterous, cheeky and smelly," she laughed, "and that's just *my* boys. The grandchildren are lovely, little munchkins all of them." She glanced over Eddie's shoulder and let out a loud sigh. "Oh god, darling. There's Jerry now." She patted her hair and hitched her handbag on her shoulder, as a black Jaguar slid into a parking bay across the road. A portly man looked out the window with narrowed eyes. Recognising Eddie, he blew a kiss. She waved and returned it; she'd always liked Jerry.

"Must dash darling, lovely to chat. Text me some dates and we'll arrange a proper catch up. Could go for lunch? Mwah." They air-kissed and Audrey was over the road and climbing in the Jaguar before Eddie could respond. She waved as they drove out of sight then settled back on the bench. She cast an eye around to see if anyone had been listening. It would be good to meet with Audrey. She'd been a good friend once and perhaps it wasn't too late to rekindle that friendship. She'd been the only one willing to break rank and tell Eddie the truth, that Rex had been spotted in a London restaurant when he'd supposedly been away on a photo shoot. Eddie remembered it clearly. Heather had been eight and she knew that because Rex had missed her eighth birthday party, arriving home late. The following week Audrey had shared the incriminating details. He'd been with a young woman, who'd been dressed in a figure-displaying black dress. Eddie excused him, suggesting that it had been a work colleague, but Audrey had described their lingering kiss before Rex had paid the bill and laughed with the waiter. Audrey had been supportive and offered a place to stay. She'd been horrified when Eddie had said she wasn't going to leave him. Now, Eddie wondered how many at the Golf club had turned a blind eye. How many knew of his wandering habit yet hadn't been as loyal as Audrey? She cringed inwardly and bit her lip, recalling their argument. She'd accused Audrey of being jealous of their marriage. What a joke. She felt quite nauseous thinking about it now. She'd apologized afterwards, sometime later, and they'd called a truce. But it hadn't been the same after. Their friendship was something else that Rex had ruined.

📷 Chapter Ten

THAT AFTERNOON Eddie was weeding her garden. She thought back to her conversation with Amir, and what he'd said about the camping shop and his father. She'd hate it if Heather couldn't talk to her if she was unhappy. She decided on a whim, to call her and unusually for Heather she picked up straight away.

"Hi Heather, it's mum here."

Heather sighed. "I know it's you, mum. Your name comes up on the screen, remember?"

"Sorry love, I forget." They'd been on the phone for two seconds and Heather was already exasperated. "How are you? How's everything in the big smoke?"

"Mum, I'm fine." She sounded tired as she told her about the deal she'd been working on all weekend. It was all part of this company takeover. Eddie didn't understand half of it, but she did notice that her daughter, whilst saying a lot of words didn't sound particularly excited by any of it. Then she spoke about the picture she'd painted for baby Mabel.

"Georgie reckons I could sell them, mum."

Eddie smiled into the phone. "Well, give it a go, love. You obviously still enjoy it." There was a pause on the line followed by a non-committal grunt. "Heather," she added quietly, "don't let what your dad said put you off."

"I wasn't thinking about that."

"It's *your* life, Heather. You've got to be happy." She heard her daughter sigh. It sounded as if she had the weight of the world on her shoulders. Bloody Rex. Bulldozing in and quashing her dreams.

I'm fine mum," Heather sniffed. "What have you been up to anyway?"

Eddie was happy to let that part of the conversation rest, as for once she had something else to say. She talked about the Wanderers and their ramble. Heather laughed when she got to the bit about Mike's gadget, Grumpy and the bird hide but went quiet when Eddie spoke about the tanks and running away.

"That could have ended badly, mum," she whispered. Eddie tried to put her mind at rest, explaining that the ammunition wasn't live.

"I'm not sure whether you're joking or not," Heather said, "it sounds unbelievable."

"I kid you not," Eddie chuckled. "It's absolutely true. You've never met a more mismatched group of people in your life. In fact," she said, "I'd love you to meet them."

"What? You're planning to see them again? They sound a right bunch of nutters." Heather had a point. But the trouble was, Eddie really hoped she *would* see them again.

"That reminds me, did you ever know anyone called Amir?"

"Nope, don't think so. Why?"

"Nice lad, he's about your age. Works in the local shop."

"Mum." Heather's voice held a warning and Eddie smiled down the phone.

"He's lovely. Well, when he's not being sullen."

"Great."

"He's clever. He goes to university and works in Shah's. But he secretly wants to run a camping shop."

"Grumpy? Shopkeeper? Just my type! I wish you'd stop trying to match-make. Even if I wanted to, which I don't," she growled, "I'm going to be up against it for a week or so. Far too busy to do anything else."

Eddie's heart sank. She missed her daughter. "Heather?"

"Yes mum," Heather let out a loud breath.

"Are you happy?" There was silence on the line.

"Er, s'pose so."

Heather wasn't convincing her. She got the distinct impression she was holding something back.

"It's just, after my conversation with Amir."

There was another tut down the line.

"No, hold on. After listening to Amir, who's too scared to speak to his dad about the camping shop. Well… it made me think."

"Uh huh." Now she was humoring her.

"I know we've not always seen eye to eye but I'm still your mum. You can always talk to me, you know?"

"Okay mum," Heather muttered, "noted."

"Seriously, Heather, I'd like us to be friends. I love you."

"Look mum, I'd better go. Love you too. I'll give you a bell soon, eh?"

"Okay. Bye love." Eddie blew a kiss down the phone, but the line had already gone dead.

Chapter Eleven

*E*DDIE FELT better having had a chat with Heather, although she still didn't believe she was fine. For weeks Heather had been busy and irritable whenever they spoke, usually on a Sunday evening. Just like her father she clammed up when any conversation turned personal. Getting information from her was difficult and for years their relationship had been like a finely balanced seesaw that could tip at any point. Distractedly, Eddie wiped the kitchen worktops for the third time as their conversation replayed on a loop in her mind. Realising the kitchen was spotless she rinsed out the cloth and popped the kettle on. She glanced at the clock and nodded. She could watch 'The Chase'. That would stop her thoughts from racing. She did worry about that girl.

The kettle boiled and a teabag was stewing in the mug when the doorbell rang. Negotiating the stairs, Eddie opened the front door to find Jack on the doorstep. The hot May sunshine backlit his feathery hair and gave it a halo effect.

"Hi Eddie, grandad brought me straight from college." Jack pointed to the green Rover idling at the kerbside and, as if it knew it was under observation, it puffed black fumes out in greeting.

"We wanted to check you were alright after last Saturday."

She raised her eyebrows in surprise. "That's thoughtful of you, Jack."

He chewed his lip and looked at the floor. "Well, it was grandad's idea really. He wanted to come round yesterday but I was busy."

Her stomach did a little flip. Tolly's idea, eh? "Well, I'm fine, thank you. My legs ached a little but I'm back to normal now."

"Cool." He shuffled and flashed a nervous smile. He seemed reluctant to leave. "And, er, you said I could look at your camping gear?"

"Oh yes, when would be good?"

He glanced round at his grandad.

"Oh, do you mean now?"

He nodded slowly. "Only if it's okay, if you're free?"

Tolly watched from the car, and she lifted a hand to give a quick wave.

"I'll phone him when we're done." Jack pushed the fringe off his face. "He'll come back and get me."

"Is he okay after the weekend; his hip?"

"Yeah, all cool- I think."

"Is he going somewhere?"

Jack shrugged. "Dunno, probably just home."

"He can come in if he wants?"

Tolly watched, straight-backed, behind the wheel. His stomach muscles must be strong to maintain that pose. Eddie took a couple of steps down the driveway towards the car. The gravel was sharp under her sheepskin slippers, and she rose up on tiptoes.

"Why don't you-?"

The buzz of the electric window interrupted her, and she waited while it lowered.

"I was just saying, why don't you come in?" She motioned back towards the house as he leant across the passenger seat to listen.

"I didn't want to get in the way."

"Don't be daft," she rolled her eyes, "besides, we'll need help to get the kit out the garage."

He switched the engine off and joined her by the front door as the doors of the Rover locked behind them with an audible thump.

"And there was me thinking you wanted me for my tactics and survival skills," he joked as he followed her through to the garage.

"Ner," she replied, "just your muscles."

"Ha! Good luck finding those, Eddie." Jack laughed, as an indignant Tolly turned and ruffled his grandson's floppy hair in revenge.

They stood in the garage peering up at the various bags and boxes neatly stacked above their heads.

"Wow, this is organized." Tolly stared around in wonder, visibly impressed. The double garage had racks built along each side with plastic boxes neatly lining the walls. Labels on the front of each box explained the contents and above their heads, the space had been boarded, providing even more storage. A red two-door car was parked to one side and the floor had been recently swept, a broom now standing sentry with an assortment of other tools.

"It wasn't my doing," Eddie answered honestly. "It was Rex's domain in here. I've just given it a quick tidy up."

Jack put his hands in his pockets looking awkward. "You know Eddie, we can leave it for now. It doesn't matter."

"It's fine, Jack." She smiled at his embarrassment. "It's nice to look through things. It brings back so many memories." She had nothing but happy memories of their camping trips. As newlyweds she'd gone camping with Rex, pitching up where there might be wildlife for him to photograph. He'd been happy, unconstrained, during these brief trips. There'd been no one for him to impress. That had been the real Rex.

"You'll be doing me a favour. I need to have a sort-out. Honestly, it's fine!" So what if it was a little white lie. There was no urgency to sort anything out but no real need to keep it either. Sensing a dip in the mood she clapped her hands loudly, the noise echoing around the breezeblocks. "So, now we've agreed, let's get going."

With Jack balanced on top of a stepladder and Eddie directing from below, they retrieved several bags. They found two tents, a six and a four-person, both in pristine condition. Jack balanced on the rafters for a better look and found a plastic storage box. Neatly packed, its lid was firmly clicked in place to protect three sleeping bags, a couple of roll mats and a thin blow-up mattress. Another box concealed a gas stove and canister together with an assortment of cooking utensils, freeze-dried foods, rehydration salts – "in case of diarrhoea" Eddie explained - and water purifying tablets – "to stop you getting diarrhoea in the first place," she added. "You need to be careful with your water supplies. We camped in a forest clearing once, collecting water from a stream. I would have drunk it straight, but Rex insisted on either boiling it, which was a rigmarole, or using those. So much easier and better than possible cramps or sickness." She handed them to Jack who carefully repacked the box.

"What's in here?" Jack pointed at two cardboard boxes then, holding one up, he pulled out a large plastic tube.

"Gosh, I'd forgotten about those." Eddie took the tube from him and smiled as a memory returned. "We went on a sailing holiday and Rex insisted we buy these emergency flares. He was convinced we'd get in trouble and drift out to sea."

"And did you?"

"Oh yes," Eddie replied, straight-faced. "There were four flares originally. We had to use two." She counted on her fingers. "One, we fired at a shark which got too close to the boat."

"Really?"

She nodded. "The other one was used to attract the navy who rescued us after we outran Somali pirates."

The men stared at her, mouths hanging open.

"Seriously?"

"No Jack, *not* seriously," she laughed. "We bought two and there are still two there. We didn't have any trouble, just a really nice holiday."

Tolly burst out laughing.

"Honestly, you two… talk about gullible," she chuckled while Jack stuffed the flare back in the box.

"So lame," he muttered, doing his best to ignore her as he carried on with his sift through the rest of the equipment. Eddie pulled a face at Tolly, she hoped she hadn't offended him by being so flippant, but the smile he flashed back told her it was okay.

"Am I allowed to borrow a tent, Eddie?"

"Of course you are, Jack. In fact, let's take it out to the garden and you can have a good look through."

Half an hour later Jack sat on the grass, surrounded by camping paraphernalia. Deciding to leave him to it Eddie took Tolly upstairs to the living room. She threw away her stewed, cold cup of tea and fixed them both a drink, inviting her visitor to take a seat. From their chairs by the window, they watched Jack outside.

"This is kind of you, Eddie, he seems to listen to you. Takes more notice than of anything I say, anyway." Tolly nodded down to the lawn. "Although I've no idea what state it will be in when it's returned."

She batted away his comment. "It doesn't matter. I doubt I'll be needing it again. Heather's not interested anymore … she used to love it as a child." Her hands wrapped around the crystal glass and the cubes of ice chinked against the side. She'd forgotten how nice it was to have company in the evening and to enjoy a civilized gin and tonic.

"Does she come home much?"

Eddie shook her head, her mouth downcast. "She's not been back for ages, but I spoke to her earlier," her mouth tugged upwards. "We had a chat. I must have caught her on a good day when she wasn't running around. She's always *so* busy." She turned to him, "she's a management consultant in London. She keeps inviting me to visit but, you know," she took a sip of her drink. "I don't want to go to London."

"Why not?"

His eyebrows knitted together. Why had she said that? She used to love London, the excitement, the noise. "I'm too busy here." And even to her own ears it sounded a weak excuse.

"Well, perhaps you *should* go?"

She smiled. He was trying to be kind. But she had too much to do here, she couldn't just up and go for days on end.

"Maybe she'd like to show you around? It's different when you live somewhere. She could take you to a show -"

"That's what she said."

"Why not? You could catch the train? Get her to meet you at the station."

"I don't know. It's a palaver, isn't it? I'd have to get a taxi to the station and lug my suitcase around. And I've got the garden to think about. I was planning a project for the next couple of weeks."

Tolly watched her, tipping his head to one side. "She might think you're not interested in what she's doing."

Eddie pulled her mouth from left to right. It could be interpreted that way she supposed. But it wasn't true.

"And then it's a slippery slope. Neither of you make an effort and before you know it you've lost touch."

"That's sad," she whispered, as emotion rose in her chest. They'd never been that close, not doing weekends away or long shopping trips like some of her friends and their daughters, but the thought of losing touch altogether scared her.

"It's easily done." He cleared his throat. "I just think family's important."

"Your family mean a lot to you?" She whispered and he nodded. She liked how he wasn't embarrassed to admit it and despite his stiff upper lip and grouchy appearance, he seemed to have a big heart beating inside.

"It wasn't always like that," he interrupted. "I was often away, and

I *did* lose that connection. It took a long time to get it back again, not sure I ever truly will with James. You have to work at it." They sat in a thoughtful, companionable silence and watched as the ducks glided past on the water. Tolly shifted in his chair.

"You know, I could give you a lift to the station. And if you're worried about the house or the garden I could pop over, keep an eye on everything?"

She looked at the fuchsia pots and geraniums on her tiny patio below.

"Thank you. I'll think about it," she said quietly, and he raised his whiskery eyebrows. "I *will*!"

Satisfied with her response, he turned back to watch Jack in the garden. Eddie studied him for a few moments. It was strange having a man in her house, having *anyone* in her house, again. She'd got used to her own company and the sound of the TV but was surprised how comfortable it was with him. She felt at ease. The silence hung gently between them as a narrow boat glided past and simultaneously they raised their hands to wave at the skipper.

"It's restful here, isn't it?"

"It is quiet," she paused, "sometimes a bit *too* quiet."

"That's good, isn't it? Oh, I see," he picked up on her intonation, "you'd like more excitement?"

"Maybe … perhaps a little."

His bushy eyebrows dominated his face. They tended to be the first thing you noticed about him but underneath his grey eyes didn't miss a thing. Now they looked directly at her, the creases deepening as he smiled.

"Well, now you've joined the ranks of the Happy Wanderers you'll have too much excitement to handle."

"Excitement like that I can do without."

"Didn't you enjoy it?" His face fell.

"It was great!" She patted his arm and felt the warmth from his skin. "Sorry, the glass is really cold."

"I don't mind," he glanced at where she'd touched him. "Did you really enjoy it or are you just saying that?" He had an air of vulnerability as he waited for her reply.

"It was the most fun I've had for years," she whispered sincerely. "Really good fun." The setting sun appeared from behind a cloud and illuminated the living room as if a low wattage lamp had been turned on. It could have been romantic if Tolly's stomach hadn't chosen that exact second to emit an enormous rumble.

"Trust me to interrupt. We'd better be going. Jack must be hungry." He walked over to the balcony and knocked on the window. If Jack was hungry, he didn't appear bothered. He was much more interested in the four-man tent he'd set up in the garden. Sad at the thought of them leaving, Eddie had an idea.

"What if I order pizzas? We could have supper in the garden with Jack?"

"I don't really know what I'm doing with a pizza, I'm afraid."

She lifted her eyebrows in surprise.

"I tend to stick to meat, potatoes and gravy… although I tried lasagna recently," he tailed off. "It wasn't a great success."

"I could help you order something?"

"Alright," he agreed. "But only if we can have some chicken nuggets too?"

Eddie's eyes widened.

"Oh yes," he said, seeing her surprise, "Jack introduced me to those when he stayed after my operation." He straightened up, warming to the idea of this new cuisine and patted his tummy. He didn't have a spare ounce on him. "If you're sure we're not disturbing you though?"

Eddie shook her head.

"In that case, it would be rude to refuse. I'll just text my daughter-in-law to let her know." He pulled an old flip-cover mobile from his corduroy trousers and squinting at the screen, began to prod the keys.

Eddie leaned out the window and shouted to Jack, his face eventually popping out the tent as he held out a camping bowl.

"Look," he rattled it. "I left this on the path while I was in the tent, and someone's dropped money in!"

She laughed and put her thumbs up. "Great, you can pay for the pizzas. I'm just about to order. Anything you'd like in particular?"

He shrugged and disappeared back inside the tent as Tolly put his phone away.

"Did you see - someone left him money?"

Tolly sighed. "He's been so excited about this. He'd been counting down to his expedition last year and then caught glandular fever. Was really incapacitated too, so he missed everything."

Eddie listened as she walked to the kitchen and sifted through the leaflets on her fridge. Lifting off the pizza menu she was walking back when another idea struck her.

"What if *we* go?"

"What? Camping?" Tolly pursed his lips. "It would take a bit of preparatory work."

She nodded so hard she could almost hear her brain rattling.

"Yes! We could get in touch with Mike-"

Tolly groaned.

"We could meet somewhere local on Friday-"

"Friday?"

"Camp out Friday and Saturday. Give Jack a real experience." She hesitated, "unless, sorry," she dropped her arms and the pizza menu creased in her hand. "Unless you're not fit enough."

"Actually, it appears to have improved this week," he wiggled from left to right. "I think the exercise was good for it."

"We could take our cars, load them up with comfy chairs and pillows." She was thinking out loud and looked around for a pen. She needed to make a list. "Do a small walk on Saturday." She continued - this was exciting. She loved planning trips. "It could be fun."

Slowly Tolly started to nod. "It *could* be fun, you're right. And the weather is supposed to be nice." His stomach rumbled again, and she remembered what she'd been doing before this insane thought had struck.

"Let's order food first, then we can talk properly," and thrusting the menu at him she practically skipped to the phone.

Two hours later the suspension of the Rover was almost scraping the floor. The boot was packed, and the backseat was rammed full of camping equipment. The front seats had been pulled so far forwards that Jack's knees were wedged against his chest. Despite his contorted position, he sat happily reading the label on the flare box totally oblivious to the two of them who stood side by side on the drive.

"He looks really uncomfortable," she whispered and Tolly chuckled. They watched Jack turn the box over in his hands.

"The blood supply to his legs must be cutting off."

Tolly nodded and shifted slowly from one leg to the other. He turned to Eddie, and she tucked her hair behind her ear, suddenly self-conscious.

"You'll have to go slowly over any speed bumps too," she added, then instantly wanted to kick herself. Why did she feel the need to natter?

He nodded then tipped his head towards Jack. "I'd better leave, before he sets that thing off and burns the car to a crisp." He took a step towards her and reached for her hands then paused as if wondering whether to speak. He leant over and gently placed his lips on hers. Eddie closed her eyes and savoured the sensation. His lips were softer than she'd have imagined and warm. They felt nice and she took a tiny step closer, but he pulled back and let her go.

"Sorry. I shouldn't have -" He rubbed the back of his neck anxiously. "I don't know what-"

Eddie caught his arm and pulled him back. She stroked his cheek. "You've had a shave," she whispered then leant in for another kiss. As they separated, she glanced at the car, hoping Jack wasn't watching. "You'd better go," she pointed to the Rover. "The flares… burning to a crisp?"

"Hmm?" Tolly was looking at her lips, a soppy expression on his face. He shook himself and pecked her on the cheek. "Roger that. I'll pick you up on Friday; sixteen hundred hours."

"Sixteen hundred hours, precisely!" She saluted as he climbed in the car.

"I'll look forward to it."

And as the green car disappeared coughing down the cul-de-sac she whispered, "I will too."

Before switching off the kitchen lights that night Eddie remembered to plug in her mobile phone and as the screen lit up, she thought of her conversation with Tolly earlier. He'd made sense, talking about losing contact with family. She pictured him as a young man… he must have been very dashing in his uniform. Did Heather have a boyfriend? There was always a persistent niggle that something wasn't right, and she did worry about the girl. She could plan a trip to London for a few days, find out more about Heather's London life. Maybe she needed to make more of an effort and as these thoughts ran through her head, she picked up her phone.

Hi darling, mum here.

It was slow going, prodding each letter on the tiny keypad.

How was your day?
Hope you not working too much – all work and no play ☹

Had lovely visit from Tolly and Jack tonight.
Tent in garden and take-out pizzas.
Love you to meet them.
Lots of love ☺

She sent it and smiled. Now Heather would know she was thinking about her when she read it in the morning. Feeling good, Eddie went up to bed.

One hundred and twenty miles away in London Heather was in bed, crying, when her phone beeped. She wiped her eyes and picked it up from her bedside table, to see a message from her mum. Instantly alert, she opened it then smiled. She was pleased for her. She deserved some fun and, selfishly, if her mum was busy that was one less thing for her to worry about. She must visit her soon. She'd really neglected her; too tied up with work. A memory of a camping trip flitted into mind. The details were sketchy - tents and camping chairs in a row - but she remembered the laughter and the feeling of being so carefree. It had been such a simple holiday. The only thing they'd had to do was sit in chairs and watch as nature unfolded. Why was it so difficult now? She sighed, knowing she wouldn't be able to sleep. She got up and padded over to her desk. She ran a finger over the lid of her paintbox then picked out a pencil. Turning to a fresh page in her pad, she sketched the outline of a crescent moon, clouds and a cobbled street beneath. She smiled, relaxing into it. She forgot about her gritty eyes and feeling sorry for herself. No longer a useless, stressed-out flake whose life was going down the pan, she was now in control and the pencil did her bidding. At work today she'd fled to the toilets after a colleague had asked her a question about her latest client. The pencil paused. She recalled the clamminess of her skin as her blood had drained away and she'd struggled not to faint. Back in January, these episodes had been infrequent but now they were happening more often. Panic attacks, her doctor had diagnosed and whilst it was good to know what they were, it didn't stop them. Now, the only place she felt safe was here, sitting in this room at this table. The pencil shaded in some cobbles and drew a row of cottages. Heather squinted at the picture. She'd been aiming for the Pied Piper, but the moon leant a different atmosphere to the scene. She wracked her brain for another fairy story. Yawning, she lined up the pencils then crept back into bed. Lying on her back she stared out at the darkness. Wee Willie Winkie, in a nightdress. He ran over cobbles with a lantern. Before she could think of any further details, she fell into a deep sleep.

Chapter Twelve

THE ELECTRONIC beep sounded as Eddie pushed the door and went into the shop.

"With you in a minute." Amir's voice floated through from the back and, taking a basket, Eddie wandered the shelves searching for tasty snacks for camping. Outside, the sun was shining, and her spirits were high. As Amir appeared, it was obvious his mood contrasted with hers.

"You alright Amir?" She walked over to the counter and looked at him, concerned.

"Ug." It wasn't quite a grunt, but not far off. He carried a large box of assorted biscuits, which he bashed into a shelf, causing a loaf to fall to the floor. Eddie retrieved it and replaced it neatly, then followed him.

"You busy?"

He grabbed a handful of packets and put them roughly on the shelf. He followed the first ones with another fistful, shoving them against the first. What was that now? Crisps and biscuits? She made a mental note of what *not* to buy.

"Amir, I'm not being funny, but you'll get people complaining about your stock."

He glared at her and, for a split-second, she expected to get a packet shoved in her face. Then he sighed. His body deflated as his bravado left, to be replaced by sadness.

"What on earth has happened?"

"My university." He emptied the rest of the biscuits and, under Eddie's watchful gaze, stacked them gently. With the box now empty, he returned to the counter and beckoned her to follow. "I'll put the kettle on?"

Eddie nodded and glanced at the plastic wall clock. "Lovely. I've got twenty minutes before I need to go." She heard the kettle boil and the rattle of mugs, and he returned with two teas.

"Come on then, out with it."

He climbed onto the leather-topped stool behind the counter. "So, I had that exam two weeks ago?"

"I remember."

"I didn't think I'd done great. But I didn't expect…." he took a deep breath. "Well, I didn't expect to fail it."

Eddie's hand flew up to her mouth and she stared at him, horrified. "Oh no, Amir. I'm sorry." She took a deep breath. "What you going to do?"

He shrugged, clearly out of ideas. "I've been in touch with my tutor. I can retake in September. Do extra study over the summer. But I don't want to." He breathed slowly in, then puffed air out his mouth as he focused on a spot by the biscuit shelf. "It's such a mess, Eddie. I'm sick of this shop. If I wasn't paying off my dad-"

She frowned.   "What are you paying your dad for?"

He cupped both hands around his mug and narrowed his eyes. "I went travelling for a year. I told you, right?"

She shook her head. "I don't think so." She couldn't recall him mentioning it before.

"Really?" He seemed surprised. "It was great." He pulled his mug in towards his body, as if it was full of memories and he wanted them closer. "Well, I stayed on in California for six months. Los Angeles, amazing place," he fixed her with his eyes, "beaches, culture, although the hostels weren't great. I travelled along the coast too. Went whale watching from Newport and surf lessons near Malibu." His eyes looked through the window and out to some imagined destination.

Eddie waited, then coughed, and he came back to the present, taking a moment to focus. "Anyway," he continued, "my dad helped me out. I know I've got to pay him back, and I will - I don't mind working, it's just that I hate Uni. I don't see the point of it."

Eddie leant against the counter and narrowed her eyes. "I know we've discussed this before. But if you prepared a proper business plan for the camping shop, your father might take you seriously."

Amir's downturned mouth gave her all the clue she needed that he wasn't convinced.

"Maybe he suggested teaching because he didn't think *you* knew what to do? And you said you liked Maths at school-"

He groaned. "I did, man, but I hate it now."

She blew on her tea and took a sip. "Let me ask you, if you were still able to get the camping shop would you be interested?"

He narrowed his eyes at her.

"You think you know how to run a shop, successfully?"

He held his palms up and looked around the shop. "Uh, isn't this successful?"

She nodded, satisfied. "That's exactly my point. Don't be so defeatist," she smiled. "You need to write a plan; income, expenditure, stock list, cost of a website, how you'd manage online sales. You could speak to the current owners. If they've been trying to sell for a while, they might reduce the price. What about the bank? See if you could get a loan?"

He chewed his bottom lip.

"If you really want it, you've got to put some effort in."

He was silent for a moment then clicked his fingers. "You know, you might be right."

"Finally," she laughed, pleased to see the return of his lovely smile.

"I'll give it a go, Eddie. What's the worst that can happen?"

Eddie wasn't ready to go straight home, so she decided to walk to town and do some shopping. It was a beautiful, bright morning. She had a spring in her step as she walked along the High Street and headed for the camping shop. The old-fashioned bell tinkled as she shoved the stiff door open and the familiar smell enveloped her, transporting her down memory lane. The camping equipment was still stocked the same way it had always been - smaller items around the counter with tents, chairs and larger displays at the rear.

"Can I help you?" Mrs. Turner appeared from the back of the shop wearing the most enormous pair of round glasses. Her eyes, behind, were magnified and stared, unblinking, as they waited for Eddie to reply. She pointed to the relevant shelf for the gas canisters and Eddie chose two, returning to the counter to pay. She watched in amazement when Mrs. Turner wrote the items in a lined ledger and pulled a drawer out for change. The shop hadn't been altered since the 1970s and as Eddie left, she felt a bubble of excitement for Amir. If he could get the lease, she felt certain he'd drag it into the twenty first century.

Eddie walked through the town's square towards the road and waited for a gap in the traffic. A steady stream of vehicles crawled along and as she stood patiently on the kerb, her eyes were drawn to a familiar, polished green car. It idled in one of the drop-off bays opposite. A couple sat on the front seats. The driver stared out the windscreen, shaking his head slowly, while the woman talked animatedly. Eddie squinted through her scratched glasses; she really must sort out some new ones. Was that Tolly? What was he doing? He didn't look happy. The woman was beautiful and poised, like a ballerina. Her white hair was styled in a short crop and her silver earrings looked expensive, even from this distance. Eddie touched hers, a small diamond stud.

Who was she? Eddie watched as she wrapped a silver shawl around her shoulders. She kissed Tolly on the cheek then paused to wipe off the lipstick. It was an intimate act and Eddie glanced away, uncomfortable. She turned back to see the woman climb from the car. She paused to don a pair of sunglasses. As the car pulled away, she crossed the road and daintily hopped up next to Eddie.

"Sorry," she trilled. She brushed past and nudged Eddie's bag. Without a backwards glance she strode along the pavement and into the hairdressers. Eddie picked up her bags. What was Tolly playing at? Why had he kissed her on her driveway if he was seeing someone else? A car honked, making her jump and she stepped back on the kerb. She'd believed him, when he said he liked her. She'd allowed herself to be drawn in. Feeling confused, the shops had lost their allure and she just wanted to go home. It was better she found out what he was like now, than when she was too involved. Straightening up, she decided she'd go camping at the weekend and remain just friendly; maintain her distance. Like Rex, Tolly was a good-looking man, and therefore not to be trusted. Unless she wanted her heart broken again.

Heather sat at her desk. It was Friday lunchtime, and she was starving. She glanced into her boss's goldfish bowl office, waiting for her reaction. Her boss, Geri, had spent the morning reading through the latest figures for the takeover. Suddenly Geri looked up and made eye contact. Heather gulped. Her heart started to pound inside her crisp, white blouse and she wiped the back of her neck. She had a pain in her stomach. A knot of tension wound tighter and made her lean forwards, her back rounding over. Geri stood up and smoothed down her black pencil skirt. She swayed over to her door in vertiginous heels and leant on the wooden architrave, waving at Heather. *Shit!* She couldn't ignore her now. Geri crooked her finger and beckoned her over.

Taking a seat inside her office, Heather's cheeks burned as she imagined the rest of the team looking in. Were they whispering, wondering why she was there? She tried to focus as Geri struggled to make it back to her seat.

"Heather. I know it hasn't been easy for you, taking over the team and having to step up to management. How do you think it's been going?"

Heather felt sick. She was going to *be* sick. She needed to move or risk the entire office seeing her throw up. She rushed out, making it to the Ladies and into a cubicle just in time. She heaved into the toilet pan then immediately felt better. She waited for her breathing to calm then, on shaky legs, crossed the space to the row of sinks. Strip lighting was never forgiving, but as she lifted her head to look in the mirror, she made herself jump.

"Shit!" She gawped at her reflection, clinging to the sink. She was still recognizable as Heather Maguire, but Jeez she looked rough. Her blonde side-ponytail hung limply as loose strands of hair clung to her pasty skin. She had bags under her eyes from lack of sleep. Actually, they were as big as craters, and her normally clear complexion had been replaced by an outbreak of ugly spots on her forehead. The door opened and heels clattered across the tiled floor.

"Heather. Are you okay?" Geri appeared next to her. Was it her imagination or did she recoil ever so slightly? Heather remained still, the cool water running over her hands as Geri slid some paper towels towards her. Grateful, Heather dampened one and used it to mop her brow.

"You got a bug or something?"

Heather nodded.

"You should go home," Geri touched her arm, concerned. "I'll call you a cab. Put it on expenses." As she turned to go Heather called out.

"Geri?"

Her boss turned round.

"Can I take some time off? Two weeks maybe?"

Geri raised her eyebrows and folded her arms across her chest. "If you're sick-"

"I just feel I need a break. Get some rest..." Heather tailed off. There, she'd said it. She waited for her boss's reaction.

"Sure. I'll call you a cab. Go home and get some sleep. Let's talk tomorrow, eh?"

Heather wanted to walk. She'd get something nice for her dinner, food that was tasty and nutritious rather than the takeaways and ready meals she'd been living on. Putting on her trainers she grabbed her bag and keys and left the flat, slamming the door behind her.

She marched to the small park around the corner from her block and sat on a bench. She'd been through this park many times but, like the other people who now walked quickly through, she'd not paid much attention to what was around. It wasn't a bad space, probably Victorian. A patch of lawn was framed by well-tended flowerbeds and a playground was in one corner, a bandstand for summer performances in another. As Heather reflected on her morning, she cringed. How on earth was she ever going to face them again? She laughed bitterly. Just imagine if she'd been sick in Geri's office. That really didn't bear thinking about. What had brought it on? The shortness of breath and the swirling stomach weren't new but being physically sick was. It was as if she'd become allergic to work. She was permanently exhausted. Constant worry gnawed away at her insides making her *feel* nauseous. A taxi hooted on the other side of the railings, and she jumped. What was happening to her? She'd never experienced a problem in Dubai. She'd worked for one of the biggest, most-respected consultancy companies in the world, yet since returning to London she'd felt unsettled. Why was she still even here? She'd agreed to stay on after her dad had died, to support her mum. But that was three years ago, and her mum seemed fine. They hardly saw each other anyway. Then she had an idea. If she had two weeks to fill, and there wasn't a lot happening here, she could go home. Surprise her mum. Picking up the paper bag, heavy with food from the deli, she strolled home, relieved that she'd made a decision.

Chapter Thirteen

IT WAS late Friday afternoon, and the sun was still shining. The temperature was a perfect twenty-three degrees. Eddie, Jack and Tolly sat in matching green camping chairs, arranged in a cosy semi-circle. To one side a low river burbled around worn stepping-stones and provided a backdrop of white noise to the stunning scenery opposite, verdant rolling hills as far as they could see.

"Well, isn't this nice?" Eddie sat in the middle cradling a ceramic mug.

"The great outdoors, you can't beat it." Tolly held out his mug for a top up then sipped it with a satisfied smack of his lips as he surveyed the scene around him.

"I didn't realize we'd be so close to the river." Eddie nodded in its direction. "I could sit here all day and watch those ducks swim up and down. It's so relaxing."

On her other side Jack also had a coffee, but his foot was jiggling up and down, an abundance of nervous energy leaving his body.

"Relax, son. Look at those ducks, swimming around without a care in the world." Tolly paused, a thought forming. "Are they what you'd call 'chilling'?"

Jack tutted. "They're more 'chillaxing'," he said irritably, "a mix of chilling and relaxing." Eddie listened, staring wistfully at the water. "I'd like to be a duck. Floating around all day. Messing about in beautiful places like this."

Jack finished his drink and put the mug on the grass with a burp. "Can we put the tents up now grandad?"

"Soon, Jack." Tolly made a calming gesture to placate the teenager. "Once Mike gets here, we'll get organised."

Jack huffed and pulled a wind-up torch out of his pocket. He'd raided some of his savings from his bank account and had blown every penny in the camping shop. He started to wind up the battery, turning a knob on the side that made an irritating grinding noise. He'd also bought a freeze-dried pasta meal, along with a block of Kendal mint cake and a bush-craft emergency foil cape to be used in cases of hypothermia. Eddie hoped he wouldn't need that this weekend, but he was learning to be prepared – which was good news if Mike was involved in the planning! He sat winding up the torch and Eddie glanced at him.

"What?" He shrugged at her and frowned.

"Enjoy the peace and quiet," she said, "make the most of-"

Her sentence was drowned out as a vehicle came down the gravel driveway, its radio blaring heavy metal music from an open window. It screeched to a halt in the car park behind the fence and sent gravel scattering. A door opened then slammed shut to cut off the sound of dog barks from inside. Tolly and Eddie exchanged a look. Another door opened then the sharp car horn blasted and all three of them jumped.

"Good Lord," Tolly stood up and looked over. "What on earth-"

A dog shot towards them. It swerved at the last moment and plunged in the river.

"Trixie! No! Do not!" The dog bobbed in the river, its tongue lolling out. It was clearly having a whale of a time. Tolly strode towards the bank and prepared to shoo the dog away if it got too close to the ducks. They, however, decided they were having none of it and took flight, indignant quacks filling the air.

"Somebody needs to train that ruddy thing."

Out of sight, a man shouted, "Trixie." Bored of its game, the dog climbed out, shook itself vigorously next to Tolly and ran back to its owner. The door opened and muffled yapping suggested that the owner had had enough of the dog's games. "If you can't behave, you'll have to stay there," the voice warned. *Yap.*

The voice sounded familiar. Eddie was trying to think where she'd heard it before when Mike rounded the corner.

"Evening everyone. Evening." He nodded at each of them in turn. "Beautiful, isn't it? I trust you're all in fine fettle?"

Eddie nodded politely. Tolly, returning from the river, shook his damp shorts and glared at Mike.

"Are you in charge of that animal?"

"Correct-a-mundo. But she's a law unto herself." He stood in front of them, blocking their sunlight.

"You never said you had a dog, Mike. Why didn't she come out last weekend?"

"Saints preserve us, could you imagine-"

Eddie silenced Tolly with a look. She turned back to Mike who explained Trixie belonged to his mum. He was looking after her for the weekend, adding "I couldn't miss the camping trip, could I?" Trixie barked in the distance, as if she understood.

"Guess what? I fixed the sat nav." Mike wiggled his eyebrows, looking smug. He waited for them to respond. "Water had got in and the circuit board didn't like it."

"Circuit board didn't like it?" Tolly mumbled, "*I* didn't ruddy like it."

Jack put a hand on his grandad's shoulder and pulled him gently back to his chair.

Tolly shook his hand off and, with a harrumph, sat down. He folded his arms.

"As I was going to say, before I was interrupted," Mike continued. "I used a map to plot tomorrow's walk."

"A map?" Even though he was trying to appear disinterested, Tolly couldn't stop a flicker of interest passing over his face.

"I even remembered to bring it with me," Mike added.

"Will you -?"

"- Yes, Colonel, I'll let Jack have it and I'll happily teach him how to use it."

Jack's mouth twitched as, through his fringe, he watched the two men. A tense silence followed before Tolly shifted. "Well, maybe you're not such-"

"I think what grandad is trying to say is 'thank you.' Isn't that right, grandad?" Eddie feared another insult was only seconds away, so was relieved when Tolly simply nodded, as a muffled yap floated over the fence.

The light was starting to fade as the wanderers struggled to make their camp 'fit for purpose'. A small two-man tent was up. The pieces of two others lay strewn across the grass. Eddie, Tolly and Jack stood in a semi-circle looking perplexed, as Mike walked towards them carrying two bendy tent poles.

"Sorry about that," he said. "I've tied her up under the tree now."

Not content with pestering the ducks, Trixie had started to pester the humans. She had enjoyed half an hour of fun, running around the camp and stealing crucial bits of equipment.

"She's certainly playful," Jack agreed, as Mike added the poles to the others on the floor. Eddie was to have the two-person tent. She had already unpacked her rucksack and sleeping bag. Jack and Tolly were to share one of the larger tents, while Mike would have the other. Their food supplies would be kept in Mike's large, zippable porch as their makeshift kitchen. With flushed cheeks Tolly straightened up and, with a loud exhale, handed the instructions to Eddie.

She began to read.

"Insert the blue rod into the pocket and push through to form

Entrance A." She paused, her eyes casting around the ground. "I can't see a blue rod."

"Read it again, Eddie."

"Insert the blue rod into the pocket."

"What rod?" Mike was on his hands and knees sifting through the plastic parts.

"It must be somewhere," Jack dropped to the ground, to help. "We only had it up two days ago and everything went back in the bag."

Eddie checked the tent bag, there was nothing left. She'd also had another thought. "Mike, where's Trixie going to sleep if you've got the food in your tent?"

"The car?" Jack suggested but Mike shook his head.

"She'd probably yap all night and none of us would sleep."

"She could come in with us," Jack looked at his grandad, his bottom lip sticking out, sad eyes pleading. "It might be fun?"

"Well, I'm not..." Tolly tailed off under the full gaze of the other wanderers. He sighed. "I suppose it'll be alright."

"Thank you," Eddie said. "Now, what about these tents?" She stood up and put her hands on her hips, pointing to do Mike's first. It practically put itself up and in no time, Mike was knocking the last guy-rope in the ground. Sensing that energy levels were running low, Eddie was keen to keep the momentum going. Besides, the sun was sinking, and she was hungry. "One more to go," she clapped her hands.

Jack, still baffled, was scanning the ground for the missing pole as two ducks flew overhead and landed on the river. Trixie, who'd been remarkably quiet under a large willow tree, growled and, glancing over, Eddie smiled. Daft mutt. Then her smile dropped.

"Mike. What's Trixie chewing?"

Mike didn't look. He was pre-occupied threading a pole through its casing. "Who cares, so long as it's keeping her quiet?"

"But, Mike, it appears to be a piece of blue plastic, although I haven't got my glasses on."

He squinted over at the dog and, cursing, dropped his pole. It pinged from its holder and whipped Tolly across the back of his legs. Muttering an apology Mike ran towards the terrier and yanked the blue pole away from her. "Don't worry," he waved it in the air, "still in one piece. It'll be fine!" He wiped it on his trousers leaving a smear of dog slobber.

"Mystery solved," Eddie sighed. "I can go and pay for the pitches now, if you three can finish?" She headed off in the direction of the campsite shop.

The shop was a modern, single-story extension to the farmhouse. On the door a roughly cut rectangle of wood hung from a string and announced that the shop was indeed open. But as Eddie went in, there was no one inside. She browsed the shelves; the usual fare for campers – fresh eggs, packets of local bacon, artisan baked bread, all at a premium price – and along one side of the shop a precarious shelf was loaded with tins of beans, soups and chopped tomatoes. Eddie hummed to herself as she selected a bottle of wine, some individual bottles of beer and a large family bag of locally produced crisps. She dinged the bell on the counter and waited for a response. A beaded curtain hung behind the counter, covering a doorway that connected through to the house itself. Eddie was thinking about calling through when a hand appeared. Perfectly manicured nails, with baby-pink polish, swept the curtain aside making the beads rattle noisily.

"Hello. You must be Eddie?" The voice was girlish, so Eddie was surprised when a woman her own age stepped out.

"I've been waiting to meet you. I'm Tuesday Week. I run this site with my sister, Thursday." Eddie chuckled at their unusual names. Tuesday stared at her, unsmiling, so Eddie coughed to cover a rising giggle. Tuesday was small and slim, with a large chest and for one moment Eddie thought she'd come across Dolly Parton working at a campsite. A set of perfect white teeth grinned out from a made-up face, and she held her hand out. Taking it, Eddie received a surprisingly strong and vigorous handshake as Tuesday stared at her over the top of her sparkly Dior glasses. Her eyes darted over her like a nervous bird, as she took in every detail of Eddie's hiking trousers, t-shirt and boots.

"All sorted? Tents up? Found the facilities?"

"Yes, thank you," said Eddie. "It's beautiful down by the river."

The woman nodded as she started to ring the items through the till. "I was looking forward to meeting you."

"Oh."

The woman peered over her glasses and leant forwards. "So, you one big family?"

"No, just friends."

"With your husband?"

"Oh no, I'm not here with my husband."

The woman paused and glanced at Eddie's wedding ring.

"Three men and none of them your husband? Clever thing." She took the money and rang it through the till, handing over the change.

"What? Oh no, my husband died nearly three years ago."

Tuesday pushed out her lip sticked lips. "Oh dear that's sad. Well good for you, getting out and about again." She pushed the items across the counter towards her then wiggled a finger as if she'd just had a thought. "Just friends, eh? Well maybe I'll pop over and introduce myself. You wouldn't mind, would you?"

Did Eddie have a choice? "Not at all, why would I mind?"

"Well," Tuesday giggled, "I wouldn't want to, you know, give you any competition."

"There's no competition," Eddie stated and watched Tuesday toy with a strand of hair. The woman pouted.

"No, I suppose not," she looked dismissively at Eddie's hair. "I'll pop over later then, just got a delivery to sort first." And with that she drifted back through the beaded curtain leaving Eddie wondering what on earth she'd just agreed to.

Chapter fourteen

HEATHER DRAGGED her suitcase out from under her bed. It was an old-fashioned case, not a fancy one with ridged sides, and as she opened it the musty smell reminded her of childhood holidays. It had been under her bed since she'd moved to London. She'd not had any reason to move it since... until now. She had time off from work and she was going on her travels.

She threw in her toiletry bag and pulled out a random assortment of t-shirts and jumpers from her drawer. She added a smart blouse in case she went anywhere. She got a thrill from seeing the suitcase fill up and debated whether to phone her mum. She decided against it, imagining her look of surprise when she arrived unannounced.

Happy that her plans were on track, Heather changed into her slouch wear and went to the kitchen. She'd bought ingredients to make a stir-fry, wanting nothing more than nice food and to watch some TV. She smiled at the thought that her mum was probably doing the same. For the first time in a long while she didn't know what the next two weeks would bring. But rather than feeling anxious, butterflies of excitement fluttered in her stomach.

Far from watching TV at home, Eddie was walking back to camp after the unusual conversation with Tuesday. As she approached the camp she saw three tents up, forming a neat semi-circle. Tolly greeted her. She was about to tell him about Tuesday Week when he handed her a gin and tonic - with lemon and ice - and she instantly forgot about the shopkeeper.

"This looks good," she indicated the tents, "and a G&T too." She took the glass, and after clinking each other's glasses, they all settled on their camping chairs and surveyed their temporary homes. Eddie sipped the cold drink. This spot was beautifully tranquil. Tolly's stomach rumbled loudly.

"Does no one ever feed you?" She pointed to his tummy. "Actually, who is on cooking duty tonight?"

"I don't mind," Jack seemed keen although Eddie wondered if he could cook.

"I'll help you son." Tolly gasped and stood up. "I forgot. I've brought something." He disappeared into his tent and after some rooting around, interspersed with gentle cursing, he reappeared clutching a bottle of Prosecco. He popped the cork and held the bottle aloft. "Would anyone like some bubbles?" At that precise moment Tuesday tottered around the hedge, in a pair of open-toe sandals.

"Oh, I *love* a man with bubbles," she declared. She hopped towards them, daintily side-stepping clumps of grass as all faces turned to look at her. She batted her eyelashes but when no one responded, she turned to Eddie.

"Eddie?" She raised her eyebrows. "Did you tell them I was coming?"

"Um…" Eddie grimaced. "Sorry, I got distracted by the gin and tonic." Disappointment flicked across Tuesday's face.

"Oh, don't worry, another time then." She took a step back. "Sorry to have interrupted."

Eddie rolled her eyes and pulled her back. "Don't be silly, Tuesday, stay. Otherwise, I'll feel awful. This is Tuesday, everyone, she runs the campsite. I met her in the shop," Eddie glanced at her watch, "er, five minutes ago." Tuesday twirled round and giggled as Mike jumped up and offered his seat. In his hurry he slopped Prosecco on the grass.

"I'll get a chair," he offered and ran to his car. Breathing heavily, he reappeared and set it up, wedging it between his own and the Colonel's.

"What a gentleman you are," Tuesday simpered. "You didn't tell me your friends were so handsome, Eddie."

The two men grinned, already under her spell. Had they forgotten Eddie was there, or that it was time to make supper? Eddie felt a little side lined – and she didn't like it.

"So, are you doing the supper?" She tried to get their attention, but no one moved. Jack continued to scroll on his phone and Tolly was looking the other way, chatting to Mike and Tuesday.

"Jack?"

He glanced up.

"Don't you need to get on with the supper?"

"Um, grandad was going to help me." He waved over at Tolly who was now topping up Tuesday's Prosecco. Eddie took a glug of her G&T and watched them over the rim of her glass. It was a good job she still had some gin as it didn't look like he was saving any fizz for her.

"I'll start supper then," she said loudly, hoping the note of irritation in her voice would prompt them. Nothing.

"I'll tidy after," Jack said - at least he was paying some attention.

Eddie got to her feet and gave them one last chance to interject. "I'll get on then, shall I?" When no one replied, she stomped toward Mike's tent and the makeshift kitchen.

Bloody cheek! Most of the stuff in the camp was hers, the tents, the sleeping bags and cooking utensils. *Good old Eddie.* She'll sort everyone out. Now she was doing the cooking as well. She slammed a frying pan down on the flimsy, two-ring stove and rattled a fork in it for good measure. She'd do the cooking, but she wasn't going to be quiet about it. "How stupid am I… *again?*" She lifted the pan and bashed it down. She paused, listening to see if anyone was coming, but no one did. "Kissing me and seeing other women too," she hissed. She opened the packet and placed the sausages in the frying pan. "And now this." A movement over her shoulder made her look, but it was just the flysheet fluttering in the breeze. She grabbed the two ends and tied them neatly to the poles, pausing to listen to the conversation outside.

"So, what have you got planned to amuse yourselves for two whole nights?"

Eddie moved her lips, mimicking the woman.

"We've got a walk planned for tomorrow."

Eddie rolled her eyes. Why was Tolly telling her that, for goodness' sake? Tuesday would want to join in and that would really put the mockers on it.

"A walk? I love walking."

Eddie groaned. Tuesday hadn't struck her as the rambling type.

"I could come with you. I'll ask my sister to mind the shop."

Eddie waited for them to protest. No one spoke, so she cleared her throat loudly.

"Don't worry if you can't make it, Tuesday," she shouted from behind the flysheet. "You could always come over tomorrow evening for a drink." She popped her head out of the porch and they turned to look at her.

"But she'd be welcome if she could though, wouldn't she?" Mike looked at the others expectantly and they all nodded.

"Might save us getting lost if she knows the area." Tolly shrugged and Eddie begrudgingly agreed that he had a point.

"You are kind," Tuesday simpered. "I think we could be really good friends, Eddie." Without answering Eddie ducked back into the tent to check the sausages, her ears on red alert for more warning signals. She was rolling the sausages around the pan, making sure they weren't getting burnt, when Tuesday appeared in the tent.

"What time will you be leaving, Eddie?"

"Early I should think…. eight o'clock?"

Mike trailed in behind, draining the last of his Prosecco. "Not that early, surely?" He handed his empty glass to Eddie.

"What time could you leave?" Tolly joined them and the three of them stood next to her, getting in her way.

"Just after nine? I've got a delivery first."

"Shall we say nine fifteen precisely?" Tolly had decided, unilaterally, that he was I.C. operations. Tuesday nodded. She finished the last of her fizz and handed the glass to Eddie.

"Another?" Tolly lifted the bottle, but Tuesday shook her head. Eddie glared at the back of his head. If there was any going spare, she'd quite like some.

"Very sweet of you. But no, I mustn't. I need to go and get my beauty sleep," She giggled. Did she just bat her eyelashes? "I'll leave you handsome men and see you tomorrow. And you, Eddie." She wiggled her fingers and then tottered off, pausing by the hedge for one last wave. Tolly and Mike continued to stare into the now empty space. Then they snapped back to action, able to concentrate on their stomachs.

"Anything you'd like me to do for dinner?" Tolly looked around in surprise at the cooking preparation. "I thought I was doing it with Jack?"

"Yes, I thought so too," Eddie replied rather sharply. The men exchanged a nervous glance, but she didn't care. She wasn't going to be a doormat again. Mike gathered Trixie's lead and pointed at the pan. "How long have I got?"

"Ten minutes or so," she replied, stony-faced.

Mike gestured towards Trixie. "I'll just take her along the riverbank for a run." He nodded at Tolly and left.

"I thought Tuesday would be good company for you." Tolly picked up the frying pan and gave it a shake. "She's obviously on the ball, running the shop single-handed like that."

"Does she run it by herself?" Eddie snapped, taking back the frying pan.

"I bet she does," he replied, "she seems very capable."

Jack came in to collect the knives and forks for the table. He looked to catch his grandad's eye, to give him a warning.

"Is she married?" Tolly carried on, totally oblivious.

Eddie pursed her lips and pushed Tolly out the way. She lifted the sausages into a dish and placed them on the stove while she looked for plates.

"I don't think she's married," she said coolly. "But she has had *plenty* of boyfriends from what she was saying." Her tone expressed her disapproval.

"I'm not surprised." He snorted in quite an unbecoming way. "Well done with those sausages by the way. Good job you're here to look after us." He walked away and sat down at the table outside. Eddie picked up a can of beans. She was momentarily tempted to throw it at the back of his head. Hard! She opened it instead and vigorously shook the beans into a pan. Seething, she glanced up to see Mike running towards them, waving his hands.

"Stop her! She's coming. Stop her."

Suddenly Trixie appeared, dashing towards them at full pelt. Jack walked towards her, his arms outstretched and Trixie stopped, a few metres in front of him, her stubby tail wagging. "Come here girl."

Trixie dodged round him and ran towards the tent, her tongue hanging out the side of her mouth.

"She's coming to you, Eddie."

Leaving the stove Eddie found Trixie in the porch area. Her nose was high in the air, sniffing.

"Come here you crazy thing."

But Trixie had located the source of the delicious smell. She glanced at Eddie, then back to the dish.

"Don't you dare," Eddie whispered. The dog looked back at the sausages. She dodged Eddie, grabbed them and was out the tent before any human could react. She ran round Tolly and headed towards the river, the string of sausages trailing behind her.

"That animal." Tolly blustered into the tent, as Mike appeared.

"I'm on it!" He chased her towards the river. "I'm sorry, Eddie," he shouted over his shoulder.

Tolly put his arm around her shoulders. "Not to worry, old bean. It's not the end of the world."

Jack slouched into the porch and rifled through their box of supplies. "We have beans," he shrugged. "Bread. Porridge. Another tin of beans and sausages." He straightened up holding two tins aloft.

"There you go, old bean. Crisis averted."

Eddie shrugged Tolly's arm off her shoulder and glared at him. "Stop calling me that. I'm younger than you and that... other woman... probably." She handed the wooden spoon to Jack and stomped off towards the river. Tolly lifted his palms up and turned to his grandson.

"What did I say?"

Jack sighed. "I don't think she likes being called 'old bean,' grandad."

Chapter fifteen

Eddie sat on a large rock wedged in the clear shallows of the river and tugged on a bootlace. The bloody thing had snapped. She gave up and dabbed at the forming tears. She blew her nose noisily. Lost in thought, she watched the patterns in the water and found it calming. She'd overreacted. But it was all too much this week. Something had been stirred up and the little voice inside her head had been berating her for being so gullible. She'd dared to enjoy his company and now she was being mocked. A flutter of eyelashes and men's heads were turned. Tolly's blatant interest in that woman had touched a raw nerve.

She heard footsteps and looked up to see Jack slouching over. Great. A teenager was being sent to look for her. This was going to be interesting.

"Can I sit there?" He pointed to the other side of the rock, and she nodded. It was big enough for two and he settled himself without speaking. Bird song and the gurgling water were the only sounds.

"What you doing?"

"Nothing." Oh, that's great, Eddie. Who's the teenager?

Silence again.

"Grandad didn't mean anything by it, you know?"

She shrugged. "Don't care."

He looked over his shoulder at her, his lips clamped together to stifle a smile. "You don't mean that Eddie. Even I have seen how well you get on, normally… and I'm a bloody teenager."

"Don't swear Jack."

They went back to watching the water.

"He's just not good at picking up clues. He probably doesn't even realize he's done anything wrong. He can be a bit…" he cast around before adding, "dense." He bounced his hand on top of the water. "He probably didn't want to be rude. She was a bit…"

"Flirty? Obvious?" Eddie folded her arms.

"'Full on', I was going to say." He lifted his hand and flicked some water at her.

"Don't!" Head bowed, she stared at her hands, picking at a piece of dried skin.

He gently pulled her hand away. "Don't," he echoed, "you'll make it sore."

"What do you care?"

He chuckled. "You're so lame, Eddie. You sound about ten."

She took a deep breath. She elbowed him. "Sorry I just felt …"

"It's alright." He elbowed her back. "He does like you. He keeps talking about you. 'Eddie this, Eddie that," - he mimicked in a weird high voice that didn't sound like Tolly at all.

"Seems as though he likes a number of ladies." She glanced at him; her mouth downturned.

"Eddie, he was probably just flattered-"

She was thinking about the mystery woman who'd been in his car but smiled weakly. "Yes, flattery goes a long way." They stayed sitting on the stone.

"You alright Eddie, you seem a bit…" The sentence tailed off. She felt his hand on her back and he rubbed it round in a circle before lightly patting her shoulder. "It'll be okay you know." His hand fell away and they went back to sitting in silence. After a few moments he stood up. "Come on, we'd better check he's not killed Mike yet?"

She pushed herself off the stone but stumbled, she'd forgotten about the bootlace. Jack shot his arm out to steady her.

"What's wrong with your foot?"

"The bootlace, it snapped earlier."

He pulled her up the bank.

"What happened to Trixie?" She clambered up next to him and readjusted herself.

"She ran off."

"If there's any justice, she'll be lying somewhere feeling extremely sick." She chuckled, then covered her mouth.

"It's not funny."

"Well, it is." She had an image of Mike chasing Trixie along country lanes, a long string of sausages dangling from her mouth.

"Why's it always Mike causing chaos, he's supposed to be highly trained?"

"The T.A. budget must have run out before they got to him. Anyway," she changed the subject, "what are we having for supper?"

"There was talk of beans." Jack beckoned to her to hurry up.

"Too many beans aren't good for people my age."

"Brilliant! And I'm sharing a tent with grandad!"

Chapter Sixteen

THE SUN had completely disappeared, to be replaced by a bright, full moon. A campfire crackled and the Wanderers sat staring into it. They each cradled a cup of hot chocolate but as Tolly looked into the cup, the most that could be said for it was that it was hot. The brown liquid was watery, devoid of any of the usual cream and marshmallow trimmings, but it was all that Tuesday had been able to find in the shop. He waited for his supper to go down, apprehensive about what so many beans might mean for his digestive system.

"Well, that wasn't so bad, was it?" Mike tried to sound upbeat as Tolly slurped noisily from his mug. Why was he always so bloody optimistic? Tolly thought the whole evening had been a disaster and Eddie wasn't exactly speaking to him either.

"It was alright," Jack muttered. He hadn't been thrilled with the evening's meal. He'd taken photos to share on social media and they'd earned him several derisory comments from his mates. Trixie obviously agreed with Jack and gave a yap from over by the tree. She'd managed several hours of freedom before finally being caught and reprimanded by Mike. She was now tied up, ostracized from the group by way of punishment.

"I'll be surprised if she sleeps tonight." Mike was still cross that he'd had beans when she'd had so many tasty sausages.

"She'd better not keep us awake," Tolly grumbled.

Eddie quietly finished her hot chocolate and put the mug on the tray. She stood up and stretched. "I think I'll turn in for the night. We've got a long walk tomorrow."

Tolly watched her go to her tent. "Night Eddie," he called but got no reply. "Is she okay?" he whispered to Jack. "She's been awfully quiet tonight."

"She thought you were flirting with Tuesday earlier."

"What? I wasn't flirting with the woman." Tolly's brow furrowed, and he leaned closer to Jack.

"Eddie thought you were. She said something about you and a *number of ladies?*" He looked at his grandad expectantly but hushed when Eddie appeared with her towel and toothbrush. Jack's phone beeped and he disappeared into his own tent to tap out a reply.

Tolly slumped in his chair, he'd most certainly not been flirting. He wanted to call out to her, to speak and reconnect, but she didn't even glance over as she went to use the facilities. She seemed so aloof and Tolly didn't know what to say to make it better. Jack appeared from his tent dressed in pyjamas, a sweatshirt and flip-flops. He pointed towards the toilet block and as he walked past, his flip-flops slapped noisily against his feet. He gave his grandad a mock-salute.

"Last one to bed is a loser." This spurred everyone into action. Eddie re-appeared. She ignored Tolly as she swapped places with Jack. Jack raised his eyebrows at his grandad - Tolly wasn't the only one to have noticed her coolness. Jack returned to his tent and switched on his torch as Tolly continued to sit.

He didn't know how long he'd been there for, but something caught his eye. Jack's torch had lit up his tent, illuminating his outline and projecting his every move to the outside world.

"Just to warn you, Jack, you're casting shadows, so I advise caution!"

Inside the canvas, Jack twisted his fingers and a shadow of a rabbit appeared on the tent.

"Very good, son." The shadow dismantled and in a whirl of shapes another appeared. "A bird?" He was rewarded with a 'thumbs up' from inside. It was actually a good likeness.

"That's your lot, grandad."

Jack's sleeping bag rustled as he climbed inside. From under the tree Trixie barked to remind them she was still there.

"Don't forget Trixie, she's coming in with us tonight." The tent fell quiet and Tolly's thoughts returned to Eddie. Why was she being so off with him? If only he knew, he might be able to put it right.

Twenty minutes later Tolly returned from the facilities. He thought it was a very grand description for the compost loo that lurked behind the wooden door, and on returning to the tent he found an interloper curled up on his bed.

"Trixie," he whispered, "get down from there. Here's your bed." The dog slunk down and curled up on her blanket, nestled between the two camp beds. Climbing into his sleeping bag, Tolly banged his head.

"Ouch." Above him Jack's torch swung backwards and forwards.

"You'll be glad of that in the night," Jack replied sleepily and somewhere in the distance an owl hooted. Trixie barked in response and Tolly tickled her chin. Her rough tongue licked his hand and as he clicked the torch off he continued to stroke her. It was comforting. He'd owned many dogs over the years, including three black Labradors and a springer spaniel. But his favourite, by far, had been Squiffy, a mongrel terrier cross. He'd been a funny looking thing, but energetic and loyal - to him at least. He pictured Thea. She'd never liked Squiffy and the feeling had been mutual. He patted Trixie's head slowly. Funny, he'd not thought about Thea since the other day. Recently, the only woman he'd thought about was Eddie. He saw her wrapped in the bin liner in the woods, despite being cold and tired she'd kept them together and he thanked his lucky stars that he'd put that postcard in the shop.

"Night, night lovely girl," he whispered.

Jack turned in his sleeping bag. "I know you like her," he mumbled, "you're not fooling anyone."

Tolly froze. Was it that obvious?

"Doesn't he, Trix?"

Phew, Jack was talking about the dog and, breathing out quietly, Tolly grinned to himself in the dark.

Chapter Seventeen

AMIR SAT at the desk in his cramped bedroom staring at his computer screen. It was late and he had to open the shop at 5.30am to sort the papers for delivery. But he couldn't sleep. He was too excited. Following his conversation with Eddie he'd spent the last two days making notes about everything to do with the camping shop. In his notebook he'd written any questions or thoughts he'd had about the business. He'd put a survey on social media and had received nearly fifty responses from people his age, describing the type of shop they'd like and the activities they undertook. He'd been picking the brains of his Uni mates too. He'd spoken to more people in the last couple of days than he'd spoken to during the whole year at Uni. A number of his fellow students had completed the Duke of Edinburgh at college and, even more interesting, was the large number of them that would like to do an expedition while at Uni. Jed, a student who'd sat in front of him in lectures all year, but he'd only spoken to this week, had talked about wild camping. That had sparked a whole chain of thought about marketing to young people and Instagrammers. He needed to get into the mindset of his target audience and his age group was certainly a potential growth area. He'd managed to interview two women in the IT studio about website design. They'd directed him to specific websites, and he'd spent two hours investigating, whilst quiet at the shop. He was on a roll and fired up. Excited. "Boom!"

"Amir?"

Shit, his father was awake. "Yes, father."

"What are you doing, my boy?"

He heard his father's footsteps pause on the landing outside.

"Nothing father, just reading my book. Couldn't sleep."

"But you're up early. You'll be tired, my boy."

"I know, father. I'll try to sleep now. Good night." He quickly clicked off his light. He waited, not daring to move. He held his breath and listened. His father remained outside on the landing. If he came in now, he'd see the computer and the notebook. He'd start asking questions. Amir's heart was thumping. Then he heard the telltale creak of the floorboard outside his father's room.

"Good night."

He breathed out deeply, as his father's bedroom door closed. Switching his light back on he continued looking through the scribbled costings for a website. He needed to be careful and keep it all under wraps, until he was fully prepared. He scanned a list of the stock he wanted. As soon as he finished his shift at Shah's tomorrow, he was going to the camping shop to meet the owners, Mr. and Mrs. Turner. He'd had a long conversation with Mr. Turner on the phone already but wanted to know more. He'd been compiling a folder of information and thought about it, hidden in his wardrobe. Twenty-five years old and hiding things from his father. It wasn't as if it was anything bad, just a folder full of dreams.

His conversation with Eddie had stirred something within him. Now, instead of the shop being a pipe dream he was beginning to think it could become a reality and his confidence was growing. He knew Eddie had been having a tough time lately, as Janet, on the occasions when they overlapped at work, didn't exactly keep the details to herself. He liked Eddie and enjoyed their chats; she made a lot of sense. He realised they were good for each other, a mutual support system. Wasn't she away camping this weekend? He wondered how she was getting on. She'd certainly been happier last time she was in the shop. Now he had to do what made him happy and that *definitely* wasn't Maths! He hid the notebook and checked his bedside clock. He was going to be *so* tired in the morning, but knowing his notebook was filling up with plans and ideas made it all worthwhile.

Amir was up early. Instead of his usual slouch to work, he had a spring in his step as he made his way across Riverview Estate. He'd had just three hours sleep but he didn't care. He rubbed his eyes, gritty from lack of sleep, but the rest of him was buzzing. He walked past two young men carrying knapsacks. Dressed in blue overalls he guessed they worked in one of the factory units in the business park. Simonton was a strange town; it had a traditional High Street with a wide range of shops. There was everything from national chains to small independents run by the same families for decades. Radiating out from the High Street were offices and smaller businesses, whilst a new business park provided larger units and now housed well-established manufacturing and engineering companies. The park had been successful in bringing a range of white and blue-collar jobs to the area and, even this early in the morning, the place felt vibrant. Amir considered the demographics of the town, as he turned a corner and Shah's came into view. There was a good mix of every age group, retirees to young people, and all the ages in between. There would be plenty of potential audience, if he wanted to do a marketing campaign. *Explore the great outdoors this summer.* He pictured the flyer and imagined wandering the streets pushing them through doors. Better still, he could put them in peoples' newspapers. That was a good idea, he needed to write that in his book. *Explore the great outdoors - plenty to see this summer.* That sounded familiar. Was someone already using that? He laughed and flicked his fingers. One session talking to IT students at Uni and he was all over it. Boom!

He unlocked the shop and sighed. Like entering a black hole, he felt his energy being sapped as he crossed the threshold. How many more days before he could open the door to his own business? *One step at a time, Amir.* This was his new mantra. He dragged in the two piles of papers from the doorstep and glanced at the clock. He summoned his energy. He needed to get a move on as the paperboys would arrive in twenty minutes and he wanted a brew first. Strictly speaking, he flicked the kettle on, they were delivery 'people'. They had papergirls and retired people too and, whistling an unrecognizable tune, he started to sort them into piles, ready for delivery. He finished his tea and had just arranged the last paper when he heard a rattle at the door. He scooted round the shelves to lift the latch and threw the door open.

"Here they are! My little battalion. Ready to uphold the reputation of Shah's convenience store."

"What y'on about?" Three young lads stood on the threshold, staring at him.

"Y'alright Amir?" Another came over and felt his forehead. "You coming down with summat?"

Amir brushed away the hand, scowling. He stood to one side to let them in.

"Good timing. I just finished them. Entre dans le shop."

"Cutting it fine, ain't cha?" A thin little lad, Dillon, with blonde spiked hair, pointed out that, yes, Amir had cut it a bit fine that morning. He'd been too busy sauntering along the estate, dreaming about his potential new business, but didn't admit *that* to Dillon. He simply handed him the bulky, overstuffed, florescent paper bag. Dillon slung it on his shoulder as if it contained feathers, then turned and winked.

"See you later Amir, same time same place."

Amir and the others watched him depart. For someone so small and wiry he was strong. He picked up his battered bike and, one handed, cycled up the road before disappearing from view. Amir glanced at the clock. Four hours to go, then he could be on his way.

📷 *Chapter Eighteen*

Jack and Tolly sat at the rickety camping table in silence, eating their breakfast cereals as Eddie emerged from her tent. She was dressed, ready for the hike, but hopped around in socks.

"Has anyone seen my boots?" She scanned the floor around the camp, sure she'd left them in her porch the night before.

"Grandad?" Jack nudged the older man's arm.

"Yes, righto." Tolly cleared his throat and jumped up. He was still chewing his mouthful of cereal. "Sorry, I'll just get them." He strode over to his tent and returned with a pair of boots. They shone, catching the early sunlight as he handed them over. "I forgot to put them back last night. I put new laces in, you see."

Eddie turned the boots over then looked at Tolly. "You've polished them too?"

"Yes, I thought I'd give them a quick shine. Hope that's okay?"

She maintained steady eye contact with him then dipped her head. "Thank you, that's very kind."

Tolly waved away her thanks and returned to his bowl of cereal. Eddie joined them. She slid her feet into the boots and secured the laces, nodding her approval. The boots were as good as new. She turned her attention to food and poured out a large bowl of cornflakes. A tent zip opened with a flourish and Mike stepped out.

"O.M.G!" Jack's mouth dropped open, as Mike strutted towards them modelling a pair of eye-dazzling, tomato-red corduroy trousers. "Do you like them?" Too dazed to speak, the others merely gawped.

"Too bright?" His smile faded as disappointment registered. Eddie wondered if this might be one of those occasions when a little white lie was allowed, to save hurt feelings.

"Um…" She tilted her head to one side. "Normally, hiking gear tends to be a little more subtle-"

"Yoo-hoo-"

Thank God. Mike's attention was diverted as Tuesday tottered towards them, waving.

"Good morning, everybody," she trilled. "How did you sleep?" She came to a stop in front of Mike. "Oh I say, Mike, I love your trousers. Very swish." She ran a hand down his thigh on the pretense of feeling the thick corduroy. She giggled as he blushed, his cheeks turning the same shade as his trousers.

"Now they are what I call 'dancing pants," she tittered. "It's such a shame we can't go to a club later. There isn't one for miles."

Eddie sighed inwardly. She noticed that Tuesday was wearing a strappy top and tight pink trousers. Maybe she had changed her mind about coming with them but, knowing it was mean, Eddie still crossed her fingers under the table.

"Are you not coming with us?"

"Yes, I'm coming." Tuesday frowned. "Why?"

"Oh, I… you don't look dressed for a long walk." Eddie pointed at her ankle boots, blue suede with kitten heels. They were nice, actually, but not for rambling. "You're not going to get very far in those."

"These?" Tuesday lifted up a foot and tipped it from one side to the other. "These are really comfy, I'll be fine." She brushed away a speck of mud. "I couldn't bring myself to wear boots. No offence," she added quickly, looking at Eddie's sturdy, polished hiking boots, "but they are quite ugly. They'd make my legs look fat too."

Eddie gritted her teeth as the insult washed over her. The woman really needed to think before she spoke.

"But they're comfortable."

Tuesday laughed. "Comfort? Oh, I haven't reached the stage where I buy clothes for comfort, Eddie." She smiled at the men. "Once you start doing that it's only a short step to beige cardigans, elasticated waistbands and then the grave."

There was a moment's silence before Jack stepped forwards. "But we *are* going quite a long way."

Tuesday waved her hand dismissively. "I'll be fine. And if I'm not," she giggled, "you strong men will help me out?"

Eddie had to look away. Her jaw was beginning to ache from clenching her teeth so tightly. It promised to be a very long day, but she was determined not to let Tuesday irritate her. She opted instead to change tack and plastered on a smile. She turned back. "It'll be useful having you with us, Tuesday, as someone who knows the area."

The woman shuffled from one leg to the other. She swatted a fly from her leg and rubbed at the candy pink material where it had been sat. "I wouldn't say I know it *that* well. I don't tend to go out in the country much." She leant in towards Eddie and whispered, "I prefer town any day. More lively and it doesn't smell of cow poo."

"But I thought you were a country girl, Tuesday?" Tolly took a step closer.

"Colonel," she giggled, "whatever gave you that idea?" She smoothed her trousers over her tiny waistband. Jack glanced away, catching Eddie's eye.

"Shall we get going?" he said then paused. "Where's your bag, Tuesday?"

She lifted her arms and let them fall by her side, pouting.

"You not bringing any water?"

She shook her head.

"A jacket?"

"I'll be fine. Don't worry about me."

Jack shook his head slowly. He held up a hand and disappeared into his tent. He reappeared with a billycan and held it out for the woman to take. "Here. I filled it earlier. You can use it."

Tuesday shrugged again. "Jack, sorry. I don't really like water."

"Tuesday, when you're thirsty later on, you might change your mind." Eddie took the can and held it out, but Tuesday didn't take it. Instead, she ran her hands around her hips and back to demonstrate she had no pockets.

"You're both so sweet," she simpered, "but I've nowhere to put it." Getting annoyed, Jack snatched it back.

"You are a good boy, Jack." She linked her arm through Tolly's and gave a gentle tug towards the river path. Reluctantly he moved off, but not before he glanced back and mouthed 'sorry' to Eddie. Tuesday pulled him along.

"It's just being sensible," Jack whispered under his breath, as he shoved the water in his backpack.

"I'm not sure 'sensible' is a word she's familiar with," Eddie replied, as she waited for him to swing his pack on his shoulder. Up ahead Tuesday daintily sidestepped a fly-covered cowpat. "One thing I *am* sure of though, is that those fashion boots aren't going to stay looking like that for long."

Chapter Nineteen

HEATHER'S TRAIN was just starting to pick up speed again. It stopped at every provincial station and allowed a trickle of passengers to get off each time. She watched curiously, as they manoeuvred cases and bags down the platform towards the Exit signs, then turned her attention back to anything happening inside the train. She hadn't done this journey for a good few months and she'd forgotten how long the last stretch of the journey took. She recognized some of the place names and glanced at her watch. It would be at least another forty minutes before she arrived in Simonton.

At midday Amir was still at work when the phone rang. He lifted his head out of his notebook. For a couple of seconds, he looked around, confused. His mind had been focused on his camping shop and he'd been able to compile six pages of questions.

"Hello. Shah's convenience store. Amir speaking." He recognized Mr. Shah's voice immediately and his heart sank. "I'm really sorry Mr. Shah but I've got somewhere to be." He paused, listening. "I'll be gone for an hour. Yes, I could put a sign on the door, that is no problem. What time will you- okay. Another couple of hours then." He rang off. Janet was sick again. What was going on with her? He worried about Mr. Shah, who wasn't well himself. How would he cope with the shop when- if-Amir decided to leave? Not his problem, but nevertheless it played on his mind as he grabbed his coat and checked the pockets for keys.

Locking the door behind him he swung his coat on and marched towards the High Street. He was late now and instead of being able to grab a quick sandwich he needed to go straight to the camping shop. He didn't mind, he was too excited to eat anyway. He'd been dreaming about this meeting for days now and a spring had returned to his step as he turned on to the High Street and headed south.

Heather continued to read the self-help book she'd bought at Waterloo earlier. It had kept her glued to the pages and she'd completed some of the exercises, trying to find out what her 'calling' was. Apparently to feel truly fulfilled you needed to do what you felt passionate about - and it was making her question what that was for her. She gazed out the window and thought about her desk at work. She took a deep breath, feeling her heart rate quicken. Work wasn't fulfilling anymore; it wasn't *good* for her anymore when just thinking about it made her anxious. Whilst she earned good money – *really* good money - she realized that wasn't enough if you were miserable all the time. She watched the countryside zoom past the window in a blur of blues and greens. Her mind wandered; how would she mix a yellow paint to be as vibrant as that rapeseed field? She put her nose back in the book, as an idea began to form.

With perfect timing, she finished the last page as the guard announced the next stop was Simonton. The book seemed to have been written specifically for her journey. *Serendipity?* She began to tidy her things and got ready to go. Once out on the platform it was easy to drag the case along. Leaving the station, she emerged at the end of the High Street and stood in the sun, savouring the warmth on her skin.

There were no taxis on the rank, so she turned down the High Street. Further along, towards the library and the camping shop, was another Pick-up area. She'd try there. She pulled her case over smooth new paving slabs and came to a stop in front of the old camping shop. She looked in the window. What had her mum said recently? Something about someone... oh she couldn't remember. Her mum liked to go into minute detail about people Heather had never even met. Then she scolded herself; she wanted to leave the city as she no longer liked the veil of anonymity and was keen to get to know people and share details of their lives. She envisaged putting down roots somewhere and this was as good a place as any. As she turned from the window, she banged into something and staggered. She found her footing in time to see her case rolling towards the road.

"No!" She lunged for it but was grabbed back as a dustcart roared past. It missed her - and the case - by inches, and she turned to see a man pulling at her jacket. "What are you doing?" She shook him off, "let go."

"I'm stopping you getting killed," he replied, tersely, "here, let me help you." He checked the road was safe then stepped down into the gutter and yanked the suitcase up. He held it out and she grabbed it pulling it towards her. Dark skinned, with short black hair jelled up into a quiff he smiled, revealing a row of straight, white teeth - a small gap between the front two. He held out a hand.

"Amir. Pleased to meet you."

She shook it and frowned. He seemed familiar. "Do I know you?" She held tightly onto her case as she paused then glanced away quickly, not wanting to stare.

"I don't think so, I'm sure I'd remember."

What did that mean? Self-conscious, she reached up and pulled her plait over her left shoulder. The suitcase started to roll back towards the road and Amir leant over to grab it.

"You need to keep hold of it. See, the camber isn't right here." He pointed to a hump in the pavement. "Little old ladies keep losing their trolleys into the gutter… they should fix it really."

"You comparing me to a little old lady?"

His face broke into a smile. He glanced down at the floor, thick long eyelashes sweeping against his cheeks. God she'd kill for lashes like that. He looked back up and right at her.

"So, *I'm* Amir," he repeated pointedly.

"I know," she replied, keeping her voice serious, "you've already said!"

He nodded his head towards her and raised his eyebrows quizzically.

"Nice to meet you Amir… and I'm Heather."

"Finally," he replied with mock exasperation.

She chuckled. "Do you work here?" She turned to see where she was. The camping shop. Something definitely niggled at the back of her brain.

"No, I don't." But she noticed he grinned. "It's a long story," he added, "maybe I'll tell you one day."

"Okay," she said slowly. Was he coming on to her?

"So do you live here, in Simonton, Heather?" He looked at the suitcase.

"Long story," she replied, equally as mysteriously. "Maybe I'll tell you one day." It made Amir laugh.

"Touche." He was about to say something else when a banging on the shop window interrupted them. An elderly man inside was waving at Amir.

"Heather, sorry, I need to go. Mr. Turner and I have got a meeting. It was nice to meet you. Maybe see you again soon?" He seemed keen but as he went, she realised they hadn't swapped numbers.

"See you around," she whispered and yanked her suitcase towards the taxi rank.

Chapter Twenty

*E*DDIE LOOKED at Tuesday's feet and winced. Sitting on a big stone, Tuesday contorted to place one bare foot on her lap as she placed a final plaster over yet another blister. Tuesday had used every plaster that the group had been able to muster between them. Her hair was now flat, with leaves and clumps of moss caught in it and her constant chatter was wearing everyone down. Eddie enjoyed the outdoors for its peace and tranquility. Despite the challenges they'd faced on their last walk they'd got along. They'd admired the fantastic views and stopped to listen to the different birdsong. There'd been *none* of that this morning! The only twittering had come from Tuesday and quite how Tolly was putting up with it, Eddie had no idea. Initially she'd felt the green-eyed monster reappear as they'd walked off together. She'd told herself he was nothing to do with her and he could walk with whomever he wanted. Now, she just felt sorry for him. He was too polite and would never tell Tuesday to shut up. He did however throw occasional glances Eddie's way, as if appealing for help or at least a little respite. Even when he'd mouthed 'help' to Jack they'd pretended not to notice and now, as the lines on his face looked deeper and more etched, she felt a pang of guilt for not helping him out.

Mike caught them up. They were walking around a huge, fallow field, following a public footpath. Hedges framed the area, interspersed with a low stonewall and through a tiny gap in the distance they glimpsed the copse they were heading for. It would be somewhere to rest and have a snack.

"Hey Eddie."

She smiled as Mike joined her and they walked side by side.

"Apparently my great grandad was a baker in the army during World War One."

She glanced across. Was this another joke? He looked back, grinning.

"Yeah, apparently he went in all buns glazing."

Eddie frowned. *Buns glazing?*

He laughed. "Buns glazing!"

She couldn't help but giggle. "Actually, that's quite funny," she said, nodding her head. "You're definitely getting better."

Mike stuck his chest out, pleased with her assessment.

"Mike? What do you get if you drop a piano on an Army officer?" she whispered and he raised his eyebrows, waiting for the punchline. "A flat Major."

He groaned.

"What? It's not bad," she appealed. "Short and succinct-"

"But it needs to be funny too."

She opened her mouth to complain then realised he was laughing, and she gave him a shove with her elbow. "You!"

They tramped on in a comfortable silence. She glanced across at Mike, he looked very thoughtful, and she wondered whether he was trying to remember more jokes. Lifting her gaze, she spotted Trixie in the far corner of the field. The daft dog seemed to be running around in circles. A larger animal appeared from behind the hedge and ambled over to her. Were they playing?

"Is that a cow?" Eddie squinted to look. She really needed to get some new glasses. It certainly looked like a cow. But as she stared, hairs rose on her arms. "Mike, is she worrying that cow?" As she pointed, Trixie began running round and round the larger animal. "She should be on a lead, Mike. If a farmer sees her they can shoot, you know."

That got his attention.

"Really?"

She liked Mike but sometimes she wondered if he'd been born with any common sense at all. "Ah panic over, she's coming back."

Sure enough, Trixie was running at full tilt towards them, her tongue hanging slack from the side of her mouth. Jack lifted his binoculars to get a better view and took a moment to focus. "Oh, oh," he said in a low, warning voice. "I don't think she's coming back because she loves you, Mike." Jack continued watching. "I think she's being chased." They were joined by Tolly and Jack handed him the binoculars. With a trained eye he found the subject straight away.

"What d'you reck, grandad?"

Tolly held his breath to steady himself as he peered down the field glasses. They waited for his verdict.

"I think we have a problem."

They waited for more.

"It's been a few years since I did biology, but I don't think that's a cow."

Jack grabbed the glasses back.

"Oh my God, it's a bloody bull," he said, panicking. "And she's leading it right back to us."

"We need to move!" Eddie bellowed and looked around the field. It was huge. There were no trees to climb or vegetation to protect them. *Where could they hide?* The ginormous creature was charging towards them at full pelt.

"This field's really big-"

"Thanks for that, Tuesday."

"Over there, look!" They followed Jack's finger to see a tiny stone hut. It had half its roof missing and was leaning precariously to one side. It was definitely in danger of collapsing at any moment. Eddie couldn't see anywhere better though – it was their best, their *only* option.

"It's not very salubr-" Tuesday didn't finish her sentence as Mike grabbed her hand and started running.

"Save your breath," he yelled and, dragging her along they sprinted as if their lives depended on it. Which they probably did.

Jack was the first one in. He burst through the rotten wooden door and held it open for the others. Once they were all through, he slammed it shut as he and Eddie, thinking the same thing, stared at it doubtfully. It had clicked into place and looked closed but one good shove and it would easily give way. It was hardly going to offer any resistance to the solid lump of muscle that was, at that moment, charging towards them. Eddie groaned. Jack gulped. She felt a sudden rush of affection for him as he braced himself against the door. Eddie peered through a small crack in the wood, then instantly wished she hadn't.

"What's happening Eddie, I can't hear anything?" Tolly stood to the side of her, breathing heavily. She could feel it moving her hair.

"It's still coming. Oh. My. God," she whispered, "it is SO fast." She lifted her head up from the crack and looked around at their terrified faces. "Sorry, that's probably not helping, is it?"

They shook their heads.

"It's still coming. Fifty metres. Forty metres. Thirty metres…" she pushed against the door, peering through the crack. "Crikes," she whispered.

"What?" Tolly was next to her, trying to peep through the lower half of the crack.

"Oh!"

"What?" They hissed in unison, unable to bear the suspense.

"It's stopped." She pointed at the door then placed her forefinger on her lips. "Shush," she whispered. "It. Is. Just. Out. There." She jabbed at the door. "It seems to be… listening?"

Jack kept his weight against the door, just in case. "Listening?"

Eddie nodded. The others followed suit and slumped down next to him.

"Yes," she whispered even quieter now that she had their full

134

attention. "I swear it's standing just" she mouthed 'out there.' They all pulled a face, holding their collective breath as she returned to look through the crack.

"So, what do we do now?" Tuesday asked loudly.

"Shush," Eddie whispered. "It is literally Just. Out. There." She jabbed her finger again for extra emphasis. "We need to stop talking and keep quiet." Trixie yapped and Mike wrapped his hands around her muzzle to quieten her. Outside the bull cocked an ear towards the door as Eddie held her breath.

"We'll have to hunker down and wait it out." Tolly sat on the floor and pulled a flask out of his rucksack. "May as well have a break," he suggested, "it'll get bored soon and move on."

Chapter Twenty-one

HEATHER'S TAXI pulled up outside her mum's house and she peered through the window. The house looked exactly the same. She glanced at the meter and handed a note to the driver.

"Keep the change, thank you."

He looked at the tenner, chuffed with the tip.

"Thanks love. Here, I'll give you a hand." He hopped out and heaved her suitcase from the boot. "Blimey love, what you got in there? Bricks?" Without waiting for an answer, he hopped back behind the wheel and reversed out. He narrowly avoided a people carrier that swung round the corner. Heather suppressed a yawn. She grabbed the case's handle and lugged it up towards the front door. She wouldn't miss having to drag this around. With all work and no time for play she'd forgotten how tiring travelling was.

Car doors opened behind her and, checking the case was safely wedged by the front door, Heather turned round. Sophie Macintosh and her children clambered out their car opposite. Dressed in sports gear and hopping about excitedly it was no wonder her mum called them the 'busy bunch'. Heather waved and crossed the cul-de-sac to say hello. She'd known Sophie at school. She had been a year ahead of Heather, and on every sports team going. Most people in Simonton knew *of* her. She'd married young, having met a local solicitor whilst still at college. It had caused a bit of a stir at the time because of their fourteen-year age gap. But, in spite of the doubters, they still seemed happy, and their kids were adorable.

"Hi Heather. Long time, no see." Sophie made sure the children were safely away before slamming the car doors. "How's the big smoke treating you?"

Why did people call it that?

"Good thanks. Been really busy recently so just making the most of some time off. I thought I'd surprise mum and come for a visit." She looked around the cul-de-sac. "How's everything with you?" The children had gathered in front of their house. The youngest was tugging at Sophie's jumper while her two brothers jumped around the lawn, trying to out-do each other in a hopping competition.

"Who she, mummy?" The pigtailed little girl smiled shyly when Heather caught her eye.

"Shush, darling," Sophie stroked her daughter's hair while continuing the conversation. "We're good thanks. Johnny's practice is expanding. I work there in the mornings now, a trainee legal executive."

"Good for you." Heather was genuinely pleased for her.

"Thanks," she laughed, "I'm doing a legal exec exam soon. Who'd have thought I'd enjoy studying so much at the ripe old age of thirty-one?" She smiled and nodded towards Eddie's house. "Your mum seems to be doing better as well. I've seen her out and about. She's been having visitors too."

Heather nodded; her mouth clamped shut. Sophie would know better than her how her mum was doing.

"Did she tell you about the walking group?"

Heather pulled a face. "She was telling me about it last week, sounds like they got in a right pickle."

Sophie nodded. Her daughter was leaning against her thigh, sucking her thumb as Sophie continued to gently stroke her hair. "She mentioned that the other day. Tanks and bird watchers in the wood?"

"That's it!" The story was travelling far and wide. Heather was pleased her mum had stories to recount.

"Actually," Sophie tapped her chin and frowned as a thought struck her. "You do know she's away this weekend, don't you?"

Her mum? Away? This was news to Heather. She'd assumed she'd be at home and pleased to give her the hero's welcome when she pitched up.

"That reminds me, I've forgotten to feed her bloody tomatoes," Sophie whispered, then clamped her mouth shut as her daughter looked up.

"Buddy domardoes," the little girl parroted. Sophie put a finger to her lips. "Don't say that darling, it's not nice." She looked back at Heather. "You okay? You've gone quiet?" Sophie pushed her daughter towards the house. "Go and play, darling. I won't be a minute."

"Buddy domardoes." Her daughter skipped over to her brothers, hitting them on their bums as she joined them.

"She's a terror. I feel sorry for the boys sometimes." But Sophie's eyes twinkled as she spoke. "Anyway, back to you. Didn't you know your mum was away?"

Heather shook her head. "No, I never thought. I wanted to surprise her." She snorted as she realised the tables had turned. "Who's getting the surprise now?"

"I don't think she's gone far. They're back tomorrow. Can you get in?"

Heather's mouth dropped open. Oh God, she'd have to break a window or something.

"I've got a spare key. Don't worry." Sophie patted her arm. "Hang on a sec and I'll grab it." She opened the front door and waited for the children to go through. She reappeared seconds later dangling a pink heart key ring from her finger. One silver Yale key hung on it.

"Thanks." Heather turned to go across the road. "Hey, I'm going to be around for a while, so I don't suppose you'd fancy a drink one evening?"

Sophie grinned, "I'd really like that," she nodded. "I'll give you a knock once I've spoken to Johnny." She rolled her eyes. "I'll persuade him to come back early to babysit, then we can make a night of it."

"That would be great, and don't worry about the tomatoes, I'll water them. It'll save you a job."

"That would be nice." With that, Sophie waved and disappeared inside her house.

This wasn't quite the homecoming that Heather had planned. Should she call her mum and tell her she was there? She didn't know the protocol for when you turned up to surprise someone - only to find out they were away. Now she would be alone in an empty house. Surprise! She lugged the suitcase through the door. Was it her imagination or was it getting heavier? Grateful that the bedrooms were downstairs, she poked her head into the spare room. The bed was fully made up and she felt her heart squeeze at the sight of familiar knick-knacks around the room. They were the backdrop to her childhood. A photo on the bedside table caught her attention. Her mum and dad smiled out, dressed in seventies flares. They looked in love, their arms around each other as they pulled in closer. She'd seen the photo before but sometimes things could be *so* familiar that you stopped noticing them. There weren't that many photos of her two parents together. There was one upstairs of her graduation, but it had all three of them in, with her in the middle. She paused, studying her dad. Her mum didn't talk about him much. Heather wondered if she missed him. She'd never asked her. Her dad could be quite domineering, both with her mum *and* with her, but who really knew what went on in a marriage? Her mum kept her own counsel. She didn't talk about affairs of the heart, or about her dad for that matter. But then, they'd hardly had the closest relationship over the last few years.

As she unloaded her suitcase, Heather thought about her time in Dubai. Hanging items in the wardrobe she smiled at the warm jumpers and trousers. They were a far cry from the sundresses and shorts she used to shop for whilst working abroad. She'd gone straight after university, young and naïve. It had certainly been good fun. She'd followed someone out there. Just thinking about Rich made her smile. Even now. They'd been in love. They were going to rule the world and it had been like that for over five years. But realisation had dawned that they wanted different things. She wanted to come home, but he loved the ex-pat lifestyle too much. Once she was aware of the severity of her dad's illness, she'd made the move and returned.

She cleared one of the drawers for her smaller items and squeezed in her walking socks. They were something else she wouldn't have needed in Dubai. Did she miss Rich? No, not really. It was first love, and they weren't compatible for the long haul. She had no regrets and wished him well. There'd always be a place for him in her heart, she'd be there for him, if he needed her.

She heard a voice. Someone walking along the river, and she watched as they passed by. It was so peaceful here. She removed her Michael Kors trainers, taking a moment to admire the gold heel pull (a present to herself, in a bid to spend some of her wages) and shuffled up the bed. She leant against the upholstered headboard and opened the self-help book she'd been reading earlier. Along with the quizzes and inventory questions for completion, she'd doodled numerous cartoons around the edges. Each was no bigger than three centimetres tall and she cast her eyes over them. A rabbit, glasses perched on the end of her nose, and a hedgehog with a large winter overcoat stuck on top of its prickles. That made her chuckle and she thought again about her 'calling'. Was it drawing? She certainly enjoyed doing it and could lose herself for hours. She hopped off the bed and opened the wardrobe, rooting through the boxes and files housed at the bottom. She dragged them out and found what she was looking for. Good old mum, the hoarder. She'd kept Heather's sketchbooks from college when she'd taken 'A' level art. She'd hated it even though she'd received an A grade. The syllabus had been far too serious, with no opportunity to do the cartoons and comical drawings that were her forte. As she flicked through the sketchbooks the drawings brought back memories. What she did notice was that, even though there were full sized paintings or sketches in the middle of the page, every margin was crammed with doodles. She studied these now, amazed at the level of detail she'd included in each one. An idea from long ago began to percolate. No longer tired from the journey, she carried the books upstairs and settled herself at her mum's dining table. She needed paper. Where could she get some? She went back downstairs and into the little room that had been set up as a study. A square, rickety desk held an old-fashioned computer and housed underneath was a bulky printer. She yanked the paper tray out. She sighed. Three pieces of A4 paper. Seriously? What use was that to anyone? She opened both desk drawers, her fingers crossed that there'd be a new, unopened ream. No such luck.

"Agh." Infuriating. Didn't her mum realize she was coming home, and she'd need paper for her unexpected, new project? When she put it like that. She laughed and ran back upstairs. She flicked through the sketchbooks, looking for blank pages. No, if she was going to do this properly she needed to get decent materials. She glanced at her watch. It was nearly five o'clock. She'd be too late for the shops in town. It was nearly dinnertime too and she hadn't even checked if there was anything in to eat. She'd not had much since her stir-fry last night, and grabbing her coat and bag, she let herself out.

Amir glanced at the wall clock and sighed. Mr. Shah was three minutes late. Amir put his coat on the stool by the counter, impatient to get going. While he was waiting, he decided to replenish the display of cans nearest the door. The benefits of this were two-fold - it afforded him maximum warning of Mr. Shah's arrival and it would be one thing less for his boss to do, once he arrived.

The visit to the camping shop had been sweet. He'd been sorry to leave after only one hour. He could happily have stayed on. Mr. Turner had lent him several catalogues and during the quieter moments in his shift Amir had flicked through their pages, amazed at the latest stock to buy. One tent could be hung from trees, if you didn't want to be on a forest floor. Another was made from a foil material that could withstand extreme temperatures. These would be too sophisticated for the camping he wanted to do, but the 'instagrammers' and 'influencers' he wanted to attract to his shop might have trips on freezing mountains or camps in tropical rainforests to prepare for. He stopped stacking cans as his mind wandered. He must remember to take the catalogues with him, he didn't want Mr. Shah binning them by accident.

The beep sounded and, surprised, he looked up. Had he missed Mr. Shah's approach? He found himself face to face with the suitcase woman from earlier.

"Hi there," he said. "Heather, right?" Mentally, he gave himself a round of applause. Normally he was rubbish with names.

She stopped, her eyes adjusting to the relative gloom inside the shop. He saw a flicker of recognition.

"Hello. Yes, Amir, right?"

He nodded. She'd remembered him too.

"Got your suitcase with you? Do I need to be careful?" He was aiming for banter, and she screwed up her face.

"Ha, ha, witty," she replied. "It's safely stowed away and I don't intend to use it again for a week or two."

"Oh, back from your holidays?" Was that too nosey? "Sorry, it's just I'm interested in travel, so I'm always keen to hear peoples' plans…" he tailed off, she was staring at him.

"I'm just visiting my mum," she explained. "I normally live in London."

"Normally?"

"Long story."

"Ahh," he smiled, "the long story. Like my own?"

She nodded, as she recalled their earlier exchange.

"What can I do for you?"

She asked whether he had any sketchbooks and he showed her what he'd got, hovering next to her while she looked.

"They're not quite what I was after." She sounded disappointed and he was sad he couldn't help. "Do you sell printer paper?"

He shook his head then held a finger up in the air. "I shouldn't be saying this, but there's a proper art shop in town." He glanced at the cheap wall clock and bit his lip. "But I think you're too late. You'll have to wait until Monday. Hmm, the shop in town might have some. It's a bigger store and they're open 'til late."

She perked up.

"In fact, I'm going that way so I can show you."

"Don't worry, I know where it is." She edged towards the door then paused. She looked back at him. "Unless you're going anyway? It might be nice to have some company."

Amir grabbed his coat from the counter. Mr. Shah was approaching, and Amir was eager to get out.

"Will you tell me your long story?"

"Only if you tell me yours after."

"Deal." As they shook hands the electronic beep sounded, announcing his boss's arrival.

Chapter Twenty-two

"I DON'T think we're ever getting out of here alive." Tuesday stopped pacing and sat down next to Tolly. She looked on the verge of tears and leant against him. Uncomfortable with this close proximity, he tried discretely to edge away.

"This is why I don't like going to the country."

He exhaled slowly. This was becoming ruddy intolerable. It was now six o'clock in the evening and they'd been trapped in the hut for over four hours.

"I watched a programme once about how animals can smell fear. Do you think he can smell us?"

Tolly felt obliged to shrug his shoulders causing her head to slip onto his chest. He leant away and stiffly pushed it back up to his shoulder. Was he the only one paying her any attention?

"I thought it was dogs that smelt fear?" Mike piped up. He was sat against the opposite wall, stroking Trixie in a calm, distracted fashion.

"I'm pretty sure it was all animals," Tuesday pouted, her brow furrowing. "It was presented by David Attenborough," she sighed. "He's so swishy, got such a seductive voice… a bit like you, Colonel." She looked up at him with doe eyes. He adjusted her head roughly.

"Oh yes," Mike agreed, "now he *is* good."

Tolly caught Eddie's eye, but she glanced away. She was still ignoring him - no mean feat given they were trapped in a place that was twelve feet long by twelve feet wide.

"I bet he hasn't seen five people cooped up in a shepherd's hut before. Held hostage by a bull." Jack joined in the conversation.

"I wouldn't bet on it," Mike disagreed, "he's been in tricky situations himself." He paused and looked up at the holey roof. "That's what we need to do… think like him. What would David do?"

Tolly stared at Mike. He'd gone bloody mad. Was he really trying to channel David Attenborough for rescue tips? As much as he didn't want to be drawn in, he couldn't help himself. "Surely Bear Grylls would be more appropriate?"

"I don't think so, Colonel." Mike seemed affronted by the very suggestion. "Don't get me wrong. Bear would be alright if lost in the outback or on top of a snowy mountain, but David would know what to do with animals - like that big bull out there."

Tuesday straightened up and tipped her head to one side, smiling at Mike. "Yes, I agree," she giggled. She started to chant "David! David!"

Tolly flapped his hand to stop her, whispering "shush." As she quietened down, he pointed at Mike's legs.

"I reckon David would send you out in those red trousers as a decoy, then he'd scarper over to the wall."

"He would not!" Mike stuck his bottom lip out at the thought of being placed in danger by David Attenborough. "I think he'd use his coat as a cape and go out there and do a spot of bull fighting."

Tolly thumped the ground. "I don't care what he'd do," he hissed. "He's not here. We are. I'm getting tired and hungry, and the light is fading-" He broke off, watching as Eddie moved to the door to spy outside. She'd maintained a watch all afternoon, peering through the door's crack. So far there'd been nothing to report, and they'd become accustomed to her 'still there' updates. But now as she closed one eye to focus, she gasped. "I think it's going." Then she exhaled. "Sorry. False alarm. He's toying with us." She sounded deflated.

Trixie, woken from her snooze, staggered to her feet and stretched out each back leg. She turned round several times and laid back down against Mike.

"I'm sorry I keep getting your hopes up. But he keeps getting mine up too," Eddie said quietly. "The bloody…bugger… bastard… bull." She broke off, looking contrite. "Sorry! I thought I'd be good in a hostage situation but now I'm not sure. I feel I'm about to snap and go running out the door."

Tolly watched. He was concerned by her outburst although rather impressed by her use of alliteration given the stressful situation.

"You know what, I've had all I can take of this," he said calmly. "*And I really need to use the facilities.*" The others murmured in agreement. "I'm sick of being cooped up and dictated to by that bloody thing." He looked at the back of Eddie's head as she continued to watch the animal through the door.

"Hold on a minute," she whispered but they'd heard it all before. Several times. "I think it might be moving away." She waved a hand to get their attention. Taking it in turns they looked through the crack. Sure enough, the bull had turned and was ambling away. Its head was low, looking for some grass tasty enough to tempt it.

"I reckon we could make a run for it," Tolly whispered, an edge of excitement in his voice. When no one replied he tried again. "Come on. We can do it if we're *really* quiet."

"What about my feet?" Tuesday gingerly pressed the layers of plaster she'd built up. "They're so painful." She'd long since taken her boots off and had been padding around the bothy in her socks and plasters.

"Will you shut up!" Eddie hissed. "It's your own fault your feet hurt. We tried to warn you."

Tuesday pursed her lips, petulant. "It's not my fault. I'm so hungry and thirsty -"

"What the bloody hell's that got to do with your feet?"

"Nothing." Tuesday sulked. "I'm just saying my feet hurt - *and* I'm hungry and thirsty-"

"We're *all* hungry and thirsty."

"I'm only saying."

"Well don't. If you'd brought some water, we wouldn't have had to share ours."

No one moved.

"And now we're all going to dehydrate."

Tolly's mouth dropped open, he held his breath. In the distance, crows cawed. Right on cue, his stomach rumbled loudly. The fact he was starving added further fuel to Eddie's angry fire.

"And if you'd brought food instead of expecting everyone else to look after you-"

"I told you I didn't like the country!"

"Then why did you-"

"Ladies, ladies, come along." Tolly spoke calmly. "Let's not fall out. It'll do no good whatsoever." He held his arms up to placate them but took a step back when he realised he was right in the danger zone between them.

"I'd expect *you* to say that." Eddie turned on him. "Sticking up for her. 'Let's not fall out'," she mimicked.

Her eyes flashed with anger and, shocked, Tolly put a hand out to calm her. "Eddie," he whispered, "this won't achieve anything-"

"It doesn't need to *achieve* anything," she hissed, "but it is making me feel better." She stepped away from the door. "But then you're not bothered about how *I* feel are you?" She stomped across the bothy, reaching the other side in five large strides. "Bugger," she whispered. She stood facing the wall as she tried to calm her breathing. For a few moments nobody moved.

"Um, I don't know if this is a good time to mention it," Jack spoke quietly, "but the bull is *definitely* moving away."

Tolly cleared his throat and joined Jack by the door. His emotions were running riot and he was smarting from Eddie's words. But, for now, he needed to bury his feelings and get everyone out of here. Survival was more important.

"Righto, I suggest two at a time." He took command. "We run towards that gap in the hedge over there." They craned their necks to look. "Jack and Tuesday go first."

Jack shot his grandad a look of fury, but Tolly replied calmly. "Survival, Jack," and was relieved when Jack nodded his understanding.

"Second out, Eddie and me." He looked across the hut to see Eddie peeking round at them. She avoided eye contact but shuffled back to the door.

"- and if it's still safe, Mike can bring up the rear with Trixie."

Everyone nodded and began jostling for a place by the door.

"Um," Mike put his hand up, "what if it's not safe and I'm stuck here on my own?"

"Mike, we're in this together." Tolly put his hand on the man's shoulder, squeezing it for reassurance. "We'll give you what food and drink we have and if you can't get out, we'll get immediate help from the farmer. Happy?"

Mike nodded and everyone emptied out the pitiful remains of their supplies. It amounted to one apple (with a squidgy bruise on its side), a quarter of a bottle of flat Lucozade and two tablets of chewing gum.

"Yum." Mike wasn't impressed.

Tolly shrugged apologetically. "Hopefully you won't need them." He lined everyone up by the door as they prepared to face their enemy.

The door opened slowly and Tolly winced as the hinges creaked. Checking that the bull was still distracted he signaled for Jack and Tuesday to run. They sprinted towards the wall as if the gun had gone off at the Olympics 100 metres final. The rest of them watched their speedy progress.

"They're doing well," Eddie said quietly. "The bull hasn't even noticed."

Tolly moved closer to her. "Eddie?"

Ignoring him she continued to watch the runners.

"Eddie, we need to talk. Have I done something?"

She remained focused on Jack and Tuesday. "They've made it." She turned and for an instant forgot she was angry. She clapped her hands together and jumped up. "Almost as exciting as the Grand National…" then she remembered where she was and fell quiet again.

"Eddie, have I upset you?" Tolly leant in close to her.

"I don't want to talk about it."

"But I feel like it's changed something between us-"

"There is no 'us'," she stated flatly. "I know that now. Can we just get out of here, please?"

Mike looked relieved that they'd stopped whispering. He waved them over and put two thumbs up in the air. "Ready?" He pulled the door open just wide enough for them to sneak out. The bull was in the middle of the field, staring in the opposite direction. Tolly reached for Eddie's hand and, gripping it tightly, they started their run towards the hedge. He prayed for his hip to remain in one piece. The hedge now looked a long way away and the ground was deceptively uneven. Large clumps of thistles snagged on their arms and legs as they ran the most direct route. Feeling a squelch underfoot he turned to see a huge, sloppy cowpat – now patterned with his deep boot print. Past the point of caring, he pulled Eddie on and they darted through a patch of nettles before, finally, reaching the wall. They tried to squeeze through the gap at the same time and turning sideways, they came face to face. Their bodies pressed together; their hands still clasped. Tolly held his breath despite his hammering heart screaming for oxygen and he looked down at Eddie. Her dark brown eyes drew him in, her little button nose… he *really* wanted to lean in and kiss her.

"Oh, you made it." The spell was broken as Tuesday appeared, clapping her hands together. She seemed to have forgotten about her blister-covered feet and put her arms around Tolly's waist, reaching up to kiss his cheek. "I thought I'd never see you again…either of you," she added as Eddie turned to her with a stony expression and shook her hand free from Tolly's.

"Oh! Oh! No." Jack shouted further along the wall. "Looks like something's caught the bull's eye." It was wandering back to the hut.

"Do you think Mike will chance it?" Tolly was worried that if they didn't leave within the next minute the bull would get too close. The door opened and Trixie appeared on the end of her red lead. At least he'd put her on that - Tolly was still not convinced Mike had the sense he'd been born with.

"Run Mike!" Eddie was watching through her binoculars and growled encouragement. "That bull is fast." Everyone turned to watch. Even without binoculars Tolly could see it was closing in on Mike.

"Do you think it's those red trousers?" Tolly wondered aloud. Was it even true that bulls were attracted to red? "Something is definitely antagonizing it."

"Take your trousers off, Mike," Tuesday screamed, jumping up and down and waving her arms. She glanced at Eddie. "What?"

"Oof, don't need to worry about red trousers now." Jack pointed to where Mike was lying covered in mud… or perhaps? Ugh, Tolly didn't like to think about the cowpat from earlier.

"Get up Mike!" Tolly shouted, watching in horror as the gap between Mike and the bull continued to close. They all screamed at him.

"Run!"

"It's coming, get up!"

"He's not getting up, is he?" Jack removed his rucksack and unzipped his coat.

"What do you think you're doing?" Tolly held on to his arm as Jack tried to brush him off.

"He needs help, grandad."

"You can't go." Tolly shook him, "what will I tell your mother?"

"I'll be alright. I'll just distract it until Mike's out the way."

"And then what?"

A commotion in the field made them turn. Trixie with her lead trailing had placed herself between Mike and the bull, growling ferociously. Whenever the bull tried to move nearer, her growl increased in volume.

"What on earth is she doing?" Eddie lifted her binoculars. "She sounds ferocious." The bull snorted and pawed at the floor, eyes on the tiny creature in front. It lifted its head to sniff the air and Trixie growled again.

"Get up, Mike," Eddie shouted from behind the safety of the wall.

Jack hopped through the gap and sidestepped around the field, keeping a watchful eye on the animal. Now outnumbered, the bull seemed more hesitant. Snorting, it started to back off and sensing his escape Mike scrambled to his feet, then collapsed, grimacing in pain.

"Phorrr mate," Jack reached him and took his arm. "It's no wonder the bull's left, you *stink*."

Slowly they limped back to the hedge, Mike wincing with every movement. "That was a close shave." He collapsed on the ground, panting. "I thought I was a goner."

"You stared death in the face." Tuesday sank down beside him then, getting a whiff of his trousers, she edged away.

"I don't know about that," Mike replied wearily, "but I saw a bull at close quarters. And I don't ever want to do that again." Sitting up he took off his boot and peeled away the sock as Tolly squatted down to take a closer look.

"Your ankle?"

"It's killing me." Mike tried to lift it but groaned. "It really hurts."

Tolly felt around the joint and tried to move it but Mike gasped. "We could do with splinting that. I can't feel anything obvious but best not to jolt it too much. Tuesday, any idea where the nearest hospital is?"

Tolly turned, a hopeful expression on his face but it faded as Tuesday shrugged. Eddie touched his arm, holding the map.

"Didn't we come through here yesterday?" She pointed to a spot and moved her finger to another symbol. "If I'm right, that's a pub - just over that hill. I'll run ahead and see if I can get help. Can you two get Mike there?"

Tolly nodded, looking into her eyes. "But you don't need to go? I'm sure Jack -"

"I'd like to," she said, "it'll give us all some breathing space."

Chapter Twenty-three

$\mathcal{E}$DDIE WALKED briskly ahead of them. Hungry and thirsty she needed time away as adrenaline coursed through her body. She'd have to apologise to Tuesday at some point. As annoying as she was, she hadn't deserved to be shouted at like that – though she was *bloody* annoying and not the sort of person Eddie would normally be friends with. She strode on. It was good to be moving and to be able to vent some of her anger. Who was she angry with anyway? Tolly or herself? Both, and Rex too. Angry that she'd allowed herself to be toyed with for so many years, when she should have just thrown him out. She was clear about one thing now - she wasn't going to be messed around by anyone again. She pictured Tolly sitting in her living room. His bushy eyebrows and his grey eyes that crinkled at the corners. Then she saw his shocked face when she'd rounded on him in the bothy. To his credit he had tried to have a conversation with her, perhaps she needed to be honest with him when this was all over – but for now, where was that pub? She needed to get help for poor Mike

Her anger dissipated as she marched. Striding across a dry field, she came out from behind a hedge to see, like a beacon in the distance, the Three Stars pub. Cars were parked in a line along the lane and strings of lights twinkled outside, illuminating a large flat beer garden. Tears sprang to her eyes as the emotion of the day threatened to overwhelm her. If she could just hold it together for a little longer and like a traveller crossing the desert towards an oasis, she staggered towards the pub. She burst through the door and was met on the other side by a shocked young barmaid. Chewing gum and twiddling curly blond hair around one finger she immediately came round to help.

"Are you alright?"

"Glass of water, please?"

The barmaid poured one out and handed it over. Eddie glugged it in one go.

"More?"

Eddie nodded and they did the same again.

"You're thirsty." The barmaid stated the obvious. "You alright?"

Eddie nodded and wiped her eyes on a sleeve as a couple of relieved tears leaked out.

"Am now, thanks. Long story. My friends are coming. One's hurt his ankle. I need to call a taxi. Where's the nearest hospital? Can I have some crisps?" She took a deep breath. "Please."

She'd never tasted crisps like them before in her life, a true 'taste sensation' as the Masterchef guy would say. The salt made her tongue water, the potatoes were crunchy and the tang of vinegar finished it off majestically. She licked her lips and started to fold the empty packet before tying it in a knot. Flicking it into a waste bin she waited on the corner of the pub garden and the country lane. She scoured the area impatiently as she willed the gang to appear. She started to munch through a second packet of crisps. She was still hungry but at least she no longer wanted to gnaw off her own arm. Her huddle of fellow wanderers finally staggered around the corner, and she waved them over. Tolly's face lit up. He and Jack were either side of Mike, carrying his weight around their shoulders as Tuesday limped behind with Trixie on a short lead.

"We made it," Tolly shouted, as they got close enough to speak. They sat Mike down on a picnic table and, unhooking his arms, they rubbed their sore shoulders. Eddie waited for them to sit, Jack ignored the table and concertinaed to the grass. He puffed heavily, moving his arms and legs like an exhausted snow angel on the floor.

"I'll get water for everyone and crisps to keep you going."

"Water, water..." Jack did a Quasimodo impression and despite their exhausted, starved state he managed to raise a few chuckles.

Eddie reappeared with a tray of glasses, a jug of water and enough packets of crisps and nuts to sink a battleship. She was greeted with sounds of approval, and they fell on the tray, tearing open packets and shoveling the contents into their mouths. Like a plague of locusts, they ripped through the lot. Jack was looking around for something else to eat as Lucy, the barmaid, came out from the pub, carrying a second tray piled with baskets of chips, a vinegar shaker and a bowl of tomato ketchup. Before the poor girl had even set the tray down Mike grabbed a chip and winked at Eddie.

"Feeling better Mike?"

He nodded and dipped a second chip in ketchup, savouring the taste. He chewed slowly. Beneath his bravado he looked tired and definitely too pale. Eddie crossed her fingers that the taxi would arrive soon. She noticed that Tuesday was missing. She looked round the garden and spotted her in a corner. She had wandered, barefooted, around the garden with Trixie and was now standing patiently, while the dog drank from a water bowl. Eddie had to give her credit. She must be starving and thirsty, with extremely sore feet, but she didn't appear unhappy. She waited for Trixie to finish. Nobody spoke. They were too busy replenishing their depleted energy levels, weariness taking over from the earlier irritability. The sun sank in the sky but the air remained warm. Burbling conversations, from the other tables, had a relaxing effect on them.

Eddie picked up one of the baskets and a glass of water and walked across the grass. "I've brought you these. You must be starving." She held them out towards Tuesday, who took the water and downed it in one go. She then took the fattest chip, slathered it in ketchup and popped the whole thing in her mouth. A grin spread across her face.

"It's a peace offering," Eddie said quietly as Tuesday reached for another one. "I'm really sorry about what I said earlier. I was tired and hungry."

Tuesday shrugged and continued eating. Trixie lay down and Tuesday loosened the lead, putting her foot on it for security. When the basket was empty Tuesday wiped the grease from her mouth. She leant forwards and planted a big kiss on Eddie's cheek, taking her by surprise.

"I forgive you."

Eddie felt the tears from earlier resurfacing. "I was feeling emotional, and I took it out on you. I am sorry."

"Honestly. Don't worry about it. I know I'm not everyone's cup of tea," she answered. She had more insight than Eddie had given her credit for, and Eddie felt suitably chastised. Why had she disliked her so much, she didn't seem so bad?

"And, for what it's worth, he spent most of the day talking about you." She nodded over her shoulder to the men. "Got a bit tiresome after a while," she sniffed, "no accounting for taste."

Eddie thought it was a compliment but couldn't be sure, so she bit her tongue. She'd made a pledge there'd be no more fighting. But she was curious.

"Tuesday, can I ask why you live out here and run the camp site if you hate the country so much?"

Tuesday poked at the dog lead with a pedicured big toe. "Because of my sister." She bent down to rub away a splodge of dried mud from her pink nail.

"You moved to help her run it?"

"No." Tuesday shook her head. She paused; an internal debate seemed to be happening. She stood up and met Eddie's eyes, her hands doing the now familiar gesture of smoothing her bright t-shirt over her hips. "She was ill… mentally," she added. "She needed peace in her life." She shrugged. "What could I do? I used to run three beautician practices in Bristol. I sold them and bought the campsite. We moved here two years ago."

Eddie was silent as she studied the woman.

"I had no idea." She'd underestimated her. "How is your sister now?"

Tuesday's face lit up. "She's doing very well." She grinned. "I don't regret it; I just really miss the nightlife. But if being here means she is healthy," she shrugged, "I can put up with that."

Eddie reached out and rubbed her arm. She understood about sacrifices and tried to convey that with her touch. "What a wonderful thing to do, and I mean that. Perhaps you could come and see me one weekend? There's not a lot happening in Simonton, but at least-"

"Are you kidding? Simonton's a metropolis compared to round here."

The two women laughed, causing other drinkers to look in their direction.

Suddenly serious, Tuesday nodded. "I'd like that, Eddie. I could do with having a friend."

A car with an illuminated 'taxi' sign on its roof pulled along the lane and Jack waved to get the driver's attention. The men eased Mike up and took his weight around their shoulders as they made their way over to it.

"Time to go Mike. Let's get you fixed."

The driver climbed awkwardly out of the car, prising his beer belly from behind the wheel. "I'm Arty." He had a friendly grin on his face until he spotted the state of Mike. He shook his head slowly. "No, no, hold on. I can't have you on the upholstery like that. My car'll smell like a dairy farm." He opened the boot and lifted out a square of plastic sheeting, which he stretched across the back seat. "Sorry, but if you want a lift you'll have to go on that."

Eddie shrugged. It was fair enough, as even in the open-air Mike smelt very ripe.

"What's been going on here, then? I gather you need a ride to the hospital?" Now assured that his back seats weren't going to be soiled Arty was chatty and Tuesday's attention honed in on him. She smiled and fluttered her eyelashes. Arty ran a hand through his greased-back, thinning hair and pulled himself up straight.

"I'm Tuesday," she said sweetly. "This is Mike. He needs to get his ankle checked out."

"Hop aboard Mike." Arty stood by the back door, his hand resting on the plastic as Mike shuffled in. "Are you coming with your boyfriend?" Arty watched as Tuesday glanced coyly down to the floor. She nudged him with her elbow.

"Oh, he's not my boyfriend." Arty visibly brightened up. "We're all just friends here. We've been out hiking together, and we've had a few adventures, haven't we, Mike?"

Eddie wished Tuesday would get in the car, so they could be on their way. Mike's face looked awfully clammy and she silently willed Arty to speed things along.

"So, are you coming with us?"

"Shall I go with him?"

Eddie nodded and took Trixie's lead from her. "We'll make our way back to the campsite. See you there, once Mike's been sorted out."

"I don't need babysitting-"

"Nonsense Mike," Tuesday replied. "I'm happy to come with you. Now, let's go, before your foot drops off." She slammed his door shut and looked at Arty. "Shall I come up front with you?"

Eddie watched her performance as she elegantly sat on the seat and lifted her knees inside. It was all the more comical because of her muddy feet, dirty boots and dishevelled hair. But, as Eddie gently closed the door, she didn't doubt that Arty was already smitten.

"Could you call us a taxi too?" Tolly asked. "I really don't think I've got the energy to walk anymore. The thought of my camp bed is very appealing."

Arty radioed through and received a response over the crackling airwaves and static. "Ten minutes," he called then turned the taxi towards the lane.

After waving them off, the wanderers resumed their places at the table. Too tired and emotionally raw for a meaningful conversation they drank a round of rum and cokes that Tolly had purchased from the bar. He convinced them of its medicinal properties - "the rum soothes and warms, and the coke gives energy," he explained and, frankly, no one could be bothered to argue.

It took ten minutes for the taxi to arrive but by then the three of them had their heads on the table. They were gently snoring, much to the amusement of the other drinkers in the garden. Trixie stayed alert and watched over her humans. Well-rested, after her afternoon snoozing in the shepherd's bothy, she had to bark, loudly, four times before they woke up.

Chapter Twenty-four

HEATHER AND Amir sat at a table in The Black Swan. It was a nice pub, with an old-fashioned décor, nothing too flash, and according to Amir the beer was good. They had found three A4 sketchpads in the shop and Heather had one open now. She was trying *not* to think about the sticky tabletop and what it might do to the cover as she sketched cartoons while Amir queued up for more drinks. She stared at his back. He was broad and towered over the others waiting. She was pretty sure they'd never met before – she would definitely have remembered - so why was he so familiar? She was still pondering this question as he returned. She made a space on the table and as he placed the drinks down, she noticed his watch. Eight pm already, they'd been out for hours and the time had flown. She was enjoying herself and wasn't ready to go back to her mums just yet. They'd already talked about her job in London. Within a few minutes of describing her workplace he had asked if she enjoyed her work and, the alcohol having loosened her tongue, she'd admitted that she didn't – not really. She had gone on to tell him about Mabel's painting, and the offer of commissions from Georgie's NCT friends - and then he'd wanted to see some of her work.

"I need to know how good you are," he'd explained, getting up to fetch more drinks. They'd agreed that while he was queuing (there was quite a scrum to get the barman's attention now) she'd sketch something whilst waiting at the table. Normally shy about showing her work to anyone, the white wine was doing a good job of bolstering her confidence and, if she was serious about jacking in a well-paid job for what could just be a pipe dream, she had to see if she could make money from it.

He went to hand over her drink, then paused and held his hand out for the pad. "Come on."

"Seriously?" Fear fluttered at the edges of her stomach. What if they were no good? "Can I talk you through them?"

He shook his head. "No, I need to look at them cold. Pretend I'm a client."

Groaning, she closed the cover and handed it over. She watched nervously as he laid it on the table and turned the cover. She'd drawn a rabbit wearing glasses and a cheeky expression on his face.

"He's cute," Amir pointed. His eyes moved to the hedgehog, and he nodded. "Nice." The sketches were small, 3cms x 3cms and were dotted around the page. "Could you do them bigger?"

She probably could. She wasn't sure why she drew them so small, to fit more on a page?

"It's almost like you don't want them to be looked at."

Was he right?

"You seem shy, not quite confident in your ability," he looked at her, challenging. "I think they're great. They could be a kid's book, or cards, even prints. I reckon you'd be able to approach greeting card companies, no problem."

She was pleased with his feedback then checked herself. What did he know about being an artist? But he was serious.

"I've seen so much rubbish on the shelves at work. Yet it still sells… but these are good." He blew out, fluttering his lips. "Come into the shop when you get a minute and I'll show you some of our stock. Or," he took a swig from his glass, "there's a card shop in town, you could have a mooch at their stock. Maybe you could print some yourself and try distributing them." He looked at her, nodding. "There's loads of things you could do." He raised his glass to her. "Cheers! Britain, you have talent!" They clinked glasses and she grinned, a seed of optimism starting to grow for the first time in weeks, months… probably years actually. Could it be possible? Her stomach fizzed with the possibilities.

"So, Alan Sugar." She collected up the sketchpads and put them on the seat next to her. She turned her attention back to him. "What's your big plan?"

He supped his pint, watching her over the rim. "I'm not sure I want to tell you now. It sounds a bit mad when I say it out loud."

"Amir," she growled, sipping her wine. "Fair's fair. Now tell me about your plan, stop stalling."

"Okay. So, I love camping."

Her eyebrows raised but she didn't utter a word, waiting patiently.

"I've done the Duke of Edinburgh, loved it, and occasionally I still take myself off to the woods and camp overnight-"

"Wild camping?"

He took a quick swig, nodding and carried on. "The little camp shop, where I crashed into you. Unreal… that was only this morning!"

She motioned for him to get back to the story.

"That's been on the market for ages now. The couple-"

"Turners?"

He arched his eyebrows, impressed. "The very same, they want to retire but obviously have money tied up in it."

"Oh. My. God. It's you! *Amir*!" Heather stared at him. *He* was the one her mum had been talking about. "I knew something was familiar."

He had no idea what she was talking about and raised his hands. "What?"

"Eddie!" She blurted. "You gave her the number from the noticeboard? The ramblers?"

"Oh Eddie, yes. She's nice." A deep furrow appeared on his brow. "What about her?"

"She's my mum." Heather saw the surprise register on his face.

"Eddie is your mum?"

They both paused and took a drink.

"So, what about the shop?" Heather was keen to get back to his dilemma.

"Long story short, I'm trying to take over the shop full time."

"Wow, that's cool. And the premises, how would that work?"

Amir shrugged. "I'm speaking to the bank next week. There's a flat above, two bedrooms. So, I'd plan to take one and rent out the other for extra income."

"I could help you decorate," she offered spontaneously.

"Great, are you any good?" He burst out laughing when she shrugged.

"Dunno. I've never tried, but I'd happily use your place to practice."

"Cheers," he smiled. Then the smile faded as he exhaled slowly.

"What? It sounds great."

"It does and it would be," he agreed. "Apart from my dad. I've not told him about it and it's killing me. We're normally pretty close. It's just the two of us - my mum died when I was young," he explained, "so I feel bad going behind his back. Now the Turners know, you know, Eddie knows-"

"Well, tell him."

"You make it sound easy." He stared into his pint glass and blew at the froth on top.

"It *could* be easy," she reasoned. "Get your story straight and have a proper chat with him. Tell him you're not enjoying university-"

"-it's worse than that," he rolled his eyes. "I've just failed the year, so I've got to retake in September."

She tapped the end of her chin, thinking. "That might help you," she looked directly at him. "You've got to tell him about the exam results, then you could explain it's because you're not enjoying it. It's costing you too much – money *and* emotionally."

He shook his head.

"To be a success in life you need to find your Calling!"

Oh God, where had that come from? She'd definitely had too much wine! She'd only read that hippie book this morning and she was now counseling people about finding their passion in life.

"Amir, anyone can see when you're talking about camping, the shop and expeditions you come alive. As soon as you start talking about university or Maths your face changes and you close down. You become Grumpy cat."

He laughed and reaching across the table he took hold of her hand.

"Thanks," he said. "I need to do it, don't I?"

She nodded, adding "and today! Before he hears it from someone else."

He took a deep breath and let go of her hand then pointed to the glasses.

"Another, Dutch courage?"

"Okay… last one though. I'll get them." She stood up and pointed at her sketchbook. "You can use a page from my book and write out a list of what you're going to say." She searched in her bag for her purse.

"Just for the record" he said, making her look up. "This *Calling* malarkey? You're the same when you talk about your sketches, you know? Your face lights up. I like artist Heather," he winked. "Just thought you should know."

She flicked her hair and smiled, then sashayed towards the bar feeling ten feet tall.

Chapter Twenty-five

"HERE HE is! Finally!" Jack sat outside his tent playing with Trixie. He'd been throwing a ball for her to chase and return for what felt like an eternity. He was amazed how much energy she had. Whilst he'd been doing that, gentle snores had been coming from inside their tent; snores now punctuated by a trio of snorts to indicate that Tolly had woken up. Eddie wandered back from her reviving shower. She'd also had forty winks and had been a little groggy on waking. A taxi pulled up and a small, slim lad, not much older than Jack, hopped out to help Mike. A huge, blue hospital boot swung out from the back seat, encasing one of Mike's legs and he reached for a pair of crutches. Manoeuvring himself round he whacked the driver on the shin then caught him across his back with the other crutch.

"Watch out Mike." Jack held his hands up defensively as he approached, "you're lethal."

The driver crouched to the side, hands over his head, as Mike placed both crutches on the floor. With the driver pushing and Jack pulling they managed to get him upright.

"Sorry about that mate." Mike placed both crutches in one hand and pulled his wallet out, handing the driver a ten-pound note. He added another tenner.

"For your trouble," he whispered, "sorry about the crutches."

The lad nodded gratefully then got back in the car and zoomed off without a backwards glance.

"Did you drop Tuesday home?" Jack asked, helping him to a chair.

"No, she went for a night out with Arty."

"Really?" Eddie frowned, that was a bit mean. "Did she at least wait at the hospital?"

But Mike shook his head. "No, they wanted to find a line dancing place." He shrugged. "It's fine. I took ages anyway."

"Oh Mike," Eddie patted his shoulder to console him. "She wasn't right for you anyway."

He fiddled awkwardly with his crutches. "They never are, Eddie," he whispered, crossing them over and hitting his own leg before laying them on the floor. She was wondering how to answer when the sound of zips on Tolly's tent interrupted and she looked across the camp, relieved to see him climbing out. He straightened carefully, giving his hip a rub, then smoothing his hair back he walked towards them. A smile broke across his face when he spotted the patient.

"Mike! What's the damage?" He pointed at the cumbersome blue boot.

"Bad sprain. Got to keep this on for a week and not put weight on it."

"Bad luck, old Bean. Giving you any pain?"

Mike shook his head and produced a plastic pot from his pocket that he rattled. "Strong painkillers, helping enormously."

"It was a shame about that divot, you'd almost made it across. Thank God for Trixie, she really saved the day."

Mike nodded and put his hand down to stroke the dog.

"We've made a fuss of her. Bought some ham as a treat," Eddie explained, "from the shop. Tuesday's sister opened up for us."

"She's actually fairly normal compared to her sister," Tolly chuckled, then stopped as Eddie glanced at him. "Would you like a drink? Beer, glass of wine…we're about to eat too. Eddie's made a chilli."

Eddie motioned towards the tent and Tolly watched as she left to check on the food.

"I shouldn't really, not with those painkillers-"

"A small one?" Jack reappeared with a glass of red wine and held it out. "You'll be having food too." He handed Mike the glass. He sipped it then took a longer glug. "That's really nice." He leant his head back against the chair and took several longer sips before getting a refill from Jack. Mike cradled the half full glass as he closed his eyes and Tolly felt a wave of sympathy. The two of them stared at him, the poor man had had a rough day.

"What are you doing?" Mike's eyes flicked open.

"I was just looking at your boot," Jack stammered. "Wondering how you'll get to work next week?" He picked at the label on the wine bottle. "Er, what do you do again?"

Mike narrowed his eyes and scrutinized Jack.

"God Mike, is it top secret or something? I was only asking."

Mike sat up straighter and adjusted his boot. He hesitated, chewing his lip and then said, "I suppose you'd say an inventor."

"An inventor?" Tolly held a glass out to Jack. "That's interesting. Who do you work for?"

"Myself."

Intrigued, Jack pulled his chair closer. "How does that work?"

"If I have an idea I patent it," explained Mike. "Then I get in touch with various contacts and if anyone is interested, we see if we can make it."

"Have you invented anything big?"

Mike named a few things, but neither of them had heard of them. Jack glanced at his phone and began texting. Tolly tutted, marveling at his grandson's short attention span.

"Anything we might actually have *heard* of?" Jack asked, pausing in his texting to make a face at Mike.

"Definitely."

Tolly looked over. He expected to see Mike laughing. But Mike was deadly serious.

"The Modesty Curtain? That was my first real success."

Tolly frowned. "That rings a bell."

Jack's mouth fell open. "You know, grandad," he said, putting his phone back in his pocket. "Like a tube of toweling material, elasticated at one end to put over your head so that you can get changed under it…"

"Oh yes," Tolly remembered. "We've had several of them over the years, for the beach and camping. Easy to get changed into your trunks underneath." *Everyone* had a modesty curtain and they'd been *everywhere* when the kids were growing up.

"Which was your idea, Mike, 'coz there were loads of different types?"

Mike cradled his glass and grinned soppily. He was reveling being in the limelight for a positive reason. Or maybe, thought Tolly, they shouldn't have given him wine on top of his painkillers.

"Most of them actually." He nodded, pleased with himself as Jack and Tolly's mouths dropped open. "We make tough canvas ones for camping; a range of posh Barbour-branded ones for the hunting/shooting set; pink spotty ones with matching wellies for festivals… they sold *really* well, hot cakes -"

"- so, you've got a company?"

Mike nodded. "I do, factry snear Birmingham, head office in Bristol." His speech was becoming slurred.

"Wow." Jack was impressed. "But aren't you busy working all the time?"

Mike shook his head. "I work fr'home mostly, visit factry.." he waved his hand around, to mean 'sometimes'. "Got a n'office manager, she's amazin'."

Behind them Eddie had popped her head out of the tent. "What are you three up to," she shouted, "you seem quiet?"

"Mike's just telling us how he's a millionaire from all his inventions," Tolly joked.

"Right! I'll leave you to it then, only be ten minutes." She went back into the kitchen area.

"It's pretty cool," Jack raised his eyebrows, "so, what *are* you working on?"

Mike closed his eyes and lay back in his chair. For a moment Tolly wondered if he'd conked out from the tablets. Then he saw Mike bite the side of his lip. As he opened his eyes he winced. "I *was* working on something. Hey, I can't feel my leg anymore, that's good. Shame George had the weekend off," he rambled.

Tolly and Jack glanced at each other.

"Who's George?" Jack waited for Mike to focus.

"George? He's my bodyguard. I'd never have fallen over if he'd been there."

Jack rolled his eyes at his grandad. "George is your bodyguard?"

Mike looked over at him, and focused, serious. "Yes. Bobbyguard. He's great." Jack played along.

"Why do you need a bodyguard, Mike?"

Mike leant back into his chair and closed his eyes. "'Coz of the work with the miltry."

Now it was Tolly's turn to lean forwards, his curiosity piqued. "You work with the military?"

Mike giggled then clamped his hand over his mouth. "Whoops. Shouldn't say anything." He pretended to zip his mouth and throw away the key as his eyes looked around the campsite. He seemed to be having trouble focusing. "Good job there weren't tablets during my training," he started to chuckle. "Interrogation. Ha, I'd have been rubbish." He opened his eyes and saw the two men staring at him. "Whoopsie-daisy. I think I need bed." He staggered to his feet, forgetting the cumbersome boot and almost fell sideways. "George!" He put his hand on his chair to maintain his balance then tapped his head. "Weekend off, of course." Jack got to his feet. "Come on Mike, I'll give you a hand." He led him towards his tent and gently laid the woozy man on his sleeping bag. "Have a good sleep, Mike. Hopefully you'll feel better in the morning." He zipped the tent up and returned to sit by his grandad.

"Do you believe any of that?"

Tolly shrugged. "It would explain how he has so much time on his hands. And all the latest kit." He paused. "He's never mentioned any of it before-"

"He's never taken strong painkillers on top of several glasses of wine before."

"True."

Eddie came over, clutching a glass of wine. "Where's Mike?"

"I put him to bed," Jack puffed his cheeks out. "The booze and painkillers weren't a good mix."

Eddie pulled a face and shook her head. "They must be strong. He already seemed a bit wobbly when he came back in the taxi. He was talking all sorts of nonsense."

"What?" Jack was interested. "About being a millionaire. Don't you believe him?"

Eddie shook her head. "If he's a millionaire then I'm the Queen of Sheba." As she topped up her wine glass and disappeared to check on the chilli, Jack caught his grandad's eye and shrugged. He wasn't so sure. There was something different about Mike tonight and the two of them remained silent.

📷 Chapter Twenty-six

THE TAXI ticked over as Amir saw Heather to the door.

"I can see myself in, Amir. You didn't have to come with me." She motioned to the taxi driver who watched them through the window. "I reckon he thinks we're going to do a runner."

Amir glanced back and caught the driver's eye. He waved, wishing the man wouldn't be quite so obvious. "I'd better go," he said reluctantly, and Heather nodded.

"No more stalling." She fixed him with a knowing look. "You're thinking that if you stay out long enough your dad will go to bed and you'll be able to put off 'the conversation'," she made air quotes, "until tomorrow morning."

God, she was good, she'd got his number already.

"Are you in the shop tomorrow?"

He nodded and took a tentative step towards her. "I've had a really good time, Heather." He glanced down the path at the driver. Still watching! He was leaning on the steering wheel, peering through the windscreen with a bored expression on his face. He was probably urging Amir to get on with it and kiss her. Amir *wanted* to get on with it. She looked so cute with the streetlamp shining on her face but he wasn't sure she'd appreciate him lunging at her.

"Look, we're being watched. I'd better go," he said, chickening out from any lunging. "And you're right," he added. "I *am* putting it off. But I do need to grasp the nettle and get it over and done with." He pulled her gently towards him and leaned in, kissing her softly on the lips. He felt her tense and took a step back. "Shit, sorry. Is that okay?"

"Of course it's okay," she laughed, "it just caught me by surprise. I've been waiting for you to do that for ages."

"Really?" His face lit up. "Can I do it again?"

She nodded. He leaned in and planted another kiss on her lips. She felt amazing, her lips were soft and warm, and he pulled her closer. He heard the car engine's fan click on behind him. He paused. "Sorry," he stepped back. "Can you hold that thought until tomorrow? I'm not sure what time I'm working, but I'll be done by the afternoon. Can I call you?" He started to move away, down the drive.

"Actually, I was thinking I might pop in tomorrow morning to pick up a paper for my mum."

"Oh, your mum gets hers delivered on a Sunday."

"O-kaay. Some milk then."

He was about to disagree again, then clicked his fingers and pointed as the penny dropped. "I *get it*. You just want to come and see me. That's so sweet." He blew her a kiss and Heather chuckled, pointing behind him. The driver, still watching, was now grinning with both of his thumbs up.

"Go inside and lock up," Amir whispered. "I'll wait." He stayed on the drive until, satisfied she was safely indoors, he climbed in the taxi. "Thanks for waiting, mate." He gave the driver his address and noticed the dashboard clock. Just past eleven - his father would still be watching football on TV. Amir leant back in the seat and summoned up his courage. He was ready to face the music.

As the taxi pulled up outside the new build, semi-detached, Amir thought it looked dark inside, until he noticed the glow from the living room TV. He paid the driver and was feeling his way along the hedge when the outside light flicked on. His father must have heard the taxi. Amir lifted his house keys to identify the one for the front door. Finding it tricky to focus, he emitted a groan. Why had he drunk that third pint? He should have stuck at two but then he wouldn't have had the courage to kiss Heather, or for this next conversation either. As he finally slid his key into the lock, the door was pulled open and his father stood on the step in his slippers, glaring out.

"At last. He returns! Been in the pub, Amir?"

"Hi father," he brushed past him. "Sorry, I really need the toilet." He slid his shoes off and ran upstairs, going first to the bathroom, his highest priority then into his bedroom. Opening his wardrobe, he grabbed the notebook and folder.

"I think I have something you might be looking for." His father's voice carried up the stairs and Amir paused. What did he mean? He flicked through the folder and hurried downstairs. As he pushed open the living room door it dawned on him what his father had been shouting about.

"Would you like to explain this, Amir?" His father sat in his favourite spot on the sofa, holding the letter. He sounded calm, a good sign, but Amir knew that could change in an instant. "Because … to me… it looks like you have failed all three of your mathematical degree modules for the year and I am really hoping that is *not* the case." He stopped talking and Amir sat down on the opposite end of the sofa. He hung his head, his mind whirring over how best to answer.

"I'm afraid it is exactly as you say, father, I've messed up the exams." His father remained silent. "But it's not that bad-

"Not that bad? Amir, you're a bright boy. I don't understand how this has happened. Maybe you shouldn't have been working so many hours at the shop?"

"Father, I've got a plan."

The older man turned to him.

"I've been in touch with the university and there are retakes in September-"

His father lifted his hands up and clapped. He looked relieved, thinking they'd found the solution.

"-but I don't want to retake." Amir risked a glance over to see his father's reaction. The older man looked tired and rubbed at the stubble on his chin. Maybe it was the shadow cast from the overhead lampshade but the bags under his eyes appeared deeper than usual. Amir felt a pang of guilt for causing him such worry. He produced the folder and notebook and held them on his lap. He motioned for his father to slide across so they were sitting side by side, then he opened the folder.

"Father, you know I love camping and being outside? I love planning trips for myself and others too?"

His father nodded. They'd taken plenty of trips together in the past and they had loved being outdoors. His mum had been a free spirit and they'd had good times together. Although not so many since her death and he missed that.

"The camping shop in town-"

His father sucked air in through his teeth. "Amir, let's not go through that again."

"Please, just hear me out." Amir slowly turned the pages and pointed to the spreadsheet. He explained each line, going over the costings, the rental and the bills he'd incur. With a forensic eye he went over everything, desperate to convince his father that he could do this. Hesitant at first, as if waiting for his father to catch him out, his voice became passionate as he talked about his dreams for the business.

"I've even been through this spreadsheet with Mr. Turner," he continued, "and he thinks it is totally do-able."

"He would say that, wouldn't he?"

Amir looked at him sharply. "Father, he isn't like that! You *know*

him. We've been going in there for how many years? He just wants a fair price for all the years he's spent building his business. He's not being unreasonable, and he thinks my ideas are good. He said it could take off. Father, he *said* that."

"I don't know, Amir, it's a risk." His tired eyes looked back at him. He seemed smaller, less intimidating which in turn made Amir sit up straighter, knowing he had another trick up his sleeve. It was the piece de resistance that could well prove to be the clincher (from his father's point of view) and Amir was determined to keep going.

"The business also comes with a flat."

As predicted his father's eyebrows rose by the tiniest amount.

"Two bedrooms. I could move in and rent the other. That would help with cash flow. You're always saying what a good investment property is, aren't you?"

His father nodded, begrudgingly. "Would you *want* to move out?"

Amir shrugged. "To be honest, I haven't really thought about that but, at some point, I'll have to." He rubbed his father's arm to reassure him. "But if it's too much all in one go, I'll stay here and we can rent out *both* rooms?" He tipped his head to one side, watching as his father thought it over. "Whatever I do, the property is a good thing." He paused, falling silent as his father slowly turned over a page in the folder.

"And what's that?" The older man pointed to the notebook, now wedged down the side of the sofa.

"Ah, these are my ideas." Amir flicked to the first page. "I'd want a new website with online sales. That way we can advertise a range of stock and double the number of customers - online *and* people walking through the door." He paused, his breathing picking up in speed. Just talking about it made him excited.

"Double the staff though?" His father looked across at him, his black eyebrows raised in interest.

"Not necessarily, perhaps the shop staff could mail the packages during downtimes." He wasn't sure about the detail yet. "I don't know father, needs more planning but you get my drift. If I've had an idea, no matter how crazy, it'll be in this book."

"Well Amir. It's a lot to take in. You could lose a lot of money - and you've not exactly got money to burn, have you?"

Amir clamped his mouth shut. He was fizzing with excitement but needed to control himself. This was the first time his father was hearing this.

"I have to say, I am impressed by your research." His father tapped the book. "Obviously, you'll be good at the numbers," he looked pointedly at his son but there was a hint of a smile on his lips. Amir started to feel more hopeful but what was his father really thinking? *Grasp the nettle* he'd said to Heather, so he took a deep breath and grasped it himself.

"What do you think?"

The older man breathed in deeply through his nose. He paused, holding the breath then released it slowly. He stared at an old photo; himself, his wife and Amir laughing in a huddle. It hung on the wall over the fire. He breathed in again while Amir sat patiently waiting.

"I think you are a very bright boy who doesn't appreciate just how clever he is."

Seriously? Amir deflated. He waited for another lecture about studying hard and becoming a teacher.

"I would like the opportunity to look over the figures. I don't want you to sign something which will leave you further in debt-"

Amir snorted. "I've done that already… the student loan company?"

His father nodded sagely. "I am aware how much debt you've accrued but humour me, Amir. I do not want you to get into something you cannot get out of." He paused. "But I think it could be a good idea *and* I like the way you keep saying 'we'."

A smile broke out over Amir's face. "Really? Because I've got a call with the Bank this week to find out about loans."

His father nodded. "Really. Let's get all the relevant information and then we can think how *we* take it forwards."

Amir turned sharply. "But it will be *my* business though, won't it?" He wanted to make sure that was understood by all parties. "You can work for me, anytime, but it will be *my* enterprise."

Pandering to his only son, his father nodded. "Yes Amir. You will be the big shot businessman… I will just be your lackey."

Chapter Twenty-seven

THE POTS were tidied up, the chilli eaten. Only Tolly and Eddie remained sitting next to the campfire. An awkward silence hung between them as Eddie finished the last of her wine and cradled the glass on her lap. Tolly looked at her.

"Eddie, have I done something to upset you?"

She stared at the fire, not trusting herself to speak. She needed to keep strong and couldn't lower her guard again.

"Eddie. Talk to me. Is it because you thought I was showing an interest in Tuesday?" He paused and when she didn't answer he sighed wearily. "I'm not interested in that bloody woman if that's what you're thinking."

She glanced across. He was staring into the fire, his mouth downturned. She wanted to believe him, but she wasn't sure.

"We've had a lovely time this last week," he whispered. "I know we haven't known each other very long Eddie, but I like you," he said in a quieter voice.

"What about the other woman?" Slumped down in her chair, Eddie's voice didn't carry very loudly.

"What?" Tolly's brow knitted in confusion.

"You said you're not interested in *that* woman but what about the *other* one I saw you with?" She hadn't meant to say anything but resentment bubbling in her stomach had forced the words out.

"What 'other' woman?" He leant towards her, a look of bewilderment on his face. "What are you talking about?"

"I saw you in your car on Thursday with a woman. Looking very cozy." She could almost hear his brain whirring, so decided to help him out. "Short grey hair, large silver earrings, elegant?"

His eyebrows rose in surprise. "That was Thea."

"She kissed you."

He shook his head then stopped when he saw Eddie about to argue. "I mean she did, yes. A peck on the cheek. That was all." He laughed with relief. "Even that's too much contact with her." He reached for Eddie's hand and took it in his. "I gave her a lift to town. She's always been touchy-feely, makes me uncomfortable, if I'm honest." He caught Eddie's eye and smiled. "You know what you said about me not caring about your feelings? I *do* care. I care quite a bit actually. I think you and I could be good together Eddie."

She didn't respond. She wasn't sure what to say.

"You must know that I would never hurt you."

She softened. His explanation was plausible.

"They are just words Tolly. I've been told similar before. The actions and the words need to marry together."

"They do, Eddie. I've never deceived you or said anything untrue."

"No," she said thoughtfully, "you haven't." She glanced sideways and, for a fraction of a second, they held each other's gaze. She turned back to the fire, her face neutral.

"Did someone hurt you, Eddie?" His voice was so gentle, she wanted nothing more than to tell him about Rex and confide in someone. But that would mean opening up old wounds and then she'd be vulnerable.

"My husband had affairs, several of them. I don't want to rake over it again. Honestly, it's better this way." The flames danced in front of her. She was tired of thinking about Rex and why he'd had such blatant disregard for her feelings. Her mind flicked back to the present as Tolly got off his chair. He dragged it next to hers and sat back down, nodding towards her hand.

"Can I?" He held his out and when she nodded, he took hers.

"You don't have to say anything," he spoke quietly. His breathing was rhythmical and soothing, the physical contact was nice. "We can just sit here, if you want. Look, the stars are out in force tonight. Let's enjoy the moment." He leant his head back against the chair, still clutching her hand and stared up into the black, star-speckled sky. "Ow, good God, ouch. I can't sit like that for long." He pulled his head back upright and rubbed the side of his neck. "I've given myself a ruddy crick in the neck."

Eddie chuckled. He did have a way of cheering her up and she felt her mood shift.

"He was very deceitful," she said eventually, her voice quiet. "On the surface we were a successful, loving family but underneath," she laughed bitterly. She shifted next to him, turning to talk more easily. Mike and Jack weren't far away in their tents, and she didn't want to air her dirty linen to everyone. "Three affairs…that I knew of. There could've been more."

"Did you know at the time?"

She nodded and a tear fell onto her lap as sadness washed over her. This was what she'd been battling, allowing the humiliation to be washed away by hurt, then anger. Another teardrop fell and she sniffed. She shook her hand free to find a tissue. Once she'd composed herself, Tolly's hand took hers again. He gave it a squeeze.

"You forgave him afterwards? That must have been very hard."

She nodded. "I tried to justify it. I loved him. He was *so* amazing, and I was *so* lucky to have him that I had to be prepared to share."

"Why did you think that?"

"Because that's what he told me. He convinced me I was greedy because I wanted him to myself." Listening to herself as she said it out loud, she wondered what on earth she'd been thinking. "I had Heather to consider. Being a single mum wasn't something I'd envisaged, and I didn't want Heather to blame me, for splitting up the family."

More tears fell and Tolly passed over a clean, ironed handkerchief. She hesitated. "It's so white and neat, I don't want to use it."

He waved away her comment. "Plenty more where that came from," he chuckled. "My Sunday evening routine, ironing."

He was so organized and in control. She admired his solidity, his character.

"Do you think I'm weak?"

"No Eddie. No," he said vehemently, turning to look at her in the firelight. "You're not weak at all. In fact, you're one of the strongest, most sensible-"

She rolled her eyes at his flattery.

"- lovely, clever women I know. Even after this short time I think of you as a dear friend."

She wiped her face with the hanky and clutched it in her hand.

"You must never think of yourself as weak. It was *him*. He manipulated you." He stopped. She could hear his angry breathing being drawn up through his nose and out through his mouth. "I know what it's like to be hurt," he said, patting her hand. "When Thea left, I was shaken. She hadn't appeared unhappy." He shook his head. "When it all came to a head, I tried to persuade her to stay." His hands stopped moving and his grey eyes stared off into the distance. "You know what she told me? She said she just couldn't bear the thought of being with me any longer." He snorted and his eyes moved back to Eddie. "That doesn't do a lot for your self-esteem, I can tell you."

He gave a resigned smile and Eddie nodded. They certainly had a chequered history between them.

"I also owe you an apology," Eddie said. "My behavior was childish. I'm sorry I was so nasty to you – and Tuesday too. When I saw you smiling at her it must've touched a raw nerve…brought it all back."

"I'm sorry too. I should have ignored her and not been so flattered. I can be a silly old fool sometimes." He squeezed her hand. "I should have made it more ruddy obvious that I only wanted to flirt with you." They resumed their companionable silence, watching the embers glow in the campfire. Tolly chuckled and straightened up. He went quiet then laughed again.

"What's got into you?" Eddie looked at him, amused. His cheeks were rosy, a combination of the exercise and wine, and he cradled his glass as he stared at the flames.

"I was just thinking about Mike."

"I know," she whispered. "Perhaps we shouldn't have let him have a third glass of wine… not on top of those painkillers." She put a hand over her mouth to suppress a giggle.

"Good job you managed to persuade him to go to bed," Eddie whispered.

"He didn't need much persuading," Tolly shook his head. "He was about to pass out next to the fire if Jack hadn't got him to his bed when we did."

She sipped her wine, remembering the funny events from the weekend. She should start a journal. They seemed to have mishaps, among the adventures, on every trip. Was it the same for other rambling groups?

"It was a good day."

Tolly raised an eyebrow. "You must be remembering a different day to the one I had!"

"Okay, eventful," she conceded, "but still, it was a good day."

The night was warm. They finished their drinks as the flames died to glowing embers.

"Yes, it was a good day," whispered Tolly, "I haven't had that much fun for ages."

Eddie raised her glass in the air. "Hear, hear. And how is your hip?"

"It's been okay. I wonder if the exercise is good for it. You know, Eddie, you've made a real difference to our little band since you've joined."

She glanced over. "Really?"

"Yes. Honestly. It is much more fun with you in the group. Mike would never have brought Trixie before. I think I scare him."

"I think you're right. Maybe you could ease up a bit?"

Tolly appeared thoughtful. "Jack doesn't complain so much either. He didn't enjoy it before, and who could blame him? Poor lad. Piggy in the middle between Mike and myself. But now… well, you've seen him." Tolly cleared his throat. "I like you, Eddie."

"I like you too, Tolly."

"No, I mean, I *really* like you." He took another gulp of wine. "And um, I was wondering what someone like you might say if someone like me invited someone out for dinner? Say one evening, mid-week?"

Eddie swirled the last bit of wine around her glass. "I couldn't really comment."

Tolly's face fell.

"I mean, if it was me being asked by you, I'd say yes. But that's me, not someone *like* me. Then I'm assuming it's you and not someone *like* you. So, I guess I'm not sure."

Tolly frowned. He decided to give it another go. "I'm going to be direct and ask you straight. Would you like to have dinner with me?"

"Yes, I would." Eddie stared at the embers. "I really like you too. I just need to take it slowly, one step at a time."

"Yes. Slowly. Excellent!" His face broke into a wide smile. "We can do slowly… I *need* to do slowly with this ruddy hip." He stretched in his chair and gave it a rub. "We can go as slow as you need, for as long as it takes. Until you realize you can trust me, one hundred percent. Where would you like to go?"

She tutted. "I thought we were doing slowly?"

Suitably reprimanded he sank back in his chair. "It's just… we could go out, a little pub in the country? Or I could cook at mine. I could do the full restaurant treatment Chez Tucker?"

She liked the sound of that.

"The Chez Tucker option. That would be lovely. No more beans though?"

Tolly was watching her lips as she spoke. He leant across, puckering his own when right on cue a loud fart sounded from inside Mike's tent. Trixie yapped. Tolly wrinkled his nose in disgust.

"It isn't conducive for romance around here, is it?" Defeated, he sank back into his chair.

Eddie reached for his hand. "No. But you have to admit, it's funny."

He lifted her hand to his lips and kissed it tenderly. "So, as we were discussing, which evening would be better for you?"

"You're as tenacious as Trixie with her sausages."

"Extremely tenacious," he replied seriously. "Especially if it's something I like." He winked and kissed her hand for a second time.

Chapter Twenty-eight

ON SUNDAY morning Heather was awake and listening to the dawn chorus. The window was ajar and she lay in bed, appreciating the sound of nature. Her life already felt different in just the space of twenty-four hours. Unable to wait any longer she made herself a cup of tea and returned to bed with a sketchbook. She pulled the curtains back to give a view over the back garden and blew on the hot drink. The movement outside was constant; birds flitted past the window to land on the bird-table or to peck on the patio. Beyond the garden people strode past or jogged along the riverbank. She climbed out of bed again and approached the window for a closer look.

A pair of blackbirds hopped across the grass below the patio table. A robin flew in and perched on the back of a chair. Its black, beady eye spotted her behind the curtain, and it vanished. Recalling what her mum had told her about Grumpy and the bird hide, she had an idea. It would need setting up, but she was confident that Amir would help. It could be fun. Finishing the last of her tea she glanced at the clock. Nearly eight o'clock. It was still early for a Sunday morning, but there was no time like the present.

Approaching Shah's convenience store she spotted Amir through the window. He was ringing items through the till while an elderly lady leaned awkwardly against the counter. On spotting Heather, he waved and pointed to a tartan shopping trolley outside the door. Heather waited until he appeared, a wire basket in one hand and the customer holding onto his other.

"Alright Mrs. Pettigrew," he said, "we're nearly there." He mouthed 'hello' to Heather as the wispy haired Mrs. Pettigrew tottered next to him.

"Hello dear." Watery eyes gazed up at Heather, taking a moment to focus. "Are you alright out here?"

"She's waiting for me, Mrs. Pettigrew. This is my… friend."

"Girlfriend, eh?"

Amir turned to Heather, his eyebrows raised. "Would you say you're my girlfriend?"

"Erm, I don't know." She felt her cheeks heat up, as Mrs. Pettigrew's eyes swiveled between them, keeping up with their conversation.

"Do you not fancy him, dear?" The tiny pensioner leaned in closer. "I think he's rather dishy myself. I'll snap him up, if you don't." She turned to Amir. "Don't you worry dear; you can come and live with me. I know you're a good boy." She patted his arm and gave an exaggerated wink, as he loaded her shopping into the trolley.

"There you go Mrs. Pettigrew." He pulled the lid down and zipped it shut. "Now you mind how you go. Take it slowly, okay?" He turned the trolley round, so it pointed in the right direction, and she started to trundle home.

"She's a lovely old dear -"

"She's got the hots for you," Heather laughed. Amir folded his arms across his chest.

"A number of them do, you know," he said indignantly. "Anyway, *girlfriend*," he emphasised in an American accent, before adding "is it okay to call you that? I don't want to move too quic-" He couldn't get any more words out, as she reached up and silenced him with a kiss.

"Let's see what happens. I'm only back for two weeks, remember?"

"Yes, course," he said holding her close. "Are you coming in for a cuppa? I've got lots to tell you."

"Me too," she added and followed him into the shop.

Inside, he motioned for her to sit down while he put the kettle on.

"Mr. Shah doesn't like people behind the counter," he explained, "but you can sit there, and we can talk."

He grabbed a pack of pain au chocolate off the shelf and offered her one. "Perks of the job."

"Come on," she made a winding motion with her hand, eager for his news. "Did you speak to your dad?"

He nodded, chewing. "Sorry," he pointed to his mouth, "I'm starving, hang on." He moved his head up and down as if this helped, then while she remained quiet he told her about the conversation with his father. Swinging her legs backwards and forwards on the stool she was desperate to find out how it ended.

"So," he pretended to do a drum roll on the counter, "we're going to meet the Turners next week and I'm talking to the bank tomorrow. The fact that there's a flat above the shop tipped it in my favour, although I got the impression he's not keen for me to move out just yet."

"Why not?"

Amir slurped his tea. "I think he's lonely," he said honestly. "I'll have to move out at some point, obviously, but it doesn't need to be just now."

"How do you feel about that?"

He shrugged. "One thing at a time, eh? Get the shop up and running. Having tenants would help the cash flow and then," he held his hands out wide. "Who knows?"

Heather wondered if she'd be able to live with her mum again. She only planned to stay for two weeks holiday, but what if it was for longer? She shook her head. She couldn't move back here. Her life was in the city, and she'd have to go back to work at some point. But ideas swirled round her head.

"So, you wanted to ask about something?"

She came back to the present. "Did my mum tell you about her trip last week, when she scared a rare bird away?"

"Yes, she did. She said it was creepy that those people were in the Hide watching."

Heather pointed at him. "Exactly. I wondered if I could set something up in the spare room, so that I can sit with my binoculars and study the birds."

"That wouldn't be hard to do-"

The bell tinkled and an elderly couple came in. They walked arm in arm, chatting animatedly.

"Morning Amir," they waved to him and disappeared towards the fridge.

"Pint of milk and Danish pastries," he whispered. Within a couple of minutes, the couple came back to the counter, still with arms linked. They carried a pint carton of milk and two pastries in a bag.

"Sunday Mail too?" He rang the total on the till and took a fistful of coins from them, not bothering to check the amount. "Thank you. Have a good day," he called as they waved and went out the door.

"Married for fifty years." Amir looked out the window to see the couple disappearing round the corner.

"Ah that's sweet." She liked that he knew so many people and their stories. He was part of their daily routine, part of the community. She thought about her anonymous existence back in the city.

Heather couldn't stay at the shop forever so, after an hour of keeping Amir company, she left to return home. As she walked along the riverbank she passed other people, out for a stroll. Pausing to sit on a bench she noticed a plaque with an inscription -'For Bet and Jim, who came here to stop and stare.' What a beautiful sentiment. She remained seated, doing the same. Two swans glided past serenely and she watched where they went. If her Hide was a success perhaps she could move it outside and draw the Simonton swans. Her mind was forming a plan, on how to get closer to nature. Standing up, her body felt at ease. Her head was clear, and her niggling backache had disappeared. She had smiled and laughed more in the last twenty-four hours than in the last six months put together. She still had nearly two weeks of holiday, and as she continued her way home, she paid more attention to the river and the activity around it. The days were much lighter already and she'd be able to work for hours. She should call Georgie later too, to find out whether she'd been serious about the painting commissions for her NCT friends, she'd be able to do one or two. Winter would be different of course, if she stayed. Already picturing the sketches of wintry scenes and animals in warm coats and gloves, she speeded up. She needed to get back to write down her ideas. A ball of excitement fizzed in her stomach. Could she really make enough money from her artwork? Well, she had two weeks to find out.

As she turned into the cul-de-sac a green Rover chugged around the corner. It pulled to a stop outside her mum's house and the doors popped open.

"Heather?" Her mum spotted her. "What on earth are you doing here?" She rushed down the road towards her and pulled her in for a quick hug.

"Is everything alright?"

Heather nodded. "Of course. I've got a few days off, so I thought I'd pay you a visit."

"You should have said. I wouldn't have gone away."

"It's fine mum. It was a last-minute thing, don't worry." Heather knew her mum was suspicious, but a noise behind made her mum turn. Lingering behind her was a tall, upright man wearing some, frankly, hideous safari shorts. His bushy grey eyebrows were the next thing Heather noticed, followed by his enormous smile.

"These are the friends I was telling you about." Her mum beckoned the man over. "This is Tolly. Colonel Bristol Tucker." Heather thought her mum's eyelashes fluttered as she introduced him. She was shaking Tolly's hand when a long pair of legs appeared from the back seat of the car. She spotted the similarity as the teenage boy unfurled.

"Jack," her mum called, "this is my daughter Heather."

The teenager raised a hand in acknowledgement then was distracted by his phone.

"So how was your trip?" Heather asked as her mum steered her towards the house. "Where have you been?"

"It was eventful," she laughed. "Let's get the kit in. I'll make us a nice cup of tea and tell you all about it." She grabbed a tent bag and heaved it up the drive. "And you can explain what you're doing here."

The four of them sat at the table and made easy conversation. Heather heard about their weekend and spent most of the time with her mouth open, incredulous at their adventures.

"I'm starting to think this group is a liability," she said. "How, or *why*, does it always happen to you?"

Tolly shrugged his shoulders. "I blame Mike to be honest. He's an idiot."

"Grandad!" Jack looked at Heather and grimaced, "sorry. He's not very PC."

"What's to be PC about?" Tolly argued. "He wore those red trousers, and he brought the dog along. He *is* an idiot."

"Thank goodness he *did* bring the dog," Eddie countered, "otherwise he'd have been toast."

"But if he'd not worn those ruddy trousers in the first place... like I said, a bloody idiot."

"Give it a rest," Jack laughed and slurped some tea. "Anyway, he can't be an idiot," he turned to Heather. "He's got a successful business as an inventor - what was it, grandad?"

"Mobile comms device, used by the military." Tolly lowered his voice. "It's most impressive actually, but don't tell Mike I said that."

A ripple of amusement ran around the table before Jack became serious. "He's a clever bloke. Worth a fortune too." Mike did seem to have gone up in everyone's estimation.

"The Sat Nav wasn't quite so impressive."

"True." Jack tipped his head to one side. "That does need a bit more w-" The last word was smothered by a huge yawn, and he covered his mouth. "Sorry, I could do with a nap. I'm really knack… er, tired."

Tolly stood and stretched his arms above his head, hitting the ceiling light. He stilled it and motioned for Jack to sup up. "I think that's our cue to leave."

"Thanks Eddie. And, you know, thanks for the kit." Jack stood awkwardly and grinned.

"You're welcome, Jack." She rubbed his arm. "I'm glad it's had some use."

"Ah, about that," Tolly paused, "shall I leave the rest in my car, Eddie, and we'll sort it out in the week?"

Eddie nodded. "I'll pop over tomorrow to check it out. If that's convenient?"

As Heather and her mum stood on the drive watching the green Rover cough its way out of the cul de sac Heather turned to her mum. "You're going over tomorrow to check *what* out?"

Catching the glimmer in Heather's eye, Eddie bumped her with a hip.

"I'm going to check out the *camping equipment*," she said firmly. Heather nodded, keeping a straight face.

"Course you are, mum. The camping equipment."

Smiling, Eddie looped her arm through her daughter's and pulled her towards the house.

"And I think it's about time you told me why you're home."

Heather watched her mum place her knife and fork together and look across the table at her.

"I'm lost for words."

"Is that a 'if you're not happy, move straight back here and give it a go' lost for words or a 'oh Heather, are you sure you've thought this through. Don't walk away from a well-paid job' lost for words?" Heather could feel tension creeping up her spine. In the space of just a few minutes she'd watched her mum's initial happiness at having her home for two weeks turn into concern.

"I've not been happy for months. Why are you nodding?"

Her mum was staring at her over the crockery. "I know you've not been happy."

"How did you know?"

"I could tell, love. On our infrequent calls you were always stressed and rushing around. You never mentioned anyone other than work colleagues. It didn't sound like you had a life outside work-"

"I didn't…don't," Heather agreed. "It's not what I imagined, mum. Since coming back from Dubai it's been a culture shock. I've got no friends left in the city, they've all moved away. I've met more people here in twenty-four hours."

Her mum patted her hand. "You're welcome to stay here as long as you like."

Heather cradled her head in her hands. "I don't know what to do mum. I just feel as if something needs to change."

"Tell me some more about your plan. How would you make money?"

Needing no further invitation, Heather ran to the bedroom and grabbed her sketchbooks. Reappearing at the table she spread them out and turned the pages. She showed her mum the different animals she'd drawn and the photos on her phone of her nursery rhyme paintings.

"I'd need to do more research," she gushed. "Amir said I could look at their greetings cards to get some ideas."

"Amir?" Her mum stopped in surprise. "You've met Amir?"

Heather nodded, feeling a rush of heat to her cheeks.

"Heather." Her mum scanned her face, her brow furrowing. "What are you not telling me?"

"I met Amir yesterday. I literally bumped into him in town outside the camping shop."

Her mum's eyebrows rose.

"I thought he seemed familiar. But later, when I went to the shop to buy a sketchbook, it clicked. We got talking-" she smiled, "he didn't sell sketchbooks, so he offered to walk into town with me. He was going that way," she added seeing her mum's eyebrows rise even higher. "He was. We went to the pub, had fish and chips and a taxi dropped me home." She paused for breath. "He was the perfect gent."

Her mum didn't say a word. Heather waited for her to speak.

"Are you seeing him again?"

"I went to the shop this morning." Heather ran a finger over her sketches.

"Blimey. What time did you go?"

"As soon as it opened." The women burst out laughing.

"What have I told you about appearing too eager," her mum waggled a finger in mock-annoyance. "I'm pleased for you, Heather," she added. "You already sound happier and you've only been here for twenty-four hours. What's going to happen if you stay for a week?"

"Or two?" Heather's intonation suggested a question.

"Indeed," her mum agreed. "It could be life changing."

Chapter Twenty-nine

MONDAY MORNING dawned bright and early. Heather woke as the sun nudged into the spare room. She needed to stop thinking of it as the 'spare room' if she was going to be staying. But that rather depended on what happened today.

Breakfasted, showered and dressed she waited for the minute hand on the bedside table to land on two minutes past nine. Taking notice of her mum's words from the day before, she didn't want to appear too eager. She punched the numbers on her phone. It rang once and was picked up.

"Good morning, Balloon Co. How may I help you?'

"Oh hello," Heather put on her best phone voice. "I wonder if I could speak to someone in the Design department, please."

"Certainly, who may I say is calling?"

"My name is Heather Maguire. I'm an artist and I'd like to speak to someone about designing for your company." She held her breath. She could hear the woman scribbling notes, the pen scratching against paper.

"Certainly. Hold on one moment. I'll find out who's best to speak to you." The receptionist covered the receiver with her hand, sending a crackle down the line.

"Johnno?"

Heather could hear her every word.

"Caller. Wants to talk about designing for us. Who's best to speak to her?"

There was movement in the background and muffling of the line, then a deep voice spoke.

"Good morning, I'm John Kingston. You wanted to talk about designing for the company?"

"Er, yes." Even to her own ears Heather sounded unsure. "That's right, yes. My specialty is cartoons. I draw countryside animals but made to look like humans. Hedgehogs wearing coats, a rabbit with shades on."

"Oh, right."

"Think Beatrix Potter, but more contemporary. Could I send you some sketches?"

There was a definite pause on the line, and she held her breath. What was he doing? She slumped, he was probably yawning, in an exaggerated fashion, to amuse the receptionist.

"I've been doing my market research," she piped up, "and I think I'd be a good fit with your company. I've seen some of your cards, they're funny." Was she waffling? She didn't want to sound desperate.

"Okay," he sounded distracted. "Can you scan a couple and send them over?"

Heather wrote down his details and promised to send some over by lunchtime.

"You mentioned market research? Can I ask, where did you see our cards?"

It could be a trick question to catch her out, but Heather was able to answer honestly. "Shah's convenience store in Simonton."

"Ahh." He sounded amused, as if he was smiling. "I know it well. Does Amir still work there?"

She looked at the phone, amazed. "Yes, he does."

"Wondered whether he'd have moved on by now. Do you know him?"

"Yes, I do actually."

He chuckled. "Tell him Johnno says 'hi' if you see him. We've been delivering there for years, I started as a rep there," he reminisced. "Anyway… Heather," he came back to the present. "Send over your stuff and we'll take it from there." After saying goodbye, she hung up and punched the air. She was proud of herself. It was premature to be celebrating but he hadn't laughed at her either. It wasn't a bad start for number one on her list of ten companies. Now what? She looked at number two and glanced at her sketchbook. This called for a coffee break.

Upstairs, her mum was pottering in the kitchen. She was wrapped in a pink fleece dressing gown, that covered her from head to foot. The blue light of the kettle glowed, and the noise was rising as the elements heated the water. Heather walked in and kissed her mum on the cheek. "Good morning." She stretched and held the pose for a couple of seconds. "What a good morning it is too."

Her mum narrowed her eyes at her.

"You know, you're a very untrusting mother." She took a mug from the shelf and added it to her mum's, next to the kettle.

"I'm just wondering why my daughter, normally so stressed, is full of beans at this early hour?" Her mum tugged at her dressing gown belt and twirled the ends distractedly.

"Well, mother, the early bird grabs the worm and I've just got through to a greetings card company."

Her mum's eyebrows rose.

"- and they have asked to see some of my sketches." Her mum dropped the belt and stepped in, hugging her.

"That's great. What have you got to send them?"

Her brief moment of glory faded, and Heather frowned. "I'm not sure. If I get my sketchbook, will you help me?"

"Go on," Eddie tutted "Get your books and I'll make the coffee."

Two sketchbooks lay open on the table. Eddie had flicked quickly through all the pages once and was now back at the beginning. She turned the pages slowly, studying certain drawings in detail. She'd always loved the Rabbits and Heather had expanded the family to include new designs of grandparents and three naughty children. Each one was different; one wore a hat with a bright red pom pom, another had a long multi coloured scarf wound round his neck. The youngest wore round, wire glasses. Eddie frowned. He had a look of Harry Potter, if Harry Potter had long rabbit ears and a button nose. The granny rabbit had three curlers on her head, held in place with a headscarf tied under her chin.

"Scan those." Eddie pointed at them. "They've always been my favourite. Although I do like the birds." She paused with her hands on the table as the two of them looked between the rabbits and the birds. "You should have gone to Art college," Eddie whispered, as she ran her finger down the page and flicked the edges.

"Was never really an option, was it?"

"I know love, I'm sorry. I should have stuck up for you. I could see how much it meant to you."

Heather straightened in her chair. She pulled at her t-shirt and brushed it over her hips, as if brushing away Eddie's comment.

"Art's only meant to be a hobby, mum."

Eddie flinched as her daughter repeated what Rex used to say. "It could have been different though, could have saved you a lot of soul-searching if you'd followed your passion when you'd been younger." Eddie thought of the rows she'd had with Rex. He'd always dismissed any notion of Heather attending Art School. He'd insisted she needed a 'proper' degree, something sensible, whatever that was.

"He didn't always know best," Eddie said quietly, "but he'd put up a fight if you tried to disagree." Heather nodded. She remembered the arguments they'd both had with him and wondered what the house had been like once she'd given in and gone to university.

"He shouldn't have been so…" Eddie struggled to find the right word then felt the weight of Heather's hand on her arm.

"It doesn't matter mum. It's water under the bridge." Heather patted her hand. "I'm doing it now. It just took me a few extra years, that's all."

Eddie nodded and turned over another page. The sketch of a hedgehog made her chuckle and she glanced up to see Heather smile.

"Were you happy together, mum?"

Eddie paused, her eyes still on the page. She'd thought about this conversation many times. She'd imagined what she'd say to Heather and how much information she should know. Heather was a grown woman now but Rex had still been her father.

"We were, in the beginning," Eddie replied cautiously. "I wasn't that keen on him to start off with," she added, smiling, "I thought he was too… nerdy. He was so clever. But he didn't have any sense of humour, which I found really hard to fathom." She laughed to herself. "I had to explain jokes to him."

"He was pretty serious, I remember that." Heather paused. "Why did you change your mind?"

What had swayed her? "I suppose I was flattered. It must seem old fashioned now, but he pursued me. You know he was sixteen years older than me? He was sophisticated, very different to the boys I'd grown up with." The truth was that Rex had swept her off her feet. He'd sent her gifts, books and clothes, and even insisted on meeting her parents. She paused, her throat tightening as her eyes watered.

"Sorry mum, I didn't mean to make you cry." Heather rubbed her arm, but Eddie caught her hand.

"No, I want to. We've never really talked about him. Perhaps we should, to clear the air." She blew her nose. Heather looked wary, and it reminded Eddie of when she'd been a little girl. "He'd been married before I met him… he was still married."

"Married? Dad? I never knew that."

"It wasn't something to be proud of."

"It happens, mum."

Eddie got up to fetch a glass of water. She stood at the window and looked out to the cul-de-sac as she drank. She returned to the table. She'd started this conversation so needed to carry on.

"Nancy. That was her name. According to him, it had been a huge mistake." Eddie tried to keep the skepticism from her voice. They met at college." She twirled the gold band around her finger and noticed the groove it had made on the skin underneath. "As soon as I found out, I finished with him. But, you know dad. He normally got his way. He asked Nancy for a divorce, and she was glad to be finished with him. He proposed to me. And the rest…" she tailed off.

"Well I never. Why have you not mentioned this before?"

"Never seemed to come up."

Heather shrugged, looking non-plussed. "It's not a big deal though."

Eddie disagreed. It had been to her. "It was more of a big deal back then and, to be honest, I always felt bad about it."

"Why? It wasn't *you* that was married." Heather squeezed her arm and Eddie knew what she said was true. But it didn't stop her feeling guilty. She'd often wondered if she should have seen the writing on the wall. Leopards never changed their spots.

"Was she from here?"

"No, I think she was from the Midlands. She moved back there after their divorce. I can't even remember her surname." She'd never met Nancy and whilst there'd been the names of several women after that, Nancy hadn't been one of them.

"Well, you learn something every day, don't you?"

"You certainly do." Eddie managed a weak smile for her daughter, her beautiful daughter. She seemed to have taken that revelation in her stride. How would she feel if she knew about Rex's affairs; would she be as forgiving of that? Maybe she'd tell Heather about those another time, about how he'd chipped away at her self-confidence and hardly had time for either of them. But that wasn't a conversation for today.

"Now, what about these sketches? I think the robin's one of the best." Eddie stuck her bottom lip out as she flicked between the pages. "They're all good, you must have spent ages doing them."

"I love it, mum and if I could get paid to do it, well that would be perfect."

Eddie was relieved they were back on safer topics of conversation, and together they chose a couple of pages.

"Can your printer scan?"

"I honestly don't know, love." Eddie shrugged, "but you're welcome to try." It was lovely to see Heather so happy, her cheeks flushed pink with excitement.

"Could I put some of my stuff in your study? I need to set up an office and you've got that desk in there, even if it is a bit rickety," she whispered.

"Hey! Beggars can't be choosers." Eddie crossed her fingers. "Although, if the Balloon people like these, you might not be a beggar for long, eh?"

Chapter Thirty

HEATHER WASN'T the only one getting organized. Amir sat with his phone pressed to his ear, listening to piped music while he waited for Simone, the Loans Officer at his bank, to return. He was on hold while she was going through the checks needed, to make a decision about his business viability. The music was catchy, in a classical, lots-of-violins way and Amir's foot tapped jauntily. He had a good feeling about this. Simone came back on the line.

"Amir, I've done the checks -"

His senses were alert, waiting for her to confirm the money.

"-and unfortunately, your application has been declined. I'm very sorry."

"What?" He couldn't believe what he was hearing. "Declined! But why?"

Pages rustled at the other end of the phone as Simone flicked through the information.

"Unfortunately, it falls within the high-risk category due to the lack of collateral-"

He took a deep breath to interrupt.

"-*or* previous experience," she added.

"But that's crazy," he raged. "I have *loads* of experience from working in Shah's convenience store, I told you about that."

"You did. I'm sorry Amir. They won't include that as experience within the camping and leisure sector, which this new enterprise falls within."

He let out a heartfelt sigh, his hopes and dreams disappearing down the plughole.

"That's crazy, right? It's still retail, still stock control. I know about profit and loss and dealing with the public. I've got experience by the bag full…"

There was silence at the other end of the phone, and he paused. He was ranting. Poor Simone was only the messenger. Deflated he sighed. "Sorry Simone, I know it's not your fault. Is there anything I can do to make them change their minds? What if I ask for a smaller amount?"

"It would have to be a significantly smaller amount, and then we'd need to justify why you'd sought to change your application."

Amir slumped to his bedroom floor and leant against his bed. He'd been so close then …whump, the rug had been pulled from under him.

"Back to square one then. Thanks anyway," he said quietly. "I'd better not waste your time anymore."

"I'm very sorry Amir. You'd stand a better chance if you stuck to retail where you've got experience. If you had some savings, or collateral, to offer against the loan…" she tailed off. They both knew she'd said this several times already.

"But I don't."

Promising to contact her again if his circumstances changed, he hung up. He remained on the carpet, feeling winded, with no energy to move. He picked at the pile, staring but not really seeing. His options had narrowed drastically in the space of just one phone call. On any other day this rejection might fire him up, but today… he glanced at his watch and sighed. He was due at Heather's in half an hour then straight over to Shah's for an afternoon shift. Pushing it out of his mind, he'd think about it again once he was safely behind the counter at the shop. Right now, he needed to avoid his dad and get to Heather's. In socked feet he crept down the stairs, knowing exactly where to step to avoid the squeakiest floorboards. He was almost at the bottom when he hit the second step in the wrong place, and it let out a loud groan. He paused. Like a spider waiting for a fly to appear, his father came out from the kitchen.

"All finished?" His eager eyes stared at Amir. "So?"

Amir shook his head. He watched his father's smile disappear, to be replaced by a frown.

"What? You didn't get it?"

Amir shook his head again. "No father, I didn't-"

"But why?"

Amir lit his phone up to see the time. "Can we talk later? I'm going to be really late." He shoved his feet in his trainers knowing that his father would assume he was going to Shah's.

"Did they not think it was a good business?"

"They thought it was a great idea. They just weren't prepared to lend me all the money. I'm high risk so they need savings or something as collateral... blah, blah, blah." He tailed off, bending over to tie his laces. When he stood up his father was looking at the ceiling. Amir's eyes followed. A huge cobweb hung in the corner and his father tutted.

"I know what you're thinking, father but we can't risk this place. It's your home."

"*Our* home, Amir."

Amir nodded, moving towards the door. "Whatever. I still won't use it as collateral, so don't even go there. Right, I'll be back for tea. We'll talk properly then. Sorry, got to go."

His father nodded somberly. "Okay Amir."

They looked at each other and Amir saw a defeated smile on his father's face.

"It'll be okay father, we'll sort something. The dream hasn't disappeared yet... it's just on hold."

As Heather opened the front door her face lit up.

"Finally! You're here." She closed the door behind her and reached up to give Amir a kiss. "Guess what, guess what?" She made him smile and instantly he felt brighter. Like a little kid she was jumping up and down as her eyes blazed with excitement.

"What?"

"Let's go in the garden and I'll tell you." She took his hand and they walked down the side path to the back of the house. In the garden she paused. "I made a call this morning to the Balloon Company and they've asked to see my drawings." She stared at him, waiting for his reaction.

"Wow, that's amazing." He pulled her in for a hug and they rocked from side to side. "What do you need to do?"

She paused, then pointed at him. "Actually, I've got a message from Johnno."

Amir was surprised to hear that name. "Johnno? I haven't seen him for years."

Heather told him about her conversation with Johnno and how they'd talked about Amir. "I think it's partly because I know you that he wants to see my drawings."

"Well, you need to send in something amazing to seal the deal."

She nodded in agreement. "I'll get on to that this afternoon."

They stood in the garden facing the river and Heather looked at him suspiciously.

"You okay?"

"Fed-up."

He sat on the grass and patted for her to join him. "The bank declined my loan application for the shop."

"Oh no. I'm sorry." She bit her lip. "What does that mean?"

He shrugged. "I don't know really. I'm going to think about it this afternoon and speak to my father tonight. I think I've got two options, either retake my exams, and go back to uni-"

Heather made to interrupt.

"-which I don't want to do, or I quit uni and work full time to save the money."

"How long will that take?"

"A year, maybe longer."

Heather rubbed his arm in sympathy. "I'm really sorry Amir. But good things come to those who wait."

He glanced across at her and smiled. "What about he who hesitates is lost?"

She tutted. "Patience is a virtue? For every saying there is an opposite one. Personally, I prefer what Buddha said, 'what we think, we become' so you've just got to hang in there and keep thinking about being a camp shop owner."

"Talking of which, I've got to be at Shah's by 12. Shall we make this hide, so you can sit in it and think about being an artist?"

"Touche," she laughed. She pointed to the pile of netting and bamboo sticks already pilfered from the garage. "Let's see what you can make from that."

Chapter Thirty-one

JACK CYCLED up to Highwood Estate. Like most people he knew where the private, gated community started - the entrance was marked by electronic gates and a dazzling white guardhouse – but, probably like most people, Jack had never ventured inside. A fizz of excitement welled in his stomach as he approached. He gently squeezed the brakes to slow down. A guard, wearing a dark blue uniform and a peaked cap stepped outside his hut.

"Can I help you, lad?" The guard stood in front of the entrance gate and held up a hand, signaling Jack to stop. His brakes squealed as he pulled the bike to a halt.

"I'm visiting Mike, er…" He patted his pockets, feeling for his phone on which he'd stored the address.

"Jack Tucker?"

Surprised, Jack jerked his head up.

"Just a minute, I'll open the gate." The man returned to the hut and immediately the gate began to swing open.

"How did you know who I was? Ah…" Jack's voice tailed off as the guard held up a clipboard, several pages of visitor details fluttered in the light wind.

"Tells me here, lad. The residents put names on the list, so you are legit. Now," he tapped the clipboard with his forefinger, "know where you're going?" He stepped outside when Jack shook his head. "Up there, left at the fork. Mike is third on the left. There's a white fountain in the middle of his drive, you can't miss it."

Jack waved as he passed through the gate and peddled up the hill – no wonder they called it Highwood Estate. It was certainly woody and - as his legs began to complain – high, too. After a hundred metres or so he reached the fork in the road and, taking the left-hand side, he was relieved to see the road flatten out. He settled into a gentle rhythm, pushing his peddles round. He had the opportunity to gaze about and coasting round a bend he glimpsed a pad to his left. It was huge. The estate reminded him of being in the wood with the Wanderers. There was no traffic noise, no sounds of life other than birds tweeting above the whir of his tyres on the smooth, clean tarmac. Where was Mike's? Was he even in the right place? A driveway appeared on his left and he passed a second detached house. Slowing to glide along the deserted road, a third drive opened in front. This must be Mike's. Sure enough, his black Land Rover was parked up. It looked lonely on the huge sprawl of immaculate tarmac drive and Jack pulled to a stop. His mouth dropped open in awe. The sweeping drive formed a circle in front of a mega house. In the middle of the circle was a lawn (as big as the whole plot of his grandad's bungalow) and on the grass was an elaborate fountain. A white marble fish balanced upright on its tail; a high arc of bubbling water sprayed from its mouth before cascading down three intricate tiers. Jack pushed his bike down the drive. A tiny shiver ran down his spine. It made him think of returning through UK Customs, after a Spanish holiday. He glanced around; was he being watched? He'd not made it halfway before the front door burst open and Mike stepped out, slowly negotiating the front steps with his blue boot.

"Jack, you found me! Bit of a maze around here, isn't it?" He fished a key ring from his pocket, twirling it until he had a white plastic matchbox between his finger and thumb. Pointing it to his left, one of three garage doors started to rise with the quiet hum of a well-oiled pulley system.

"Push your bike in there and then we can go in."

Jack ducked his head and went into the cavernous garage. He propped his bike against the wall then turned to see three cars parked neatly in the other half of the building. Mike joined him.

"Jesus, Mike, is that a Ferrari?" Jack, like his grandad, and his great grandad before him, loved cars. He'd been lucky enough to ride in a McLaren formula one car once when visiting the Motor Museum at Beaulieu. He could still remember the smell as he'd been strapped in the seat, the mix of oil, grease and leather.

"Correct-a-mundo. I bought it last year." Mike leaned in conspiratorially. "I've only used it a couple of times though, stresses me out too much."

Jack laughed. "Seriously? Why?"

"Well, around here there are so many speed bumps."

Jack could hardly believe what he was hearing. He'd *never* get out of it, if he owned it.

"I'll take you for a spin, if you fancy?"

Jack's mouth fell open. "God, yes… please," he stammered. "That would be so cool." He looked down at Mike's foot and Mike tutted.

"Damn it. I keep forgetting about that. Rain check? I promise a spin as soon as I can."

Jack nodded. This was so cool. Wait 'til his friends heard about it.

"Right well, let's have a drink and do some map reading instead."

Not quite the same. Jack tried to hide his disappointment as they paused on the drive watching the garage doors close. His eyes travelled up and he noticed black boxes on every corner of the building.

"Are they cameras?"

Mike's eyes flicked up and nodded. He went in, waiting for Jack to follow him into the vast, circular entrance hall. Their footsteps echoed, the bare cream walls and marble tiles did nothing to dampen any noise. It reminded Jack of the Town Hall - he'd been once on a school visit.

Two curving staircases rose either side before coming together on the first floor.

"Wow, Mike. How long you been here?" Jack tipped his head back, gazing at the empty space around him. There were no personal effects, no pictures. Maybe he'd not had time to decorate yet.

"Five years now."

Well that blew that theory out the water.

"It's huge."

Mike shrugged; the impact of his surroundings lost on him. "Let's go through." He pointed down a hallway and Jack counted at least six doors.

"Where do all these go?" He asked as he followed Mike's blue boot.

"Cloakroom, bathroom, housekeeper's flat-"

"You've got a housekeeper?"

"No, but it leads to a one bed flat in there… if I did."

It would keep you fit, walking these long corridors every day.

"And that's a small office, that's the laundry room…" Mike continued as they arrived in an open-plan kitchen. At the back of the house, a wall of glass overlooked an impressive patio. Mike limped towards another doorway.

"That's my study, come on."

Jack was expecting a small study with maybe a desktop computer and an office chair, like his dads at home. Instead, the 'study' was more like the Head Quarters of a Tech start up firm. Multi-coloured beanbags gathered around a whiteboard in one corner. One wall was completely given over to expensive-looking bookshelves whose every square inch was crammed with books and folders. The adjoining wall was covered in a bank of … Jack counted… six CCTV cameras, each revealing clear black and white images of the entire surrounds outside. Finally, and most surprisingly, a large four-man tent was pitched in one corner, with a lopsided airer to one side. From the airer dangled some clothes; several pairs of boxer shorts and two t-shirts. Jack didn't know where to look first. Peering closer at the CCTVs he saw the back garden from several angles.

"What the…"

Jack glanced at Mike. All the doors into the garage – front and back – were covered by cameras. Hidden among the trees was another office building, a wooden shed and an old-fashioned greenhouse. The images swapped continuously between the various views.

"Oh, it's nothing." Mike waved his hand backwards and forwards. "I had a spot of bother. Someone tried to break into the office."

"Jeez, what are you housing in there," asked Jack, "the crown jewels?"

"You're quite funny when you want to be," Mike deadpanned. He pulled up a chair and motioned for Jack to sit down. "Would you like a drink? Can of coke?"

With an open mouth, Jack turned and nodded. "Please," he added, remembering his manners. He waited for Mike to go through to the kitchen. He wanted a few moments to have a good look round, so was taken aback when Mike limped over to the tent and ducked inside. He shuffled around, there was the sound of a fridge opening and closing, then Mike sighed loudly.

"Sorry Jack," he shouted, "I can't manage everything. Could you help? There are crisps in that cupboard," he pointed, as Jack appeared. Inside, the tent was crammed with things - a total contrast to the sparseness of the house outside. There was a comfortable camp bed in one of the bedroom compartments. A plain duvet cover was topped with a homely blanket of tiny patchwork squares. A fully equipped kitchen, with fridge and cooker, was in the porch and a two-shelf, bookcase displayed framed photos of people having fun, along with a line of well-thumbed paperbacks.

"Mike, do you live in here?" Jack gazed around. It was homely, a personal space. He could easily live here, and he bent down to retrieve the crisps from the cupboard.

"Not 'live' but I do tend to sleep here."

"Why? You must have a master bedroom upstairs?"

Mike pulled a face. "I've not slept there for ages. I still keep my clothes and things there. When Pamela and I weren't getting on, if we'd been arguing, I used to come down here. It was always peaceful. I had this tent up for work purposes, so one day I set up the camp bed."

Jack looked nervously towards the kitchen and lowered his voice. "Pamela's not still here, is she?"

Mike laughed softly. "No, she's not, and we get on fine… now she's moved out. I've just not had time… it's easier to stay here." He looked about him. The tent was cluttered. It could probably do with a spring clean. "I normally see visitors in the office garden," he offered as an explanation, "so no one comes in here." He put two ice cubes into a glass and poured coke in, waiting for the fizz to settle.

"Good job," Jack whispered, "I couldn't help clocking all your undies on the airer." He took the glass that Mike was holding out.

"Maybe I should tidy up a bit," Mike mused. "Anyway, come on… map reading!"

Half an hour later they were both craned over the map, smoothed out on the desk, when an alarm screeched into life.

"Warning! Unauthorised entry. Warning! Unauthorised entry." Suddenly alert Mike looked at the bank of CCTVs. He sighed and pressed a button under the desk and the alarm stopped instantly. Silence returned. A man in a shirt and tie was coming out of the garden office. He locked the door then looked at the camera and waved.

"Just John, finishing for the afternoon," Mike said distractedly then turned back to the map. He ran his hands over the creases to flatten it whilst Jack watched the man on screen.

"Who's John?"

Mike paused. For a moment he seemed to have forgotten what they'd been talking about.

"I told you I'm an inventor, didn't I?"

Jack nodded, a smile spreading on his face. "You did. In fact, you told us a lot of things."

Mike searched his face for clues but finding none he held his hands out. "Like what?"

"About George?"

Mike jerked his head to look at him. "What do you know about George?" His brow furrowed as he waited.

"You said he was your bodyguard."

Mike ran his hands through his hair then rubbed his temples and groaned. "When did I say that?"

"At the camp site. Those painkillers loosened your tongue... or made you talk nonsense. We weren't sure which."

"George is my security."

Jack looked around at the CCTV, wondering where he was. As if able to read his mind Mike continued, "he's in his flat, above the garage. Because of this thing," he lifted his leg up and knocked on the blue casing, "I'm not going anywhere so he's having a quiet week."

"But why do you need security?"

"Because of my line of business - communications mainly. I work a lot with the military in the UK."

Jack nodded again. He hoped he looked intelligent and as if he understood what Mike was talking about.

"At the moment I'm going through the final stage of creating a prototype for them and John's been helping me with the electronics. A comms device... sort of. More like a drone."

"Sounds great." Jack had been thinking about what to do after college. He didn't really fancy the university route, preferring something more 'hands on'. Maybe Mike knew someone taking on apprentices. He liked the idea of working with tech or electronics.

Mike gave an exaggerated sigh. "Come on," he said, "stop asking me questions and let's get you up to speed with this map reading, shall we?"

"Oh. My. God. Grandad." Jack was making a cup of tea in his grandad's kitchen. He could hardly contain his excitement as he topped the teapot up with boiling water. Once full, he put it on a tray along with three mugs, milk, sugar and a teaspoon and practically ran through to the living room. Eddie and his grandad sat quietly side by side on the sofa, looks of amusement on their faces as they waited for his return.

"Seriously! I've never seen anything like it. His house is *massive*! I don't know what he's inventing in that office of his, but it must be something amazing if he's that much in demand. He said the military are waiting for him to finish. They're desperate to get it into production, according to Mike."

Tolly poured three mugs of tea and handed them around, pondering what Jack had been saying. "He certainly is an enigma, isn't he?" He seemed thoughtful as he took a first sip of the scolding hot drink.

"And he lives on his own?" Eddie leant forwards to put a teaspoon of sugar in her mug. "I'd have thought someone would have snapped him up."

"He's been single since Pamela left," Jack nodded. "He really threw himself into his work when she left. Seems really busy now. Did you know he spent a week last year training in the Black Forest with the SAS? He was telling me about the satellite systems. There are three layers, he said. The nearest ones are the low earth orbit one, the

LEO. There's also GEO and MEO but I can't remember what they stand for…"

"And George brought you back in a Ferrari?" Eddie laughed, getting caught up in his excitement.

"Yes. He said it was an old one," Jack continued, "can you believe it? Even so… a *Ferrari*!" He paused, his eyes wide and shining. "That reminds me, he said I could go back anytime to fetch my bike. Maybe you could drive me, grandad? Oh, and he gave me these for you." Jack fished a box out of his rucksack and threw it to his grandad.

"What is it, son?" Tolly opened the box cautiously and pulled out several thin pads, each the size of a small handkerchief.

"He said they were heat pads, designed for medical use. You snap them to set off a chemical reaction and stick them to your skin. He had loads lying around, designed them for a pharmaceutical company or something. He thought they might be useful for your hip."

"Well, well, well. An inventor and a millionaire. But he's still happy to go out rambling with you two?" Eddie stirred the sugar into her tea. "He can't be that bright then, can he?"

"Oi," said Jack, frowning at Eddie. "He was asking whether we're going out at the weekend actually. For some strange reason - which I don't quite get - he does seem to like spending time with us, doesn't he?"

At four a.m. Tolly woke and stared out into the pitch black. Deronda Close was silent. For a moment he wondered why he'd been roused from his sleep until he felt a familiar throbbing in his hip. He pushed himself up and gently swung his legs out of bed. He gasped as his hip protested at the movement and, gingerly, he slid his feet into his leather slippers. How much longer did he have to put up with this? Every morning he woke early, needing more painkillers and, bone-tired from the weeks of broken sleep, he stumbled through to the kitchen. He rolled his eyes at the dent in the fridge and pulled the door open to retrieve the milk ready for his tea. On automatic pilot he reached for the medicine box. He was reliant on these pills but what else could he do? The throbbing was unbearable. Compromising, he swallowed one instead of two and chased it down with a glass of water. Waiting for the kettle to boil, he stretched against the counter. He spotted the box of heat pads and frowned. Mike was still an idiot but if the Army were working with him he must have some redeeming qualities. Back in bed he plumped up two pillows and carefully eased back. He looked at one of the plasters, turning it over in his hands. It was worth a try, and he peeled off the backing. He placed it over his hip, adjusting his pyjama bottoms over the top of it, then closed his eyes and practiced the deep breathing exercise the physio had shown him. He'd only breathed in and out four times when he realised, with surprise, that a warmth was spreading over his hip. Was he imagining it? He placed his hand on the plaster. He could definitely feel heat. It was nice and soothing. He smiled. Well, well, well. Mike was a mystery. He sank into his pillows as his body relaxed. When he next woke up, sunlight was seeping through his bedroom curtains. He pulled his bedside clock closer, nearly nine o'clock. He'd slept for over four hours which was unheard of since his operation. His cup of tea was stone cold beside him, but for once he didn't mind at all.

✦ Chapter Thirty-two

ON WEDNESDAY evening Eddie walked along Deronda Close. All the bungalows were identical in design, apart from the occasional porch or extension and all were immaculately kept, with the exception of one. Number six was neat but it didn't have the full array of colourful bedding plants that those on either side did. Eddie wondered if Tolly liked gardening, or maybe he'd not been able to do much since his hip operation. She walked up the drive, sidled past the trusty green Rover and pressed the doorbell. She waited, turning her back to the door until she heard it being unlocked. Tolly's face broke into a broad grin when he saw her on the doorstep, and he opened the door wide to let her in. He looked different. For a moment they stood looking at each other. Was it his hair? It had been cut and he was clean-shaven too. Eddie smiled. Had his eyebrows been trimmed? He certainly looked very handsome.

"Eddie, come in come in."

She stopped staring and handed over the bottle of wine she'd been clutching. He took it gratefully and bent down to kiss her cheek.

"Oh superb, Shiraz. That'll go beautifully with the dinner. Beef casserole, is that okay?" He led her through to the living room. It was tastefully decorated with cream walls and carpet; a floral sofa and two matching chairs added a splash of colour. A tall bookcase sat against one wall and a dark wood sideboard ran along another. Various family photos sat on top, and she smiled at a silver pot, filled to the brim with mint imperials.

"Can never have too many mint imperials," he said with a twinkle in his eye. He pointed to the bottle, adding "I'll just pop this in there, and then I'll be back for your coat." She moved towards the wide patio doors, to look at the expanse of lawn at the back. It was long, divided into sections by willow screens and framed on all sides by a green wooden fence. Her pots and greenhouse would certainly be in safe hands, if she ever did go away. A neat shed was positioned halfway down, opposite an empty vegetable patch.

"Gin and tonic?" His voice floated out from the kitchen, and she followed it to find him. She stopped on the threshold and gasped. The kitchen was a scene of devastation. Every surface was covered with kitchen utensils - some of which Eddie didn't even recognize – used once then discarded. Carrot peelings and cabbage pieces were scattered everywhere, some still lay where they'd fallen on the floor. She glanced in the oven; a glass casserole dish was visible with its contents bubbling away. On the shelf below was a tray of roast potatoes.

"Impressive." She meant the oven's contents and was choosing to ignore the general state of the kitchen.

"Sorry about the mess," he said sheepishly, "you weren't meant to come in here."

"Want me to help you?"

He shook his head as he popped the ice cube tray. Two errant cubes flew up. They narrowly missed his eye then fell to the floor to join the peelings.

"Bloody gravity," he sighed. "I swear the only exercise I get during the week is bending over to pick things up."

Chuckling, Eddie put her coat on the back of a chair. She began to collect the dirty equipment, carrying it over to the sink.

"You don't have to do that," he scolded, "I'll tidy up later."

Now she shook her head and shrugged. "I may as well do this and chat to you in here, than sit through on my own." He started to protest, but she interrupted, "we don't need to stand on ceremony." He relaxed. It was strange how he could help organize a camping expedition, get them safely away from tanks and a charging bull, but an invitation to dinner at his bungalow had put him in a tizz.

"It smells delicious." She squirted washing up liquid in the sink and ran the tap. She found a cloth and tidied up the peelings, making sure she'd got the bits from the floor, she didn't want him to slip on those after a glass of wine. "You seem quite proficient in the kitchen; do you enjoy cooking?"

He paused.

"Be honest," she cautioned, "we'll find out later, won't we?"

He chuckled. "I'll have a go; I quite enjoy it but I'm not particularly good. Did I tell you that I blew up the microwave?"

She shook her head with a laugh.

"A couple of weeks ago and I haven't replaced it yet. I didn't follow the instructions on the packet and the door blew off–"

"Goodness!" She was shocked. "That could've been dangerous."

He nodded. "It flew across the room and wedged itself here." He pointed to the dent in the side of the fridge and laughed when her mouth dropped open in a large 'O'.

"I wondered what that was."

He set the table while she busied herself washing up. The plates were out, and the bottle of Shiraz was open and breathing. While the vegetables simmered Eddie told him about Heather, glowing with pride when she said that Heather had been phoning companies about working for them. "She went, with Amir, to meet the website developer. Apparently, they got a good deal to design two websites, one for the shop and one for 'HM Animals'." She screwed up her nose. "It's a working title. We've been throwing ideas around … 'brainstorming' I think they call it."

"Ah. We used to do that for military projects. Rooms full of people, flip chart at the front." He stood up straight as he puffed his chest out.

"Do you miss the Army, Tolly?"

He paused, contemplating. "Not really. I still carry the training with me, probably always will. I like order and cleanliness. I can't help but get up early-"

"Oh, me neither. All those years being woken by Heather as a baby and now, when I could stay in bed, my back aches."

"The joys of getting old-"

"Alright! Thank you."

"Oh, I didn't mean-"

She held her hands up, laughing. "I know you didn't, it's fine. We *are* getting old. I think we've got to embrace whatever happens next."

He watched her over the top of his wine glass.

"I know what's going to happen next," he wiggled his eyebrows as he leant across the table and puckered his lips for a kiss. He was so lovely, and his eyebrows were *definitely* tidier. Eddie rose to meet him halfway just as the doorbell rang. They hovered in mid-air before, with a sigh, Tolly stood up.

"Hold that thought," he said and went to see who was calling.

Eddie sat back down and took a sip of the wine. She swilled a mouthful, trying to pick out the various flavours before giving in and reading the label. It was tasty. Amir had recommended it when she'd popped in the shop earlier. She could hear voices in the hall and tipped her head towards the door. Tolly was speaking then a woman replied. They were getting louder. They were coming this way.

"Thea, you can't just-"

A woman burst through the door. She stopped when she saw Eddie sitting at the table. Her eyes took in the candles and the wine bottle. Then the eyes turned to Eddie.

"Oh hello."

Tolly rushed in behind her.

"Thea! You can't just burst in like this."

The woman flapped a hand for him to stop talking but he ignored her.

"I said you could have the ruddy vase. I'll drop it round when it's convenient. But this is *not* convenient."

"I can see that."

So, this was Thea. She walked over and held a hand out. "I'm Thea. Pleased to meet you."

At least she had manners. Not that Tolly thought so, as he stood behind her with a thunderous glare on his face. Eddie half-rose to shake hands. Thea looked her up and down.

"Ah I recognize you." Her voice was clipped and confident. "You were in the High Street the other day when I crossed the road."

Eddie was amazed that anyone noticed her, let alone this glamorous woman.

"Tolly, I don't want to be here all day," Thea continued. "I'm off to Spain tonight. Shall I just get it?"

"No, you will *not*."

"I know exactly where it'll be." She waited; her head cocked to one side as Tolly glanced at Eddie.

"It's fine," Eddie urged. "Do what you need to do. I'll keep an eye on dinner."

"I can get it, Tolly." Thea backed towards the door. "It's probably still in the same place I left it."

But Tolly moved her out the way.

"We've discussed this before, Thea. You can't just swan in like you own the place-"

"Well, I do… technically." She pulled a face as Tolly stopped in front of her.

"But you don't *live* here." He stared at her then pointed his finger. "You wait here, *I'll* get it." He hurried out, leaving Thea to gaze around the kitchen.

"He *has* done well." The woman looked through the oven door and nodded, impressed. "That looks quite edible. He never used to cook when I was here. He must be getting domesticated in his old age." She leaned against the counter and spread her hands along it with a proprietorial air. Why did Thea have a claim to the bungalow? Eddie had assumed it was Tolly's place. Maybe they had come to an arrangement when they'd divorced.

"Mind you, he's been getting some practice, from what James tells me." Thea paused. She waited to get Eddie's attention. "He likes to entertain when I'm not around," she whispered, glancing towards the door in a conspiratorial fashion. "You must realize he doesn't want anything serious. Just a bit of fun while I'm not here. So, Edith-" she brightened her tone.

"- my name's Eddie."

"Oh!" Thea looked puzzled. "Sorry, Eddie," she repeated, tapping her chin with a manicured finger. "I thought his friend was called Edith?" She pondered, as if trying to remember where she'd heard that name before, then shook her head. "Anyway, it's all a bit of fun so I wouldn't get too enamoured. I am *still* his wife."

Eddie stared. She put a hand on the table, feeling suddenly lightheaded. She repeated, "still his wife?"

With a look of satisfaction, the woman smiled. "Yes, we're still married. Are you alright, you've gone a little pale?"

"What? Yes, I'm fine." Still his wife! No wonder she had a claim on the property if they were still *married*. They heard Tolly returning down the hallway and Thea put a finger to her lips.

"Shush, don't mention Edith," she whispered, "he doesn't like gossip."

With her mind racing, Eddie turned her attention to the pan of vegetables, as Tolly burst into the room carrying a hideous, orange and green wonky vase. He handed it over then went to a corner cupboard. He reappeared with a square of half-popped bubble wrap.

"Here, take this. It'll keep the monstrosity safe on the journey."

Thea took the wrapping and carefully wound it around the object.

"Thank you Tolly. I'd forgotten I'd put that in there." She put the vase under her arm and hitched her tiny, expensive-looking handbag on her shoulder. Placing her hand on his shoulder she leant in and kissed his cheek. "Goodbye darling. I'll be back in a month or so-"

"Thea, next time we need to have a proper talk."

She waved him away," of course darling, I'm sorry I can't be more help this time." He smiled weakly then cast a glance over to Eddie.

"Until I'm back, please let Diana and James help you, then I won't feel guilty about deserting you."

"I'm alright Thea, don't fuss."

"I'm not fussing, Tolly, I just worry about you when I'm not here." She rubbed his arm. "I'll let you get on with your little dinner. Don't bother seeing me out." She turned to Eddie and nodded then went, leaving a changed atmosphere and a cloud of expensive perfume in her wake. For a moment neither of them spoke. The front door slammed and with the spell broken Eddie lifted the pan and drained the vegetables. The faster they had dinner, the faster she could get out of here and back to the safety of her own home. She needed to think.

Chapter Thirty-three

HEATHER WAS waiting for the microwave to work its magic on a bowl of chilli con carne. Her mum had plundered it from the depths of the freezer. She hadn't been too sure how long it had been in the frozen wasteland, reasoning anywhere between two weeks and seven months. Because of this lack of clarity around the 'Manufacturing date' her mum had cautioned Heather to 'nuke it' (her words) in the microwave before attempting to eat it. Not normally squeamish about what she ate Heather was nevertheless following her mum's advice. It had now been in the micro for six minutes with another two on the clock. Surely that would be enough? She watched the bowl twirl round on the microwave plate.

Her mobile vibrated in her back pocket, and she took it out to look. She didn't recognize the number and was tempted to hang up, but something stopped her and she swiped to answer.

"Hello is that Heather Maguire?" A man's voice: she couldn't quite place it. "Hi, it's Johnno. John Kingston, from the Balloon company."

Heather instantly forgot about the chilli and concentrated on the voice.

"Listen, sorry to call you so late but we've had a couple of things happen today and I wondered whether you'd be able to help us?"

"Go on," she said cautiously, "I will if I can."

He went on to explain that they'd been offered a huge contract to supply a large national retail chain. He wasn't in a position to be able to tell her who the company was, but it would mean a lot of work to turn ideas around quickly depending on the brief they were given.

"For instance," he explained, "they might say 'Birthday card, blank inside aimed at retired Golfers'. Then we come up with several suggestions from which they pick maybe two to work on."

It was interesting to understand how the industry worked and Heather grabbed a sketchbook to make notes in the back.

"Or they might say 'Cute animal - Get well soon – and then provide a short poem or limerick, so we design the cute animal using clues from the poem."

"I get it," she said. "That'd be nice, having a brief to follow."

"I could send over say ten-" He already sounded relieved.

"Ten!"

"Five, if that's too much?" He sounded worried again.

"Email me however many you want and let me have a look. I'll see what thoughts and ideas I get for the different 'lines'," she said, using the industry speak. "Shall I phone you back, say, tomorrow?"

"Great."

Heather moved her phone to hang up, but Johnno continued without pausing.

"So that was the first thing - the second thing is that one of our regular freelancers has handed in his notice, not that he doesn't like working with us," he added hastily, "but he's setting up his own art company." He took a deep breath. "That means I'll have his work to cover as well, if you're interested?"

"What does he do?"

"Traditional stuff, cards with hot air balloons on the front, vases of flowers, tends to be aimed at the older market. I'll send you some photos over and happy to discuss making it more..." he paused, "modern?"

They swopped details then agreed to have a video call the following day.

"Thanks for the opportunity, John, er Johnno," then as she hung up Heather squealed in delight.

Amir collected up the plates while his father went to check on the dinner in the kitchen. They'd had a prawn cocktail starter, prepared by his father, and there was a pasta main course to follow. His father had been working away in the kitchen for ages, banging pots and crashing pans and Amir had been banned from entering the room since returning home from work. Something strange was going on but Amir couldn't put his finger on it. To be honest he was too tired to argue. He'd had a long afternoon shift at Shah's and just wanted to eat then sit in front of the TV. His father appeared and took the plates away, returning seconds later with a bottle of Prosecco and two glasses.

"Father, what is going on?" Amir eyed him suspiciously. "Prawn cocktail and Prosecco? It's only a Wednesday."

"My boy, we are celebrating." His father's face was a picture of concentration as he focused on getting the cork out of the bottle. There was a loud pop, and he grabbed a glass to catch the escaping liquid. He waited for the bubbles to subside before topping it up and handing it to Amir.

"What are we celebrating?" Amir was confused.

"Today, Amir, we are celebrating the fact that you will soon be a businessman." His father held out his glass and clinked it against Amir's.

Amir didn't move. "What are you talking about?"

"You have the money necessary to buy the business from the Turners, although we need to try and knock it down a little," he chuckled, taking a glug of Prosecco. "You've got enough for six months' rent too, but it won't last long." His father stared at him, excitement on his face, which faded when Amir didn't say anything. "Amir?"

Amir shook his head. "Sorry, what?" He put his glass on the table and massaged his temples. He was getting a headache and he couldn't blame the alcohol as he'd not had any yet!

"It's your birthday and your Christmas presents for the next... forever! You'd get it all when I die anyway so I might as well give it you now." He laughed. "Come on, don't look so shocked, my boy. It's a good thing, yes?"

"But, how?" Amir was finding it difficult to form whole sentences and stared at his father. "You haven't mortgaged-"

His father shook his head sharply and held out a hand to pacify him. "Don't worry. We won't be homeless." He topped up their glasses then became serious. "When your mother died, I had a payout from her life insurance. It wasn't a huge amount but even so, I didn't want anything to do with it. It seemed wrong to be spending *her* money, as I thought of it. I didn't want a payout." He picked at the label on the bottle. "I wanted her." Lost in thought, he took another sip. "Because I felt that way, the solicitor suggested I put it into Premium Bonds," he glanced at Amir. "So, I did. And I've never touched them. It was set up so that if I had a win it used the money to automatically buy more premium bonds. I'd almost forgotten about it," he chuckled. "When you were so upset on Monday, I phoned them. There's enough in there to buy the business from the Turners and help with six months' rent."

"But you'll have nothing left."

"I'm leaving myself a little, don't worry and I think this is a good way to use it."

Amir sat back, stunned. "Have you thought this through properly? What if you suddenly want to go on a cruise or, I dunno, go gambling in casinos or something?"

His father looked at him as if he'd gone mad. "That's not going to happen, is it Amir? For one thing I'll be too busy working in the shop and for another, if there's any spare time, we'll be off camping, testing our new stock for the shop."

"I don't know what to say, father-"

"Thank you?"

"Yes of course, a huge thank you." Amir hopped off his chair and ran round the table to his father. He grabbed him in a huge bear hug and kissed him several times on his cheek.

"Stop it, stop it, you're nutty!" His father laughed and Amir realised how happy he looked too. Maybe this was a good thing. It could be a fitting way to use this money - a real tribute to his mother too. Then Amir narrowed his eyes and stared at his father. "But the shop will be mine, I'll be the owner?"

His father tutted. "Yes, Amir. You'll be the hot shot, I'll just be your lackey, remember?"

Chapter Thirty-four

EDDIE HAD been wandering for hours. She'd woken early – well she'd hardly slept – and had left a note for Heather before leaving the house. Walking at a pace, she tried to tire herself out, hoping to forget Thea's words from last night. She spotted a resting place. A fallen log lay on an angle. It wasn't ideal but if she planted her right foot wide, she could prevent herself from sliding. She dug in her rucksack for the tartan flask. Pouring the hot, strong coffee into the beaker made her think of the wine from last night. Her brow furrowed as she recalled the interruption from tall, slim Thea. In just a few moments she'd managed to unsettle Eddie and had sown the seeds of doubt about her relationship with Tolly - seeds, which were now taking root. Eddie had stayed to eat some casserole, but her heart hadn't been in it after that, her appetite gone. Making her excuses she'd left early, ignoring the obvious disappointment on Tolly's face. She gazed around the wood, her foot tapping up and down as she fidgeted with the flask lid. She usually found this place restful but not today. Everything reminded her of Tolly, the woods, the birdsong. Even the log made her think of eating egg sandwiches whilst wrapped in bin liners. She could smell the spicy, cinnamon notes of his cologne as he'd leant in to tie the plastic ends under her chin. There had been a spark between them as his warm finger had caught her cheek - they'd both felt it, she was sure. She smiled then stopped. Why did he keep popping into her head? She pictured him when they'd been trapped in the bothy, making Tuesday giggle with a funny story, and in the car, with Thea kissing him on the cheek. A dull weight settled in her stomach. Perfectly innocent, he'd said, but then Rex had said the same. What if it *was* harmless and he *did* only have eyes for her? But what if it wasn't? Hurriedly she packed everything away and stood up. She was sick of thinking about it, thoughts going over and over in her head. She wouldn't be lied to again. He was *still* a married man and she refused to become the other woman; she'd been on the receiving end of that too many times. If he wouldn't make his choice then she'd make it for him. Swinging her rucksack on her back she stomped through the woods. She continued marching as the trees gave way to fields and soon found herself on Marner Drive. From there it was only five minutes to Deronda Close. She couldn't bear another sleepless night. She'd go to his house right now and explain why she couldn't see him anymore.

The doorbell rang at number six and everyone in the kitchen froze.

"Who the bloody hell's that?" Jack whispered, looking petrified. No one moved. "Someone needs to get it 'coz I'm not going like this."

"You've only got pink paint on your face," hissed Tolly. "Look at the state of your father and me. We can't possibly go…" He cocked his head, listening. "Maybe they'll leave if we don't answer." Why had he allowed himself to agree to this? *'Family time'* Diana had said and now look at them! The bell sang out again.

"They don't seem to be leaving," Jack replied and glared at his grandad. With her paintbrush hovering in midair, Diana sighed. It looked like answering the door was going to be down to her, so she carefully placed the paintbrush in a glass of water.

"Diana, just leave it. I'm not expecting anyone, so it can't be important."

She stood and wiped her hands on a rag. "I'll see who it is and get shot of them." She made her way across the kitchen. "You're all a load of babies."

"Close the door behind you," James hissed, "We don't want anyone barging in on us." She pulled the door to, leaving the three men to stare at each other as they listened to her footsteps retreat along the hallway.

Eddie was steeling herself to explain to Tolly why she was there. So, when a younger woman answered the door, she was taken by surprise.

"Oh!" She took a step back. "Hello, I was hoping to speak to Tolly please."

"I'm afraid he can't come to the door at the moment." The woman peered round the door. She seemed reluctant to open it fully and cast a sly glance behind.

"Is he alright?"

The woman paused, tucking her unruly hair behind her ears. She had paint on her fingers and succeeded in wiping it on her curls. Looking flushed, her cheeks bright pink, she definitely wanted to get rid of this visitor.

"Oh, he's fine. Just a bit… well he can't get to the door at the moment."

"Who is it?" Suddenly Tolly's voice rang out from the kitchen and the woman froze, as if she'd been caught with a hand in the cookie jar.

"It's Eddie," Eddie shouted, leaning in through the gap in the door. "I just popped round to have a quick word." She waited for a reply as voices whispered furiously in the kitchen.

"One minute Eddie. Oh, you may as well come in, but brace yourself."

What on earth was going on? Eddie had expected him to be home alone, but it sounded like he had company in there. The woman opened the door and allowed Eddie to step into the hallway. She closed it behind her and led the way into the kitchen, pushing the door open wide.

"Oh my goodness!" Eddie shrieked in surprise and her hand jumped up over her racing heart. "What on earth…" Sitting at the table, looking rather sheepish, were Tolly, Jack and, she assumed, James. Their faces were painted pink. A collection of fairies and butterflies had been outlined on their cheeks and foreheads, at various stages of painting. A strand of ivy wound along Tolly's temples, highlighted with green glitter around his eyebrows. Eddie had been at the front door wondering what on earth was going on in the kitchen, but never in a million years would she have imagined this. She laughed.

"You must never tell anyone," Tolly whispered, waggling a warning finger as the others watched meekly.

"What are you doing?" Some words finally left Eddie's mouth as the woman stepped forwards and offered her hand.

"It's my fault," she smiled. "I'm Diana. I've been persuaded to run a face-painting stall at the fete tomorrow and I needed to practice on someone. These three offered to help."

"Offered? Not quite." Jack stared down at the table. Even though he had no images on his face he still looked mortified.

"True! 'Offered' might be stretching it, but you did agree in return for a chocolate orange, remember?" Jack's face brightened; he'd forgotten there was a reward on offer.

"So to what do we owe this pleasure?" Tolly hopped up and pulled out a chair. "You look rather hot and bothered." He guided her to the seat and flicked the kettle on as she explained where she'd been walking. Their conversation was easy and Tolly knew exactly where she'd been. As they compared notes the other three sat quietly. Eddie and Tolly seemed oblivious to them until Diana cleared her throat.

"I think I'll be okay at the fete actually. Let's go and wash this paint off." She looked pointedly at her son and husband.

"We could do it there," Jack nodded towards the kitchen sink, but James pulled his sleeve. "Better upstairs, let's leave these two to chat." Diana ushered them out of the room and closed the door behind them as Tolly put a mug of steaming tea in front of Eddie. He pulled the tin of Mint Imperials from his pocket and opened it for her. She shook her head.

"No, thank you."

"Are you alright, Eddie? I thought I looked rather fetching," he joked, "but judging by your reaction…"

"I'm sorry," she whispered and watched as his face clouded over.

"What for?"

"For bursting in like this."

"You didn't burst in," he countered, "I invited you."

"I should get back."

"You've only just got here. Why did you come round?" She looked at him and tried to ignore the butterfly on his cheek. Actually, that was easier to block out than the glitter on his temple, which sparkled as it caught the light. She composed herself and took hold of his hand. There were even specks on the back of that and, gently, she brushed them away with her finger.

"I came to say that I can't make tomorrow… the garden centre?"

"That's a shame," he shrugged. "Nevermind, we'll go next week."

"Tolly, I don't think we should see each other… not for a while."

He frowned and sat straighter, pulling his chin back towards his neck. "What? Why on earth not?"

"I don't think I can do a relationship."

Tolly opened his mouth to speak. He closed it again and stood up. He walked over to the window and stared out, taking a crisp white handkerchief from his pocket. He gave his nose a quick blow, then spotting the pink and green paint on the material tutted. He wiped roughly at his face. "Bloody Diana," he cursed, then turned back. "I'm not expecting anything from you, Eddie."

"That's good, seeing as you are still a married man." She'd meant for it to sound more like a joke, but the harsh words caught Tolly off guard. He frowned, then his eyebrows rose as the penny dropped.

"What? Ah!" Realisation dawned and he clicked his fingers. "Thea. Did she say something last night? Take no notice of her."

"She's your wife, Tolly." Eddie nodded to his wedding ring.

He jammed his hand in his pocket, his face clouding over. "On paper only."

"That's what they all say," she murmured, but Tolly heard. He opened his mouth then closed it again. He looked shocked and Eddie wanted to reach out, to take the words back. But she couldn't, it was too late.

"I just want you to be honest with me -"

"-I *have* been honest." He sat down and leant forwards, elbows resting on his thighs. "I like you, Eddie. I thought you liked me too. My relationship with Thea is ... complicated-"

She laughed. It sounded bitter.

"We have children together. But I assure you," he spoke sincerely, "the marriage is over."

"According to you! She might see it differently. You *are* still married, and you have this house together."

He looked at her, confused. "Is that what this is about?"

She shook her head slowly. The temptation to reach out and clean paint from his face was huge, but she kept her hands on her lap.

"I thought you were divorced and I'm certainly not going to be the 'other woman'".

"Eddie, you're not! That's ridiculous."

Her eyes narrowed. *Ridiculous?* "You are still a married man."

"And you are a married woman."

She snorted. "*Now* who's being ridiculous? Not to mention cruel." She clasped her hands, the metal of her wedding ring digging into her finger.

"He might not be here, Eddie, but in *here,*" he tapped the side of his temple, "you're still married." He straightened up, his eyes looking at her coolly. "But I think you're right. We *both* need to move on."

"I'm sorry, Tolly." She made to touch his face, but he pulled away. "I might feel differently in a few weeks… a month."

"A month?" His hands rose in apology. "Take as long as you need, Eddie. Maybe it is time for both of us to sort ourselves out." He held her gaze and she couldn't stop a slight smile from appearing at the corner of her mouth. It wasn't funny. But seeing this man's face, with a smudged purple butterfly, wasn't what she'd been expecting.

"Before you go, I've got something for you." He walked stiffly to the fridge and took out a tupperware dish. He brought it over and removed the lid. "It was supposed to have been a surprise last night, but you left so quickly."

She peered in the plastic box and gasped. "Is that Pavlova?"

He nodded. "You mentioned at the weekend it was your favourite."

She remembered the conversation clearly. It had been after their bean supper at the campsite when they'd shared stories about the fanciest foods they'd eaten. Eddie's had been a restaurant in France. She'd visited with Rex and Heather and after a fabulous meal (not dissimilar to last night's casserole) the cook had appeared with a huge Pavlova and given each table an equal share. Crispy on the outside, chewy in the middle, it had melted to nothing in her mouth and Eddie had almost salivated as she'd recounted the story last week. The back of her throat ached, as she took the box and busied herself with checking the lid.

"It looks amazing. Don't you want it?"

He shook his head. "No, it's for you. I asked Diana to make it especially for you."

As she walked out of Deronda Close, she turned to look at the bungalow. Tolly was watching from the front door. He raised his hand to wave. His clear grey eyes were clouded and sad, the previously perfect facial drawings now smudged and messy. Eddie's heart sank knowing she'd been the cause of that, and she just hoped she was doing the right thing.

Chapter Thirty-five

AMIR STRODE along the river path. He was a couple of minutes late but congratulated himself, as only an hour before he'd been frantically searching the attic for his walking boots. Wearing them with long trousers and a zip up fleece, he looked every inch the rambler. He paused on the gritty path and turned to stare at the houses. Unsure which was Eddie's, he was pulling his phone out when he heard a familiar voice.

"Romeo, Romeo… where've you been?" Heather stood on a narrow, first floor balcony overlooking, what must be, Eddie's garden. She held her palms to the sky then pointed to the path. "I'll come down." Minutes later, she was in the garden and, opening the gate, she joined him on the path. Without a word, he pulled her towards him and kissed her gently on the lips.

"Look at you." She leant back, to check out his outfit. "Rambling Ronnie with all the gear."

Amir shrugged. "I know we've only got an hour or so, but I got carried away in the attic." He modelled the boots and held a pose, as if on a catwalk.

"And what's in the bag?" She patted his rucksack.

"Not a lot. Just a flask and some biscuits. I thought we'd head to the woods." They walked in the opposite direction to the shop. After two kilometres, the river path forked, and they took a track towards Huntsman's wood. Heading into the warm sunshine they walked side-by-side, swinging their hands.

"Have you been here before?"

She shook her head, searching the sky for birds. He watched her. She noticed the details of the animals around them and, whilst his eyes focused on the paths, trees and plants, she would point out the creatures.

"See those holes?" She pointed to muddy openings beneath the hedgerow. "Rabbits, by the look of it." As if rehearsed, a white tail bounced out from the hawthorn and disappeared back to its warren. She giggled, girlishly. Binoculars hung from a blue lanyard around her neck, and she lifted them to her eyes.

"Buzzard. Do you see?" She pointed to the cloudless sky. Amir had spotted the large bird circling, but as she handed him the glasses, he was able to distinguish the detail of its fanned-out tail. It circled, searching and riding the thermals, and he hoped the rabbits would stay hidden for a while.

"How's the Hide been?"

"It's been great," she nodded. "I've been able to catch all sorts, which I'd never have seen before."

"Like what?"

"Garden birds for a start. I never realised there were so many finches around. I was thinking about the Simonton Swans too, about doing some drawings for the art shop. I could make them into postcards?"

He nodded. That could work. "They are quite a tourist attraction."

With the warmer mornings she'd been getting up early to sit in the Hide and sketch. She'd also had good news back from Johnno.

"He wants me to do ten designs to start with," she explained. It would be on a trial basis to start, but the excitement in her voice was unmistakable.

"I've also been in touch with Geri, my boss," she clarified. "I've requested a month's unpaid leave." She grasped his hand, her face lighting up. "It's been confirmed. I'm staying a bit longer."

"That's great." He stopped, and she stopped too. He picked her up and swung her around. "I knew you'd enjoy it back here."

"I'm not saying it's forever," she cautioned, "but it does buy me a bit more time."

He nodded. He understood it was a big decision and he put his arm lightly around her. He knew what he wanted her to do, but he couldn't influence her one way or the other. It had to be her decision. As much as he'd struggle to, he needed to remain silent.

They reached the edge of the wood and stopped by a gate. He put his arms on her shoulders and pulled her round to face him. The strap from his rucksack dug into his arm and he nudged it away. He leant in to kiss her lips and she responded, as the sunlight danced through the leaves and on their faces. He felt at peace, wondering if he'd ever experience such a perfect moment again. Then he felt her pull away. He opened his eyes, to see her smiling back at him.

"Come on Romeo," she tugged his hand. "Let's go and find somewhere to have your coffee," and reluctantly he followed.

As they entered the wood, Amir couldn't hold in his news any longer. He had been to see a solicitor and contracts had been drawn up. A grin broke out on his face and Heather waited expectantly.

"So, the contracts are all signed. The Turners did theirs this morning."

Heather stopped and gasped. "That's fantastic news, Amir."

He paused for dramatic effect and took a deep breath. "I take over in ten days' time."

"What? Ten days?" She squealed. "Can you do it all in ten days?"

He nodded, a grin slowly widening across his mouth. "I think so!"

She started to jump up and down on the spot. Her enthusiasm was infectious, and he found himself joining in. They do-si-doed and twirled each other round, as if they were the only people taking part in a Barn dance.

"Stop, stop. I'm out of puff," Heather laughed and sank to the floor. Amir joined her, while their breathing returned to normal.

"Mr. Turner is going to stay until the end of the month, to show me the ropes." He sucked air in through his teeth, "and then it'll be down to me." Word had begun to get out about the change of ownership and the town's business community was rallying round to show support. Most of the community knew that the Turners were ready to retire, and with other shopkeepers spreading the word about Amir's business acumen at Shah's, the whole town seemed excited about a new owner taking over.

"Were my designs any good?" Heather had drafted three new logos for the camping shop.

Amir nodded and pecked her cheek.

"What? Did you like one?"

"It was unanimous." He'd spent the previous evening looking at them, with his father. He pulled out his phone and scrolled to find a photo. Heather saw her design. A blue sky, with a green hill and in the foreground was a small tent, with a dog sitting outside.

"That was my favourite too," she agreed. "Are you going to use it?"

"Sure am," he agreed, emphatically. "If that's okay? Do I need to pay you, copyright or anything?"

She shook her head. "Nope. Consider it a gift. To wish you well in your new venture."

"Thank you," he said. He felt humbled by everyone's support and generosity. "I can't believe this is happening so fast, to be honest." And he wasn't just talking about the business.

Chapter Thirty-six

"Look mum, why don't you just phone Tolly and see if he wants to meet?"

Eddie glanced up from her paper and frowned as Heather watched from the doorway. A knowing smile spread across her face and Eddie felt a prickle of irritation.

"Why'd you say that? I'm perfectly content," she replied frostily.

"Oh mum," Heather walked over and put a hand on her shoulder. "I've been watching you all week and you just seem a bit… sad."

Eddie felt the warmth from Heather's fingers and sagged under her touch.

"Mum, I don't know what happened when you went round to his the other day -" Eddie started to protest but Heather cut her off "- and I don't want to know, but you've not seen him all week, *and-*" she held up her hand to silence her mum, "you've been mooching around the house like a lost soul."

"I have not." Eddie protested in vain, knowing it was true. She shook her head, her mouth downturned. "We've decided to cool things."

"What? You *both* decided… or you did?"

Heather stepped back to get a better view of her mum's face. "He was really taken with you, mum. He was a nice, genuine man from what I saw. He was kind, you said yourself he was really thoughtful… what about that pavlova that he had made especially?"

Eddie nodded, a wave of sadness washing over her as she realised she might not see him again.

"He looked after you all when you got lost, walking. He's sensible and good in an emergency."

"Yes, yes, I know all that Heather," Eddie said irritably. Her thoughts were racing. Had she done the right thing? "I know he's a really nice man, of course I do."

"So why cool things?"

"Oh Heather. It is complicated."

Her daughter's arm slipped round her shoulders, and she allowed herself to be pulled in for a hug, enjoying the contact. She was so pleased that Heather had come home, and their relationship had changed a great deal in just the last two weeks.

"Mum, I know dad… well," Heather hesitated for a moment. She cleared her throat, "to be blunt, mum, dad was a dick."

"Heather!" Eddie looked at her, shocked.

"Well, he was, mum. He treated you badly."

"Not all the time-" Eddie's voice was muffled from being half hidden in Heather's jumper.

"Mum, listen to yourself. You're still making excuses for him."

"I know," she whispered, "but it's better than admitting what a fool I was." The room fell silent as Eddie wrapped her arms around her daughter. Heather continued quietly. "You weren't a fool, mum. You had me to think about and times were different then. He hurt you, he behaved badly and if he was here, I'd tell him to his face, daughter or not." A tear trickled down Eddie's nose and clung to the end before dripping onto her jeans. Heather passed her a tissue and waited while she blew her nose.

"If he was here, you'd be divorced and moving on quicker than you are now."

Eddie nodded. There was probably some truth in that.

"You've got nothing to reproach yourself for. But *now* is different. Now, *you* have a chance of happiness and I think you should grasp it… with Tolly." Heather waited for her reaction, but Eddie shook her head slowly.

"I don't know if I could face it again."

"Face *what* again?"

"Being cheated and humiliated."

Heather sat down. There was silence as they both pondered what Eddie had just laid bare.

"I get it mum, I do. I could make you cringe with some of the stories I could tell you. But sometimes you've just got to trust your instincts and dive straight in."

"But what if I sink like a big, old stone?"

"What if you bob to the surface like an elegant synchro swimmer in one of those 1930s films?"

Eddie managed a weak smile. "You always did answer a question with another question when you were a child. It was most annoying." She reached out and took Heather's hand. "I'll think about it, okay? I promise."

And so, as she walked along the river, she mulled over their conversation. She'd done nothing *but* think about Tolly since she'd seen him last week. She'd upset him by breaking off their friendship and probably deeply offended him by comparing him to Rex. She winced at the many times he'd helped her out, all done generously, for no reward or recognition. She did miss him, unbelievably so, given that they'd only known each other for a few short weeks. A commotion on the river made her look across. The mother duck sat on the bank watching as her brood of five scrapped over a strand of weed. She watched and stretched her wings but wasn't prepared to leave her resting place. Eddie smiled at the change. Only three weeks before she had rounded them up, surveying their every move. Eddie paused to watch. It hadn't been long at all, yet so much had changed.

She turned away from the river and headed towards town. She tried to turn her mind to dinner, but inevitably it slid back to Tolly. Perhaps she could text him and invite him on a walk? There was nothing to say they couldn't still be friends.

Leaving the supermarket, she put the rucksack on her back carefully, trying not to bash the pastry crust of the pie she'd settled on for their evening meal. Carrying a bottle of Sauvignon Blanc, and making a mental note to put it straight in the fridge, at first she didn't hear her name being called. She jumped with surprise when someone caught her arm, and it took her a moment to recognize Diana. Her usual unruly curls were pulled back into a tight, neat ponytail and a long cream mac covered black trousers and a t-shirt.

"Diana, hello." The two women hugged without a thought, pleased to see each other. "You look smart, no painting today?" A frown flickered across Diana's face, and she shook her head.

"No, not had time this week. Too busy at the hospital."

"Hospital?"

"With dad. And now all the arrangements," she tailed off and sighed.

"Tolly?" Eddie caught her arm, her heart starting to race.

"Didn't anyone tell you?"

Eddie took a sharp intake of breath, her hand clamped over her mouth as her stomach lurched. She stared at Diana, noticing that she was dressed all in black. Not Tolly, no? Eddie thought she might be sick.

"Eddie, I'm so sorry, I didn't think…." Diana led her towards a bench, and they sat side by side, their thighs touching.

"What happened? When did he-"

"He wasn't feeling very well last weekend-"

"I haven't seen him since Friday," Eddie whispered.

"He came for dinner on Saturday." Diana paused, recalling the evening. "He didn't seem himself. He was quiet and didn't eat much so we persuaded him to stay. For once he agreed." She smiled sadly. "Sunday morning, he had a fever and said his hip was hurting so we called the doctor, and he was taken in to hospital."

Eddie covered her mouth, her eyes wide and unblinking.

"Anyway, to cut a long story short, his hip was infected so he's on strong antibiotics and they're keeping him in to monitor. Much to his annoyance, as you can imagine."

"What? He's alive?" Eddie's eyes widened as she took in the news.

Diana laughed. "Course he's alive! You didn't think-"

Eddie waved her hand at Diana's black outfit and tried to swallow but her mouth was devoid of any moisture. "You said you were making arrangements."

"Yes," she whispered, "for when he leaves hospital…not *funeral* arrangements."

Eddie's eyes watered and she dipped her head, searching her pockets for a tissue.

"Oh Eddie, you poor thing. I didn't mean to make you think…" Diana tailed off. She rubbed Eddie's arm until, after a blow of the nose, Eddie regained control.

"So how is he now?" Her brain just kept repeating that he was *alive*. Her Tolly was alright.

"He's okay. To be honest I thought he'd be complaining more, giving the nurses a hard time. But he seems," she waved a hand around, trying to find the right word. "He seems sad. It's as if he's resigned to getting old. His spark has gone."

Sad? Eddie looked up. "Do you think I could visit?"

"Of course! If anyone can make him smile you can." Diana glanced at her watch. "Visiting time is in half an hour. I was going to pop up." She noticed Eddie's rucksack, crammed full of shopping. "I've got the car here. We could drop your shopping home on the way?"

Eddie grinned. "That would be perfect, if you don't mind?" She wouldn't make any promises to him. Not yet. But at least she could be a friend in his hour of need. And now she'd made the decision, she couldn't wait to see his face again. Kind and charming Tolly.

As they entered the hospital a sense of unease settled on Eddie. The smell of antiseptic and the hushed atmosphere gave her goose bumps. She allowed the memory in - her last visit to see Rex - then pushed it aside reminding herself it was different now. Time had moved on and this was about Tolly. Just thinking of his name gave her strength. Diana stopped.

"I'll sit here for ten minutes – give you some privacy." She pointed to the plastic chairs lining the corridor. "He's in there, last on the right." She nodded to double doors, which announced 'Maple ward'.

"I feel a bit nervous," Eddie whispered as Diana perched on the chair.

"Go on, it'll be fine. Just tell him what you told me… and be quick!" She smiled. "This chair is *bloody* uncomfortable."

The twenty-minute journey to the hospital had been tense; partly because Eddie had explained how, by keeping Tolly at arm's length, she'd been trying to protect herself from being hurt again and partly because Diana drove like a maniac! Eddie had finally been able to breathe again once they'd pulled into a space and Diana had yanked on the handbrake. Now, as Diana gave her a gentle nudge, butterflies started to flit round her stomach. She took a deep breath to regain some calm then went through the double doors.

Maple ward contained six beds, three on either side, facing into the middle. Each bed had visitors and the level of chatter was loud. All beds, except one. As she walked through the ward, she could feel eyes following her. She saw him straight away. He was sitting upright in the last bed. Even in long sleeved, cosy, pyjamas, whilst stuck in hospital, he was the epitome of smart and well groomed. He was clean-shaven too, which surprised her. What appeared to be a new dressing gown lay across his blanket and he was reading from a large, hard-backed book, oblivious to the others around him. Sensing that someone was approaching he glanced up. His double take was comical. Yet, unflustered, he placed a leather bookmark between the pages and, moving his tin of ubiquitous Mint Imperials out the way, he put it gently on the bedside cabinet. His eyes remained firmly on Eddie.

"Eddie." He lowered his voice. "What are you doing here?"

"Hello Tolly." She stood awkwardly beside his bed, and he gestured to the visitor's chair.

"Sit down, please." He waited for her to sit and unsure what to say she fiddled with her jacket before laying it across her lap. "How are you?"

He shrugged and pulled on the drip attached to the back of his hand. "Fed up dragging this thing around. It's like going on a dog walk every time I get out of bed. Apparently, it's doing me good though. I'm feeling much better." He smiled thinly, smoothing the bedding either side of his legs to keep his hands busy. "How did you know I was here?" His eyes sparkled. He seemed pleased to see her, and her stomach flipped in response.

"I bumped into Diana in town. She told me what happened. In fact, she drove me here."

"Oh?" Tolly looked expectantly towards the door.

"She's waiting outside. She thought she'd give us a few moments first."

"She doesn't need to stand on ceremony-"

"Actually, she does," Eddie interjected. "Sorry. I've got something to say, and it's probably best done without an audience." She reached out and took his hand, stilling it to stop him fidgeting with the blanket. She leant forwards in her chair. "I've been doing some soul searching over the last few days, wondering why I put the barriers up when all you've ever been is lovely towards me."

"I was happy to take it slow-"

"I know." She squeezed his hand and managed a nervous smile. "And I'm grateful for that. But I've been thinking about what *I* want?"

Tolly's hint of a smile disappeared.

"All this time I've been cautious because I've been comparing you to Rex."

He frowned, clearly not comfortable with the comparison.

"-but I've realised that you're nothing like him. You're kind and thoughtful." She paused and bit her lip. Tolly didn't speak. "All I want is someone who loves me and looks out for me," she said quietly, her eyes dipping downwards for an instant. She looked back at him. "I want someone who enjoys an adventure; someone who wants *me* with them on that adventure, but also someone who will order pizza, and is happy to snuggle on the sofa-"

"I can do that," Tolly said then louder he added, "I can *definitely* do that, and I like pizza so long as I get chicken nuggets too."

The ward erupted to the sound of clapping and Eddie jumped. The two of them looked around to see that the other visitors had been listening and were now on their feet. A woman in a garish, green-patterned jumper opposite, sniffed. She wiped her eyes and cuddled the bald occupier of the bed she was visiting.

"That's better than any romcom I've seen," she shouted, as her tears threatened to spill again.

"Oh my goodness." Eddie was shocked to see their audience. "They've been listening-" but the rest of her sentence was drowned out by chants of 'kiss him, kiss him.' Grinning, she leant forwards and her lips connected with Tolly's, to yet more applause. The double doors burst open, and a buxom ward Sister bustled in, scowling. Diana was hot on her heels. The Sister scanned the ward, her eyes narrowing, as she searched for the culprits. "What on earth is going on here?" Like scolded children, everyone immediately settled down.

"It's them two lovebirds," the green-jumpered woman pointed in their direction. The Sister strode over, her flat black shoes squeaking on the lino. She nodded briskly at Eddie and stood at the end of the bed as Diana scuttled behind her.

"Well, I'm pleased to say, Colonel, you might be able to leave today." A hint of a smile lifted the corner of her mouth. "You'll need adequate care arrangements in place first, of course."

"I'll be alright."

The Sister waved his comment aside. She wasn't taking any nonsense from anyone. It didn't matter if he *was* a Colonel. "Nope. Not happening, I'm afraid."

Tolly shrugged, defeated. "Well, another night in your luxurious bed and breakfast it is then, please." His downcast eyes summed up what it meant for him to spend another night in hospital.

"Dad don't be silly. You can come to us." Diana lifted her eyebrows, questioning, but Eddie knew he wouldn't want to impose. Sheepishly she lifted her hand.

"I was going to ask if you wanted to convalesce at mine. I have got plenty of room and-"

"I couldn't ask you to do that." He sounded adamant, but his eyes were hopeful.

"I'd like to," she replied, with feeling. "Honestly, let me take care of you."

"But you don't want to be tied down again."

"It won't be for long. Anyway, the right person can't tie you down. They give you an anchor and provide stability."

"That's beautiful… really beautiful." A loud sniffing from the other side of the ward made them turn. The green-jumpered woman was dabbing her nose. "I wouldn't be surprised if they get married soon."

She pretended to whisper to the bald man, but she was as quiet as a foghorn. Embarrassed, Eddie stared at the floor. This was all a bit awkward. Tolly squeezed her hand.

"I think we'll take it one day at a time, eh?"

Eddie looked into his grey eyes and smiled. She really liked the sound of that.

Chapter Thirty-seven

Ten days later…

MONDAY MORNING dawned and at seven a.m. sharp the Wanderers, minus Amir, were hanging around the back door of the camping shop, waiting to be let in by Mr. or Mrs. Turner. Tolly rapped on the wood four times.

"Who's there?" Mr. Turner mumbled.

"Operation New Beginning," whispered Tolly and the others leaned towards him, eager faces watching. The door creaked open and one by one they squeezed past and went in the shop.

By eight a.m. Tolly had lost count of the number of balloons he'd blown up. He sat on a chair behind the counter, recovering from a dizzy spell, and handed the remaining balloons to Jack. The enthusiasm of youth! Tolly smiled affectionately as Jack began puffing frantically. He didn't have the technique quite right, but Tolly knew he'd get his head bitten off, so he remained silent. A '*Congratulations*' banner fluttered outside. Mike had hung it over the front door, together with bunches of green balloons, which danced and threatened to blow away in the breeze. A pale-green feather flag bounced from a pole on the pavement and displayed the shop's new logo of a tent and a dog, with a hill in the background. Designed by Heather it announced 'Simonton Camping Supplies'. There was a similar logo on the new website, ready to launch at lunchtime. Tolly glanced at his watch.

"Time check," he shouted with authority. "Thirty minutes to zero hour."

Mr. Turner appeared, carrying teas and coffees. He offered one to Tolly who took it gratefully. He took a sip and sighed, glad to finally be rid of the taste of rubber balloons. Mike returned from securing the hangings outside.

"Mike, I've got a joke for you." Tolly beckoned him over and everyone fell silent. "Have you heard the US Army have introduced the first unit of specially trained, combat-ready rabbits?"

Mike shook his head, an expectant grin on his face.

"Yes, they're called Hare Force One." A groan rang around the shop and people returned to the job they'd been doing before.

"That was awful, grandad," Jack laughed. "Have you got anything better?"

"Actually, I do." Tolly replied, nonchalantly. "Why did the military arrest all the pigeons?" He looked around, pausing for great effect. "They were worried they would start a coo."

Eddie appeared next to his side, laughing and reached up to kiss his cheek. "They're getting better, Tolly. You'll soon be giving Mike a run for his money!"

Mr. Turner looked around the shop, his face beaming at the shop's transformation. "This is so exciting," he said. "I can't think of anyone better to be handing over to." His wife, equally as thrilled by their imminent retirement brought through a tray of cake. She'd been in the back room cutting up platefuls, clearly expecting to feed the five thousand later on. Not realizing he was doing it, Tolly licked his lips at the sight of the gateau. Heather nervously tidied the box of folded competition entries. She had devised a colouring competition, to engage the local schools and it seemed that every youngster under the age of twelve wanted to have a go. Whilst Amir knew they were running it, to generate publicity, he didn't realise how much interest there had been. Tolly rubbed his hands in glee as he thought of the surprises Amir had in store.

"Time check. Fifteen minutes to zero hour." They tidied up and hid in the back room and at ten to nine Amir knocked on the front door and waited to be let in. The Wanderers listened at the door.

"Morning Amir, how does this feel?"

Mr. Turner, sounding over-bright to Tolly's ears, drew back the bolts and they heard the door's hinges protest as it opened.

"Great, Mr. Turner. Absolutely fantastic and it looks amazing. You should have let me help you with the balloons." They heard Amir take off his coat and hang it on the other side of the door.

"Shall I make us a brew before we open up?"

The back room burst open, and everyone charged out. Party poppers fired into the air and Heather and Eddie blew on the vuvuzelas they'd bought especially. Poor Amir staggered backwards, clearly having had the fright of his life.

"When did you do this?" Amir downed his drink and held his glass out for more.

"We came in early to help," Eddie explained. "It didn't take long, although," she looked across at Tolly, "the balloons took a while. For once the boys didn't have enough hot air!" Tolly frowned, pretending to take offense and next to him Jack blew up an imaginary balloon.

"Well, it's fantastic," Amir beamed around him, delighted. "Thank you everyone."

Mr. Turner held the door open, and his wife came in with a plateful of cake.

"I know it's early," she said, "but go on, have a slice." Everyone tucked in as she wandered around.

"Are you sure you've got enough for later?" Eddie paused, her hand hovering. She didn't want to eat all the stock.

Mr. Turner nearly choked on his drink. "Enough?" He whispered so Amir didn't hear, "There are plates full of it back there. I'd be surprised if there's a cake left anywhere in this town."

Tolly watched. He smiled as Eddie reached for two pieces. She was always thinking of others first, putting herself second and as he gazed at her, a warm feeling rose in his chest. She needed someone to look out for her, be on her side. He really wanted that to be him.

"I've been hearing all about this group of yours." Mr. Turner's voice broke into his thoughts as he cradled his champagne glass. "It sounds good fun. I suppose I should have organized something like that, but you know… Mrs. Turner doesn't like camping."

It was a joke and Amir rolled his eyes. A scout leader for several decades, Mrs. Turner had started the shop.

"Don't believe a word of it," Amir said. "He thinks he's funny. Thank goodness I won't have to put up with him for much longer."

Mr. Turner took a playful swipe at him then held his glass up. "Unless we join the Wanderers and give camping another whirl!" A cheer went up from the group.

"You'd be most welcome," Tolly replied. "We don't always camp but we try to get out most weekends. The more, the merrier."

Amir finished his second glass of bubbles and put the glass on the counter. He slapped his thighs and stood up.

"Right, well. I don't know what the rest of you have planned for the day," he said, "but some of us have got work-" His sentence was interrupted by voices singing outside.

Ging gang gooli, gooli, gooli, gooli, watcha
Ging gang goo...

"What's that?" He opened the front door and stepped outside as the Wanderers scrambled over each other to get to the window. The local

Scouts Group stood in a semi-circle outside, singing at the top of their lungs. Heather stepped out and, moving next to Amir, she put her arms around his waist and joined in.

"Ging gang gooli, gooli, gooli, gooli, watcha."

One by one the Wanderers, with Mr. and Mrs. Turner, joined in. Amir noticed something over Heather's shoulder and leaned in. "Won't be a minute." He pecked her cheek and brushed past, and she turned to see where he was going. He ran along the High Street and caught up with someone, an older man in a blue anorak. He pulled at the man's arm to make him stop and pointed back to the crowd. Heather glanced at her watch. The Mayor was scheduled to cut the ribbon in five minutes. What should she do? She weaved her way through the gathering to the Mayor, just as Mr. Turner handed him a pair of scissors.

"Mr. Mayor," she said. "Could you just hang on a few minutes? Amir is busy; he shouldn't be long."

"That's his father," Mr. Turner said, following her line of sight. "Amir will be pleased he's come. Have you met him?"

Heather shook her head. "No. Maybe I should go and get them." She marched up the road and waved as Amir saw her. He beckoned her over.

"Heather, this is my father. I'm trying to persuade him to come and join the party."

She held out her hand. He graciously took it, smiling shyly at her.

"Ah, this is Heather. I gather you've been helping my son?"

"Well, it's down to Amir and you too." She acknowledged the part he'd played in getting the shop open. "A joint effort I'd say."

Amir tapped his head and stared at her, his eyes wide. "I forgot to ask you. How did the Skype call go yesterday? I feel awful, I've been so wrapped-"

"Amir, it's fine. Don't worry, I'll tell you later." She pointed at the shop. "Look, we need you back there. Something is planned and we can't do it without the shopkeeper, can we?"

Amir appeared to be torn. Heather sensed his quandary.

"Mr. Hussain, come and join us. Amir, you go. I'll walk with your father." Amir nodded. He patted his dad's shoulder then turned towards the shop.

"The Mayor is going to say a few words and cut a ribbon," she explained. "Amir would love it if you came to watch. It will only take five minutes." Mr. Hussain paused. He stared up the road and Heather held her breath, willing him to join in. Unexpectedly he nodded.

"I'd like that, Heather," he said. "You can tell me about your drawings. Amir tells me you're a very good artist."

Over the top of the crowd Heather waved to get Mr. Turner's attention. She pointed at Amir and put her thumbs up for the Mayor to begin. Joining the back of the small crowd she stood next to Amir's father and watched as Amir basked in the limelight.

"As you all know," the Mayor began, "we're here to see the changing of the Guard at Simonton Camping, er… shop." He'd forgotten the new name for the place and Heather sighed. She'd given him a prepared speech, but he'd obviously not rehearsed it. "Firstly, we'd like to say a heartfelt thank you to Mr. and Mrs. Turner for their years of hard work and perseverance. They have kept this shop running, sometimes under very difficult circumstances. I mean, they faced several recessions too when money was scarce. There were times when people weren't really doing 'camping'" he made air quotes and grinned at the crowd. "They kept it going, putting in the hours. Always with a friendly smile and a joyful wave."

Heather and her mum exchanged a look. What was he wittering about? Eddie shrugged and smiled. Everyone seemed happy enough. Pausing, the Mayor hitched his trousers up and fiddled with the heavy chains of office draped around his neck. He talked about the joys of camping and went off on a tangent to explain how he'd camped out with Mr Turner, as young lads.

"We took a two man tent up to the woods. It was a lovely evening." He glanced over at Mr. Turner. Was he turning pink? "We had a great time, cooking on the campfire, telling ghost stories and in the middle of the night-"

Mr. Turner coughed noisily. "Anyway, about Amir," he shouted and the Mayor cleared his throat.

"Yes. Sorry, silly of me," he adjusted his golden chains. "Now, where was I?" He praised Amir's hard work and his commitment to the shop. He mentioned the long hours he'd worked at Shah's and his love of hiking. Amir's father was watching intently, hands clasped over his heart as the Mayor continued to heap praise on his only child. Heather pulled out her phone and took a few photos to remember the day by. The Mayor droned on until finally he seemed to run out of things to say and stopped. He looked out at the small gathering and seemed surprised that anyone was still listening. To the side of him a pair of scissors appeared, a subtle hint to get a move on. Mr. Turner said a few words but kept it short and sweet, echoing the sentiment of having new blood and energy taking over the business. He shook Amir's hand, the Mayor shook his hand and holding the scissors up together they paused for photos. Heather found herself being pushed forwards and as Amir kissed her on the cheek, grinning, several flashes went off. As the ribbon was cut, everyone cheered loudly. Heather knew the hard work was just about to begin. But she also knew that Amir wouldn't mind one little bit.

Chapter Thirty-eight

The weekend

EDDIE STOOD in her living room, watching the small group gathered in her garden below. Laughter reverberated around and carried on the surface down the river. She thought it sounded delightful. Everyone was so relaxed, and the conversation was flowing. She had made a buffet and there was plenty for everyone. Even the weather was behaving for the first time in a few days and the sun came out to warm the gathering, showing off her new patio in its best light. She touched her new hairdo and scanned for the group to see where Tolly was. She was learning that he was a man of many talents and now that his hip was fully recovered there was no stopping him. He had a number of projects on the go and had offered to help her neighbours with a small gardening job. Amir had joked that he should buy the hardware shop next to his, recently put up for sale.

"You haven't got time for that," she'd warned him. "You're far too busy looking after our gardens and going camping."

"Don't forget you offered to help in the shop when I'm away," Amir had added and thankfully Tolly knew when he was beaten.

There had been several new recruits to the group, all of them bringing some excellent qualities. There was Amir, of course, a great addition. Extremely experienced in trekking and camping and he'd taken on an unofficial mentoring role to Jack, who worshipped the ground he walked on. Amir had been teaching him about the Duke of Edinburgh award and what to expect from the expedition and, for anything he bought from the shop, Amir sold it at cost price. This was proving to be an immense bonus to Jack and his family - his father already joking about extending their garage to store his kit. Eddie also knew that Amir was considering having Jack in the shop on Saturdays. But he needed to wait a few months first to check he could afford it.

The group had also welcomed Mr. Hussain into the fold. This had been a surprise to everyone including Amir himself. Amir had confided to Heather, who had confided to Eddie that he'd been concerned about his father since he'd retired. Eddie didn't know all the facts but from what she could gather his father hardly ever left the house. It all sounded rather too familiar to her own story, and they'd persuaded him to come on a walk. She'd confided about how lonely she'd been before joining the Wanderers and she didn't know if it had made any difference or not, but he seemed lighter nowadays, happier. He even joked about Amir being a nightmare to live with, asking when he was moving out.

Mr. and Mrs. Turner arrived at Eddie's invitation. They were gradually easing themselves into retirement but were happy to be called if Amir needed help. They'd been out with the group too and Eddie had enjoyed having female company - and a female who knew that proper walking boots were a 'must' and that rucksacks and water bottles were necessities.

Having Heather home had been wonderful. Watching her with Amir she was like a different person. They worked well together. Eddie had known they would be suited all along and she was pleased they'd found out for themselves. If she'd tried to match-make, Heather wouldn't have been half as keen! She was a stubborn thing at times and knowing *exactly where* she got it from Eddie smiled to herself. They were like two peas in a pod sometimes, but she was immensely proud of what she'd achieved in her short weeks home. Heather had been determined to set up her own business and Eddie should have had faith in her at the beginning. Heather had worked tirelessly to establish her website, develop a company name and logo and had now secured a contract with the Balloon company. She had also undertaken some commissions for local, artwork production and she had agreed to produce two Nursery rhyme pictures for Georgia's friends too. The Gods had certainly been smiling on her since her fortuitous phone call with Johnno and the fact that he'd known Amir was an amazing coincidence. Never had Eddie believed in serendipity more than in the last few weeks.

The doorbell rang and she put her glass in the kitchen and ran downstairs to answer it. She recognized Diana immediately and gave her a hug.

"You must be Diana's husband." She offered her hand out to the serious looking man. They had met already but she didn't think he'd want reminding of the face painting occasion. He shook her hand.

"Your hair looks fab," Diana tipped her head from side to side taking in Eddie's new cut. "Very chic, are you pleased with it? New glasses too if I'm not mistaken?"

Eddie nodded, patting at her shortened haircut. It had taken a bit of getting used. It was shorter than she'd ever had it and styled into her neck at the back, but she loved it. It was so easy to do in the mornings; a quick ruffle with her fingers and she was done.

"And those earrings look expensive!"

Eddie touched the amber studs in her ears. In the shape of a sun, with silver beams radiating out, they were still subtle but with a fashionable twist. Tolly had given them to her as a present after they'd decided he should move in properly with her. His bungalow was up for sale, and he was finalizing the divorce with Thea.

"You look lovely, Eddie." She squeezed her shoulder then looked around behind. "Is Jack here?" She seemed to be searching for him.

"Honestly, I hardly see him. He's either off in a tent somewhere, with Tolly, or here. I was starting to wonder if he'd got a girlfriend, but he assures me he just loves camping."

Eddie laughed. "I've certainly not heard talk of any girlfriend."

Poor lad, leave him alone," James grumbled, and Diana nudged him with her elbow. "Ignore him," she continued. "We've just heard Thea might be back next month to go through her things at the bungalow."

"Oh yes, Tolly mentioned it." For some reason Eddie's stomach dropped but putting on a brave face she straightened and led them through to the garden. She waved to Tolly who extricated himself from a conversation with Mr. Turner about hanging doors and walked over to join them.

"James, good to see you."

James nodded in response and shook his father's hand.

Jack had spotted his parents and, leaving Amir, he sauntered over. He allowed himself to be pulled in for a hug from his mum.

"Alright Olds," he said cheekily, "how's it going?" He listened patiently while his parents gave him a shortened version of their day. "How's the painting mum, finished it?"

Diana rolled her eyes. She explained to Eddie she was doing a landscape at sunset and that the client, a woman with expensive tastes, had asked for flecks of gold leaf to be used in the painting.

"Sounds beautiful," Eddie gazed out to the river. "I can imagine it'll look amazing hanging up. Opposite a large window, the sunlight picking up the flecks." She stopped and realised everyone was looking at her.

"Very poetic, I should get you to read over the blurb of my catalogue," Diana said, only half joking.

Eddie shrugged. "I'd like to, I'd be interested to see your work. My daughter's just starting up her own business. She draws cartoons, animals mainly-"

"- Heather," Jack pointed to the other side of the lawn where Heather stood with Amir. "She's Amir's girlfriend."

"She's just got a contract with a greetings cards company so we're very excited for her."

Amir and Heather wandered over having heard their names mentioned and Jack made the introductions.

"Your mum was telling us about your drawings," Diana said. "Sounds like you could be in demand."

"My mum's an artist too," Jack chipped in. "*Big* paintings, they can take ages can't they, mum?"

Diana nodded. "They can. Normally about three months."

"Wow, mine take about three minutes, occasionally three hours," laughed Heather. "But then they're about…" she showed a measure on her fingers, "three or four centimetres. I'd love to see your pictures. Are they landscapes?"

"Abstract nature. Trees and water mainly. We'll have to compare notes some time."

Heather nodded and, pleased they had something in common, Eddie decided to check on her other guests. "I'm just going to circulate and top up drinks," she whispered and Tolly turned to her.

"Want some help?"

She smiled at him but shook her head. "No, I'll shout if I do. Stay with your family."

She sorted out more drinks and took fresh wine, beers and a bottle of lemonade downstairs. She'd set a table up for people to help themselves and weaving through the chattering throng she cleared dirty glasses and left fresh ones in their place. She checked everyone in the immediate area, gave more drinks to Mike, Amir and his father, Sadiq, and left them talking about the mayor's re-launch of the shop. It was still the talk of the town and had made a big splash in the local paper.

Back upstairs Eddie pottered around the kitchen. She washed and tidied then filled her own glass and took a couple of sips. She watched everyone from her vantage point on the balcony. Why had she been worried about everyone getting on? They were gelling really well and even James had loosened up. He stood on the lawn talking with Amir and his father, but she couldn't quite make out what they were talking about. It felt like they were already one big, extended, blended family and she allowed herself a satisfied smile.

A pair of warm arms wrapped around her waist, making her jump and Tolly bent down to kiss her neck. "This feels strange, kissing your short hair, but I like it." They stayed together, enjoying the intimacy. "Penny for them."

"I was just thinking what a difference you've all made to my life… to our lives," she pointed at Heather who'd now looped her arm through Amir's. On cue Heather tipped her head back and laughed at something that Amir had said.

"He's something, isn't he? I've been very impressed with him and how he's taken Jack under his wing." Tolly was talking quietly next to her ear. His breath made goose-pimples appear on her arms. "I don't know what's happened to him in the last few weeks, but he's taken hold of that camping shop and is really turning it around. He's a good businessman." It was true and Amir had been coming out with the group when he could. The Wanderers were now going out more regularly on a Sunday so that the maximum number of people could come. The first time the bigger group had gone walking together it had been, well… a surprisingly uneventful day. Mike still brought his latest inventions to test on the group. Jack now worked as an intern with Mike's company during holidays and as co-navigator on any trips

Jack always remembered a map. Amir kept an eye on them to make sure they didn't go too far off track. If Eddie was being honest the latest trips had all been a bit... well *boring*! There'd been no near-death experiences, no encounters with savage wildlife, angry bird watchers or hunters... nothing.

"Oo, stop that." Eddie hunched her shoulders up, rubbing her ear. "That tickles."

"You two, you're like a pair of love-struck teenagers." They were joined by Diana. She was on a mission to retrieve a bottle of chilled wine from the fridge.

"Is it okay if I take this out," she waved the bottle, "I'll top everyone up?"

Tolly nodded before Eddie could say there was already one downstairs. Oh well, it didn't matter. Diana blew them a kiss before heading back out to the garden.

"She's lovely," Eddie whispered in case she could still hear.

"Yes, she is. I'm not quite sure how she puts up with my son. But she is a good egg, despite her wayward locks and her paint splattered outfits. She is very successful; her paintings are very sought after. It's a shame she can't knock them out faster," he laughed as he received a nudge in the ribs.

"As the mother of an artiste," Eddie scolded, "I know they don't just 'knock them out'... more's the pity if they *are* worth a bob or two." They remained standing by the window. Was it rude to leave your own party? Probably. "Come on, I should be entertaining my guests," she said, extricating herself from his grasp. She pulled at his hand. "We should be mingling."

But Tolly groaned and pulled at her hand. "I only want to mingle with you," he whispered and earned a stern glare from Eddie.

"Later," she said, "come on!"

"Is that a promise?"

As she followed him downstairs, she put her hand on his shoulder and flicked his ear. Already she couldn't imagine her life without him, and she thanked her lucky stars that Amir had persuaded her to call his number all those weeks ago.

THE END

Acknowledgements

Firstly, thanks to you, the reader, for being kind enough to give this story a go. I really hope you enjoyed it and want to read more about these characters and their continued adventures.

Thanks to all those who have helped on this writing journey, the Romantic Novelists Association and Helen Lederer and the Comedy Women in Print prize. This story has undergone a lot of changes since being longlisted in the 2020 CWIP, but the fact that they thought it had legs made me focus and finish.

Thank you also to my writing family, including (but not limited to) Three-She and the Chick Lit & Prosecco group.

A special mention and thank you to my accountability buddies, Ros and Debs, who have provided sound advice and a shoulder to moan on at various times during this whole process.

And finally, a huge thank you to my family for your continued support, cups of tea and patience (and tech skills)! *I love you all*.

If you've enjoyed this story about Eddie, Tolly and the others please read on for a free excerpt from 'The Tower on the Hill', the second in the *Happy Wanderers* series, coming out Autumn 2023.

Free excerpt: The Tower on the Hill

Chapter one

Phoebe walked back to her desk and plonked herself down. The movement woke her computer and the monitor lit up, asking for her password.

"Well?" Penny popped up over the desk divider. She widened her eyes expectantly, causing numerous horizontal lines to appear on her forehead. Phoebe looked up at the older woman and shook her head.

"Oh love, I'm sorry."

"Me too." Phoebe clamped her scarlet-painted lips together to stop her chin from wobbling. She wasn't going to give Thomas Johnston the satisfaction of making her cry at work, again!

"Here, you get off," Penny said, her voice upbeat. "Have an early lunch. Tell me about it later when you've…" She flapped her hand. The meaning was clear: *when you've calmed down.* Penny didn't *do* tears. She'd been through several traumatic experiences herself and had only returned to work recently after the unexpected death of her husband. Stiff upper lip and keeping busy was how Penny coped. And right now, Phoebe was grateful for it. If she'd been offered sympathy, she'd have collapsed into a sniveling mess. She sniffed.

"You sure?"

"Of course; and if the toss pot comes over, I'll cover for you."

Phoebe laughed, grateful for the attempt to cheer her up.

"Go on." Penny urged, glancing at her watch. "Take the full hour, I'll go at one."

Phoebe grabbed her bag. She didn't need telling twice. "Might not come back." Grumpily, she blew her friend a kiss.

"Give oyer, ye daft sod. You'd miss me too much."

Phoebe gave a watery smile. It was true, she would; but at this moment she'd like nothing more than to walk out and never return.

Outside the 1960s Council building the sun was high. Phoebe stood at the top of the impressive flight of stone steps that led into the Simonton Council offices and hitched up her shoulder bag. Office workers sat on wooden benches dotted around the pristine public gardens. It wasn't a bad place to work. The people were nice, and the pay was alright. She took a deep, steadying breath. It was the second promotion she'd applied for in the last twelve months - the first one being for the job now held by her boss, Thomas tosspot Johnston. She didn't know what she'd done to offend him, but there must have been something as it now appeared he'd put the knife in for this latest promotion she'd gone for. She smoothed down her fifties-style dress, the petticoat felt coarse against her legs, and she breathed in the fresh air. Was it so bad to want… well… more? She was hard working and ambitious. But she was also realistic. She knew that as a single mum to a nine-year-old she needed a job that was flexible too, at least for a few more years. Her stomach rumbled and brought her back to the more pressing issue of food. First stop, lunch. Then she'd find a quiet place to lick her wounds in private. She set off towards Simonton High Street.

***

A thriving market town, Simonton was all that Phoebe had ever known. It had a good mix of independent shops and chain stores and was big enough to find most of your weekly necessities. Five minutes later, having targeted the Buttery Bap sandwich shop, she stood at the side of the High Street and waited for the traffic lights to turn red. She clutched a brown paper bag; a sandwich nestled inside with a can of Tropical drink as a treat to improve her mood. When the lights changed, she stepped out in front of a shiny grey Range Rover. She was two strides across, thinking about where to eat her sandwich, when her back leg stopped.

"Ow." She stretched into a lunge. Her left foot was caught and, shuffling backwards, she inspected her now rather painful ankle. A smile flicked across her lips at the sight of her polka dot shoes - an impulse buy from a local indoor market. She sighed when she spotted the heel, firmly wedged in a manhole cover. She gave it a tug and tried to turn it. It wouldn't budge. She glanced at the Range Rover and mouthed "sorry" to the couple inside. A pensioner paused on the pavement and leant on her tartan shopping trolley. Phoebe wasn't sure if she'd stopped to watch the side show or to catch her breath, but Phoebe felt her cheeks heat up and she bent to undo the ankle strap. She stepped out of the shoe, the tarmac warm beneath her bare foot. A car tooted making her jump. The lights had turned to green and the traffic on the other side of the road was beginning to move. Her heartbeat quickened. What was she going to do? It really wasn't sensible to be standing in the middle of the road and, to prove her point, a whiny moped swerved round the Range Rover and accelerated away, missing her by inches. But she couldn't just leave her shoe sticking in the road. The Range Rover's door opened, and a man hopped down. His wife watched his movements with interest.

"You having trouble?" He smiled confidently as he approached. "May I?" He nodded at the shoe.

"Go ahead, it won't budge."

She caught a whiff of his aftershave as he wiggled the shoe. "The heel's wedged. If I pull it, you might lose the plastic tip."

More expense. Phoebe sighed.

"That'll be cheaper than getting new shoes," she shrugged and pushed a wave of blond hair away from her face. She groaned as she caught sight of the huge queue now forming behind his vehicle. "God can this day get any better?" she whispered, and he glanced up. He paused, shoe in hand, to study her face.

"Are you having a bad one?"

"You could say that."

"Well, nearly the weekend." He smiled kindly, holding her gaze. She felt a butterfly flutter in her stomach and instantly glanced away. She wasn't used to being studied in that way and she puffed at her hot face. It *was* nearly the weekend and that meant two days at home with Celeste.

"Look," she nodded at the line of vehicles that now snaked through the High Street. "We'd better leave it … thanks for trying."

With a last tug the shoe came away and the man shot backwards. Instinctively Phoebe grabbed him. His arms felt taunt beneath his soft shirt and her fingers closed, gripping his arm. They paused, then she sprang back.

"Sorry." With a nervous laugh she let go.

"Yours, I believe, Cinders?" He held up the shoe. It was still intact except for a slight scratch on the back. "Perfectly wearable."

"Thank you," she whispered and took it in both hands.

"Will you be alright now?" He leant forwards slightly, his eyes looking deep into hers.

"Yes. Thank you so much for your help." Neither of them moved. "And no damage either." She turned the shoe over in her hand, grateful she had somewhere else to focus on rather than on him. Her lone butterfly had now been joined by others and her heart was starting to thump.

"Do you want to-" he pointed to the side of the road.

"Yes, thank you," she smiled, throwing him a quick glance, before a car horn blasted. She heard him gasp.

"Oh lord, I'd better …" he pointed to the huge queue of traffic winding down the High Street. "I need to…" He waved at his passenger who was scowling through the windscreen.

"Yes, of course. You should go. Thank you so much, it was lovely to meet you…"

"Mike." He held out his hand and she shook it. They smiled at ech other, their hands hanging in the air between them as they lingered.

"Thank you, Mike," she whispered. Again, the smell of his spicy aftershave floated towards her, and she had to restrain herself from leaning in. They released their hands and, reluctantly, he backed towards his door.

"Don't forget your lunch." He pointed to the brown bag on the kerb, and she nodded. By the time she'd retrieved it, the vehicle had gone.

***

Mike glanced for one last time in his rearview mirror, watching the figure in the distinctive '50s style dress. Like a disorientated Marilyn Monroe, she hobbled back to the pavement and inspected her shoe. She certainly stood out from the crowd; red polka dots will ensure that. Reluctantly, he dragged his eyes away and turned his attention back to the road in front.

"Earth calling Mike. Come in Mike."

He glanced over, to see a glum-looking Heather staring at him.

"Sorry Heather. That poor woman, good job I got her shoe out. Anyway, you were saying, you've moved out from Amir's?"

She nodded.

"Crikey. You've moved back in with your mum?"

She nodded again.

"And how is Eddie taking that?"

"It was good at first, I think she liked having me back; but I worry that I'm getting in the way between her and Tolly now."

Mike nodded - Eddie and Tolly's story was a heartwarming one. Two retired people, who had recently been through the mill, they'd met when Tolly, an ex-Colonel, had set up a rambling group. Recovering from a hip operation, Tolly had been reluctant at first, but he had persevered to help his grandson prepare for a Duke of Edinburgh expedition. Now, a year on, Eddie and Tolly were together and trying to find their perfect place to live. It was also partly because of the group that Heather and Amir had also met, but that is where the similarities ended between Heather and her mum.

"What happened with the two of you? I thought you and Amir were sorted." For the first time Mike noticed how gaunt she looked. He liked Heather, he liked *all* the Wanderers, but he wondered how Heather and Amir's relationship could have fallen apart so quickly. He checked himself; he shouldn't ask too many questions as he didn't want to get caught in their crossfire.

"Honestly? I think we were both too busy building our businesses. We were both tired all the time, and living above his camping shop didn't help," she said with feeling. "He was always thinking about work, he never set any boundaries." She snorted, sadly. "It sounds pathetic when I say it." She tapped her chin. "Maybe I should have cut him some slack, although *I* was in the same boat as well. He seemed to forget that."

Mike's eyes stayed focused on the road in front. "No, it doesn't sound pathetic," he sympathized. "I'm divorced, remember? Pamela and I had those same arguments. I was so focused on work; I would eat and sleep it if I had an idea I was working on. Businesses demand a lot at the start, like having a new baby, that's what Pamela said, … right before she moved out" he added, with a sad smile.

Heather patted his arm.

"I just thought you were love's young dream, that's all," he added, then turned at the sound of Heather's bitter laugh. "What, don't you think there is such a thing?"

"You're asking the wrong person, Mike." She shrugged.

"Why don't you text him? See if he wants to meet."

She turned sharply, making the seat belt lock.

"No way!" She frowned. "He knows where I am."

"You know, some people aren't always very good at backing down. Why don't *you* be the grown up?"

She chewed the inside of her cheek. "But I want him to show how much he cares."

"A grand gesture? Does that really happen, outside of movies I mean?"

She went back to staring mournfully out the windscreen. "If it doesn't, it should."

An image of the shoe woman came to Mike's mind; he was dressed as Prince Charming, shoe in hand, she was Cinderella. He frowned; he hadn't even got her name. Heather shuffled in the seat next to him and the image popped.

"Anyway," he cleared his throat, "how is your mum? And poor Tolly, I heard about his brother."

Heather sighed. "It's been a sad business about Morris, very unexpected; it was a bit of a shock for Tolly, although he was eight years older." She glanced across at Mike. "He collected Morris's ashes a fortnight ago, but he seems to be okay. He's even started talking about a motorhome again," she chuckled softly, and Mike slowly shook his head.

"Oh no. He's still talking about that. Still comparing the pros and cons to a caravan?"

Heather looked over and laughed. "I think Jack upset him. He was laughing about caravan names - the 'Fleet-foot Conqueror'" she made air quotes with her fingers, "the 'Royal Ranger' … that sort of thing. Tolly likes one called the 'Swifty 500'" Mike groaned.

"Jack said it should be the 'Stationary 500'.

Mike gripped the steering wheel, laughing in appreciation.

"As it was Jack," he said, "I'm sure he'll be forgiven. That grandson can do no wrong in his eyes."

"You remember we're going camping this weekend, to scatter Morris's ashes at Gundry's Tower. You coming to join us?"

Mike screwed up his nose. "It feels like it's a family thing."

"Well, I'm not really family either."

He realised she was right.

"There'll be a few of us. The plan is to walk to the Tower for sunrise, then have bacon butties and fizz afterwards. It should be lovely, a fitting tribute."

It did sound nice, and Mike was always happy for an excuse to reunite with the original members of 'The Wanderers' walking group.

"Go on then," he said as if under sufferance, "I suppose I'll only be working otherwise."

"Great." Heather nodded towards the kerb, "and you can drop me off here, please, I need to pop into the gallery before I head back to mums." The Range Rover purred to a stop beside the bus stop and Heather jumped down. "Thanks for the lift, Mike," she waved, "and see you tomorrow."

Printed in Great Britain
by Amazon

26564142R00158